BLINDSIGHT *Oxon...*

December 24, 2002

With his previous two novels, *Monkey-shines* and *Far Cry*, Michael Stewart has become an international bestselling author in eight languages. A master storyteller, his hallmark is in-depth research at the leading edge of scientific development.

He lives near Oxford, in a fourteenth-century abbey.

To dear Barry

with an fondest

love and greater

admiration

Michael

Dec '02

MICHAEL STEWART

Blindsight

FONTANA/Collins

ACKNOWLEDGEMENTS

Especial thanks are due to: Professor Colin Blakemore, Wayneflete, Professor of Physiology, University of Oxford; Professor Alan Cowey and Dr Peter Collett, Department of Experimental Psychology, University of Oxford; the Rehabilitation Unit for the Visually Handicapped, Oxford; the Royal National Institute for the Blind; Dr David Spalton, St Thomas' Hospital, London; the Society for Psychical Research; Professor Larry Weiskrantz, Department of Experimental Psychology, University of Oxford; and, above all, Dr David Geaney, Lecturer in Clinical Psychiatry at the Littlemore Hospital, Oxford, and my ever-imaginative *confrère*, James Hale.

First published in Great Britain by
Macmillan London Ltd 1987

First published in Fontana Paperbacks 1988

Copyright©Michael Stewart 1987

Printed and bound in Great Britain by
William Collins Sons & Co. Ltd, Glasgow

'BLINDSIGHT': visual ability in a field defect in the absence of acknowledged awareness. That is, the ability of a blind person to see.

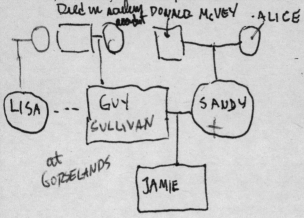

For the first time in the three years since his mother had died, Jamie felt he wasn't getting through.

He knelt in the back row of the school chapel. Twilight slipped in like a thief through the side windows, robbing him of his purpose. Wasn't humility enough? His clenched knuckles dug into his forehead, whitening the flesh. Nothing. Nothing was happening.

Pushing himself to his feet, he walked unsteadily forward to the altar. The Christ figure in the stained glass windows behind stared down at him. The wooden cross gleamed dully on the wall between them. Nothing moved.

The boy edged forward until he was at the foot of the altar, then knelt again. He looked up into Christ's eyes.

Protect him.

Protect him.

There was no answer. Nothing. What had he done wrong?

I

SUMMER

If the human brain were so simple that we could understand it, we would be so simple that we couldn't.

EMERSON PUGH,
The Biological Origin of Human Values

CHAPTER ONE

Guy nosed his battered old Ford through the gateway of Gorselands School. Leaving the main gravel drive to his left, he headed up the small track to the Victorian red-brick house that stood sentinel on a hill overlooking the school grounds and the rolling Suffolk countryside beyond. He drew up outside and gazed down the sloping shrubbery to the playing field, now white-lined for cricket and athletics, and, beyond a stand of redwoods, the sprawling stone buildings with their crazy towers and ivy-covered gables.

This had been his boyhood school. Here he'd first met Sandy, the daughter of Donald McVey, the headmaster. They'd lost touch after he'd left but they'd come across one another again at university. From where he stood, he could just make out the chimney of the small cottage they'd lived in when they were married and where Jamie had been born. It lay empty and shuttered, as it had these past three years.

'Guy!'

He turned, recognizing the headmaster's warm voice with its trace of a highland lilt. The man had appeared around the side of the house, wearing an old lumberjack's check shirt and gardening gloves. He was a tall, silver-haired Scot with an apple-red complexion and clear, pale blue eyes.

'Hello, Mac.'

'Wasn't expecting to see you today. Your half term, too?'

'That's right. How's Jamie been?'

'Fine. Got a good English report. And I think we might make a cricketer of him yet.'

'Or a tennis-player. I'm not sure he's cut out for team games.'

'Nothing wrong in that at his age.'

Guy followed the older man down the path and into the greenhouse. 'Nothing . . . else?'

'Oh, just one of his silent moods at supper. Alice got him out of it. Today he's been fine. Spent the morning helping me tie up the tomatoes.'

Guy glanced at the raffia ties on the bamboo stakes. 'Done a good job, I'd say. Is he around?'

'You'll find him down at the river, fishing.' McVey paused, looking him in the eye. 'Any more head-aches?'

'No. I've been pretty good lately. Right. See you for tea.'

'Here.' McVey picked several cherry-sized toma-toes. 'Take these with you. He's got a real tooth for the small ones.'

Guy set off down the rutted woodland path.

Sunlight filtered in dusty shafts through the beech canopies high above, spilling off the naked lower branches and dappling the carpet of leaves. Deep in the undergrowth, some invisible creature took flight as he trod on a twig. He swung his linen jacket over his shoulder, careful not to let the pill bottles fall out, and, jumping a fallen tree-trunk, broke into a jog.

It was great to get away from the comprehensive during the week. He'd gone to teach there after Sandy had died, partly to gain more experience, for the plan was he'd take over Gorselands when McVey retired, but partly also to get over the tragedy. He left Jamie in the care of his grandmother Alice, Donald McVey's wife, with whom he was very close, and he came down to spend the weekends with him.

The path soon began to fall away down the hill. He felt wonderful. He should have been alert to that sign of danger.

He slithered down a bare mud slope the boys used for dirt-track bicycle racing and vaulted a small stile. A short distance away, knee-deep in cow parsley and sedge, stood Jamie, fishing.

The boy looked round as he heard him. His thin, oval face lit up and he shook the fringe of dark hair away from his eyes. He had a pointed chin, serious brown eyes and a peculiar way of looking at people with his head slightly tilted. Just like his mother.

'Hi, Dad.'

Guy tousled his hair. 'Caught anything?'

'A couple of tiddlers.' The boy reeled in his line and cast again. 'We'll have to do a loaves-and-fishes job for supper. Or aren't you staying?'

'I'll have to get back.'

'Lisa, I suppose.'

'Among other people.' That wasn't true. 'I'll be back on Friday, early. Tell you what, let's do something at the weekend. Do you fancy stock-car racing? Or there's a circus on in Cambridge.'

'I'm happy here, Dad.'

Guy said nothing for a moment; it was then that the first lightning flash of the migraine hit him. As he instinctively reached into his pocket, he felt the tomatoes there. He handed them to Jamie, wondering how he could get the pills out without the boy seeing.

'Here. Mac sent you down these.'

'Thanks. I could live on them.'

'So, how's the project going?'

He sat down on the bank and sucked at a stalk of grass while Jamie chatted on about his term project, a wildlife survey in and around the school estate. There was a buzzing in his head and small bright flecks began writhing in the corners of his vision. He blinked and shook his head and they vanished. He looked back up.

Jamie seemed talkative enough right now. Perhaps any boy without a mother should have his father around more often. Well, in a year's time his job at the Cambridge comprehensive would be up and he'd return to Gorselands. Jamie would be just twelve. Maybe by then he'd be more grown-up and find it easier to accept Lisa.

A bumble-bee lumbered noisily past, and from the reeds downstream a pair of ducks suddenly took flight. Otherwise, the air was still, heady and slumbrous. Jamie had fallen silent. Guy's mouth had gone dry, and a curious taste filled his throat. He stared into the brown water, coruscating in the sunlight. He felt the growing throb.

'You know,' he said distantly, held fascinated by the flashes of sun winking off the surface. 'I once caught a three-pound bream right where you're standing.'

'That was before the rivers were polluted.'

'Come on, there's not a factory for miles.'

'There's acid rain.'

'True.'

They fell silent again. Even the birds seemed to have fallen quiet. It was almost too hot for coherent thought. Guy found his gaze locking on to a small point just beside the float. The more he stared at this dazzling pinprick of light, the more it seemed to tighten its grip on him. The river appeared to stop moving. Gradually, almost without his realizing it, the edges of his vision began to darken until all was blotted out but this single flickering beam. His eyelids fluttered. The migraine hit him like a hammer. He

14

couldn't do anything about it. His eyes were locked, mesmerized . . .

Railway lines. One train, stationary. The track curls away round a gentle bend, losing itself inside a hill. All of a sudden, out of a tunnel, explodes a gleaming engine with a line of coaches hurtling along behind. Flashing like an arrow in the sun. Rounding the bend. The other train still there, just ahead. The gap closing. Brakes shrieking. Too late . . .

He felt the sting of nettles on his arm and face and heard the boy's cry. He jerked out of his trance. Desperately his hand felt in his jacket. The ergotamine was in the smaller bottle.

He took two. He could barely make enough spit to swallow the pills. They stuck somewhere in his chest, leaching directly into his heart.

Jamie was shaking him.

'Dad? Are you okay?'

He sat up and stared at the sky, already growing light. Then he looked at the figure standing over him. As the silhouette regained its detail, he saw the alarm in the boy's face.

'I'm fine,' he said, struggling to his feet.

'I thought you were going to faint.'

'Just went dizzy for a second.'

It wasn't that.

'Must be the heat,' said Jamie. 'Lack of salt. Mum used to say people needed extra in the summer. Hang on.'

He wetted his handkerchief in the river. Guy wiped it over his face.

'Thanks.'

'I'll get some dock leaves.'

'Don't worry. A few stings won't kill me.'

He walked to the shade as steadily as he could and supported himself against a tree. A double dose of pills acted fast, but even so he knew it would take a good few minutes for his vision to return to normal. In the meantime, through the wriggling patterns, he watched Jamie casting and reeling in his line. He felt sick. He'd managed to stem the migraine in time, but what the hell was that horrific nightmare? He'd never had anything like that before during an attack.

'Let's call it a day,' Jamie was saying. 'The fish aren't biting.'

'Too hot even for them.'

Guy waited under the tree while he packed up his tackle, then followed him up the path through the woods. Along the way, the boy turned to him.

'Dad, are you're sure you're okay?'

'Absolutely fine. Most likely something I ate.'

'What were those pills for?'

'Indigestion. Hey, let's go back via the pond and see if there's any watercress. We'll have it with Alice's cucumber sandwiches.'

It was not absolutely fine, and he knew it.

It had begun two months earlier. He'd been coaching the football first eleven. Teaching them a new setpiece, he'd dummied inside the left back, sent his own right back down the wing and headed the return high cross hard into goal. The blow had dazed him for a moment, but he'd gone on playing until a sudden, blinding headache forced him to end the practice early. That night he'd gone to bed at nine-thirty, thinking a good night's rest would put him right.

In the early hours he'd had a bad dream and woken to find the room in pitch darkness. Fumbling for the light, he touched the naked bulb. And burnt his fingers. The light was on, and he could see nothing!

A week later, in the middle of a class, he'd had another migraine attack. Within moments the room had dissolved into jagged patterns and he'd had to leave. By the time he'd reached the corridor his whole world was blotted out. It was as if he'd put on a dark red blindfold. It lasted for about thirty minutes.

He'd mentioned it casually to the school doctor, who'd prescribed Clonidine. It was on the fifth of these migraines that he saw the doctor again and was referred to Dr Berriman, a Harley Street neurologist.

Dr Berriman performed a CAT-scan but found no evidence of lesioning in the brain. He prescribed Pizotifen as a general prophylactic, and ergotamine for the attacks themselves. Within a week, however, Guy's migraines had returned, and thereafter they grew more frequent. They began to interfere with his work. It became increasingly hard to hide them from Lisa, too, with whom he spent most nights during the week. Once she caught him taking the pills but he just told her he wasn't sleeping well. She was about to sit her Finals and he didn't want to give her any cause for worry.

After a particularly severe attack, leaving him with a painful stiffness in his neck, he'd gone back again to Dr Berriman. This time the neurologist listened to the blood flow at the back of his head through a stethoscope and detected a *bruit*. Worried that there might be internal bleeding, he kept him at the clinic while he performed an angiogram. If there was damage to the blood vessels in his brain, this would show it up. Meanwhile, he told Guy to take special care driving long distances and, above all, to drop sports coaching. That was why, this Tuesday, he had a free afternoon.

The results were now through. He'd called Berriman that morning, but the doctor had refused to discuss them over the phone, insisting on an appointment for that Friday morning. No doubt that was just to clock up more fees that he could ill afford.

He stayed while Jamie had his supper, then drove back to Cambridge into the setting sun.

He should have known. That sudden mood of happiness and elation, the foliage shining with that surreal inner brilliance, the grass glowing with that waxy luminescence – all that should have told him. Unnatural euphoria often heralded an attack. This time he'd fought it off, but how much longer could he go on doing so, and hiding it? He wasn't sure if he'd fooled Jamie. He wanted to keep quiet about it, at least until he knew what the matter really was.

In his flat, a small two-roomed apartment in an ungainly Thirties block fronting the Causeway, he took a quick shower, changed and set out on foot for Lisa's.

As he walked briskly through the familiar narrow streets, he could feel the sun's warmth still radiating from the old brick and stone buildings and, mingled with the scent of lilacs and the sweaty draughts from cellars, he caught that peculiar smell of hope and dread that reminded him sharply of the days when he'd taken his own Finals there nearly a decade before.

Then this had been Sandy's city. Now it was Lisa's. He'd known Lisa for two years; they'd met at a tennis club and fallen for each other at once. If he'd been looking to re-live his love for Sandy through her he'd chosen badly, for she was far too strong and distinct a person to subordinate herself to another's image. Very soon the city had taken on the imprint of her own very definite presence. The river now was where he and Lisa went punting, the pubs and wine bars were the ones he and Lisa frequented, and the friends he met in the street knew them as a couple. They had an implicit understanding that, in time, they'd set up home together, perhaps when she'd finished her training at the BBC and he'd returned to Gorselands. Perhaps, too, when things were easier with Jamie. That was a promise lying ahead of them. More immediately, though, she would soon be leaving to start her job in London, and this city would feel very empty indeed.

He took a short cut through his old college. As he went along the cloisters, deep in twilight, he saw the remains of a garden party being cleared away. On a trestle-table stood an ice-bucket full of flowers; as he passed, he appropriated a large yellow rose. Hiding it in his jacket, he crossed the quad and hurried over the old stone bridge into the fading afterlight.

'It's open,' called Lisa from inside.

The fragrance of bath essence met him as he squeezed past the bicycles in the hallway. From the mail on the table he could see that her flat-mate was away.

She looked up from her books as he entered the large living-room, and took off her glasses. She had a long face, a long nose with a childish snub at the end and long coltish legs clad in tight jeans. By contrast, her curly blonde hair and unpainted nails were short. She wore a collarless shirt under a man's waistcoat and a cowboy belt with a large medallion for a buckle.

He held out the rose.

'This fell off a bush.'

She took it and inhaled its scent, then drew him to her and kissed him long and hard. He shut his eyes to drink in the aroma of her hair and skin. He hungered for her. He'd not seen her since the previous week; her exams were only days away and he was trying to spare her from distractions. She broke away at last, out of breath.

'You've been practising, you reprobate,' she teased.

'You've just forgotten.'

'I wouldn't bet on that.' Her blue-grey eyes grew serious as she examined his face. 'Honestly, you look terrible. Still sleeping badly? You're going to a doctor tomorrow, even if I have to frog-march you there.'

'Sympathetic exam nerves, that's all,' he said lightly. 'Right, where do you want to go for supper?'

'We can stay in. Save it for Greece.'

'Come on, I got paid today.'

'Then let's be plutocrats and go to the pizzeria. And we'll have an early night. Or won't your exam nerves allow that?'

'They can be *very* sympathetic.'

'That's settled, then. In bed by eleven, or else.'

CHAPTER TWO

Guy woke with a jolt, panting and drenched with sweat. His heart-beat revved out of control

He felt for the bottle of ergotamine in the pocket of his trousers, which he'd laid on the floor beside the bed, ready to hand for an emergency. He'd thought to have a glass of water there, too.

Lisa stirred. She turned over, pulled the sheet after her and went back to sleep with a long, contented sigh.

What time was it? In his own flat he had an alarm-clock without a face; he'd broken the glass during an attack and deliberately left it bare. But here, there was no way of telling. Certainly not by how light it was. Was it seven? Seven-thirty? He *had* to get through it before she woke.

He lay back, shivering. Noises seemed unnaturally loud. In the street outside, a garbage van choked on its refuse. He began his counting. *A thousand and one, a thousand and two . . .*

Nothing. *He could see nothing*!

No panic. He knew what it was. Negative scotoma, Berriman called it. A normal concomitant of the attacks.

He counted another forty, then opened his eyes fully.

The cool air on his eyeballs told him they were open, but all he could see was a red-black screen covering his whole field of vision and a mass of tiny shooting-stars fizzing away in the bottom corners.

He was going to be sick.

He rolled carefully out of bed and felt the edge of the table to orientate himself. Left foot, right foot, slowly he shuffled along the corridor to the bathroom. In the hall, he knocked into a bicycle and sent it crashing to the floor.

'Guy? What are you doing?'

He'd woken her. Any moment she might get out of bed . . .

'Just tripped,' he called back. 'Go to sleep.'

He trailed his fingers along the wall until he came to the bathroom door. He fumbled for the handle. A smell of dank walls and shower curtains met him, and cold tiles stung his bare feet. He locked the door on the inside and knelt at the bowl, waiting for the watery bile to rise. After a while, he straightened and squared himself up to the basin. He looked in the mirror.

He had only half a face.

Just wait.

He waited. Gradually, like an image coming up in a developing tray, the other half began to take form, filling in from the centre towards the outside. The sight shocked him. His fair, stubbly hair was the colour of ash, the old boxing scar on his forehead had turned blue and white blotches had come up all over his broad, tanned cheeks.

In the distance he heard the alarm go off. A moment later, bare feet came padding down the corridor. The doorhandle turned, the door rattled.

'Guy?' Her voice tautened. 'Angel? You okay?'

'Of course I'm okay.'

'Open up, then.'

He wasn't ready! He felt along the towel-rail to the door and, squinting at the key, unlocked it.

'I forgot Ann's away,' he bluffed, referring to her flat-mate.

He could see three-quarters of her face now. The bright sunlight was making her wince.

'I think your subconscious is trying to tell you something, Guy.' She faced him. 'Hey, you look awful. We didn't drink *that* much. And we did have *some* sleep.'

'I lay awake thinking of you.'

'Liar.'

With a laugh she turned on the shower and slipped off the stretch of tie-dyed fabric around her waist. She cast him a sly look over her shoulder.

'It's the weekend,' she said. 'God knows what you get up to in that hot-house of vice. Talk about school for scandal.'

'I'm a monk. Ask Jamie.'

'I will. I've a mind to hire him as my spy.'

'He'll charge you. Union rates.'

'He would, too!'

He tested one eye, then the other. Vision was still incomplete. He looked at her in the steamy mirror, soaping her long body. Then he began to shave. On the second stroke he cut himself. The blood welled up among the white foam. He clenched his teeth. It was just a nick; no point in fretting at that. He'd better get himself an electric razor.

He cleared his throat. 'Do I gather it's Sheridan today?'

'How did you guess?' she said ironically. 'What have you got on?'

'Not much. It's half term, remember?'

'I've seen a dress. Will you come and look at it with me this afternoon?'

'Lisa, you've got work to do.'

She wrapped a towel round her and ran a finger seductively up his neck. 'All work and no play . . . Didn't you ever take a break?'

'I didn't go frolicking round town, buying dresses.'

23

*

While she was making coffee, he put on his clothes. He looked around the room, checking each eye in turn.

The bed was a sheet of blockboard mounted on bricks on which he always stubbed his toes. In the corner stood a Fifties-style wardrobe he'd helped her salvage from a skip one night and later they'd modishly stencilled. On the dressing-table, among the scent bottles and her collection of large flashy earrings, was a radio and an old-fashioned typewriter. Her Chinese silk dressing-gown was draped over the armchair, and the desk was piled with books, files, notes and empty mugs of coffee. On the floor by the bed, spilling out of her kelim saddle-bag, lay a copy of the *Guardian* with its crossword nearly finished. He could almost read the print.

Not bad.

Not good, either. He couldn't go through life like this. He hoped to God that Berriman had found the answer.

Lisa came in, dressed in an old shirt of his and carrying two mugs of coffee. He kissed her on the snub of her nose. She put the mugs down and wrapped her arms round him.

'See you tonight?' she murmured.

'I'll call you.'

She pulled away. 'Bastard. Just wait till exams are over. I'll devour you.'

Two days later, Dr Berriman did a routine check of Guy's retinas with his ophthalmoscope, then took him over to a light-screen on a wall of his consulting room. He clipped up a series of angiograms and picked up a pointer.

'This,' he said, indicating, 'is the vertebro-basilar

24

system. The main artery running up the back of your neck divides here, at the occipital cortex. Next to it lies Area seventeen, the primary visual area.'

Guy cleared his throat.

'Can't you just cut the science and tell me if I'm okay?' he asked.

'No, it's most important you understand.'

'I'm sorry. Please go on.'

The doctor pointed to an opaque patch on the scan.

'That's an arterio-venous malformation. A short-circuit between the artery and the vein, if you like. This anomaly is the root cause of your migraines. I fear the structure in this area is damaged.'

Sweat prickled Guy's skin.

'Just from heading a football?' he asked.

'The brain is encased in a protective sack of fluid, but the tissue is relatively soft. A sudden whiplash shock can cause contusion. That's what happened here.'

Guy swallowed. 'I see. What are we going to do about it?'

'Our first aim is to prevent further attacks. I could put you on Methysergide, but it can have unpleasant side-effects. I think we'll just increase the dosage of Pizotifen and hope that will contain it.'

'Hope? You mean it might not?'

'Come and sit down.'

The doctor led him to a leather chair and stood facing him.

'I'm afraid I haven't quite explained properly. Your migraines are the result of bleeding in the brain. The malformation I spoke of is an angioma. A vascular tumour. It's not malignant, but,' here he picked his words with tweezers, 'there's always the danger of another bleed. Sooner or later, you'll have one that's massive enough to destroy the surrounding tissue permanently. And that, as I said, is the primary visual area.'

'I'll have to wear glasses?' Guy demanded.

'Worse than that.'

'More migraines?'

Dr Berriman faced him squarely.

'I'm talking of a total loss of sight.'

'You mean . . . I'll go *blind*?'

The doctor nodded, frowning.

'In my judgement, it's only a matter of time. I can't tell you when, but it will happen. And then, I'm afraid, you will be completely and irrevocably blind.'

Irrevocably? Men played golf on the moon, yet a man playing football on earth could go blind *and they couldn't cure it*? Pills could do no more than contain the symptoms. Surgery, Berriman had said, was far too risky; it would probably send him blind anyway, and perhaps worse: if it caused damage to the brain stem, he could even die. There had to be something someone could do. Under pressure, the doctor had mentioned experimental work was being done with animals; there was a Dr Patrick Ross in Cambridge, working on sight in cats. But this was state-of-the-art research, years away from clinical application.

Guy's train back home was delayed, and as he waited at the station he sat in the cafeteria and stared numbly into a cup of tea. Was this justice? He'd lost his own parents in a sailing accident shortly after his twenty-first birthday. Then, three years ago, it was Sandy. And now this living death, visited on him . . .

He was thirty-one. The best part of his life had lain ahead. He was going to be a teacher, a *good* teacher. He was fit. He loved sports of all kinds, especially football, and despite his chunky build he'd been college squash champion. He was looking forward to taking a party of boys climbing during the summer holidays.

A blind climber? He'd read a book about one once and been moved close to tears. But he'd never read about a blind footballer or a blind squash-player.

He had played the piano a bit, too, encouraged by Sandy. She'd been brilliant. His own hands were too big and although he enjoyed it, he'd never be as good as he wanted to be. Would he still be able to play? Were Mozart and Bach published in Braille?

What about the plan to move back to Gorselands in a year's time and, eventually, to take over the school? Had anyone read of a blind headmaster?

What about Lisa?

And *Jamie*?

He had to *think* what he was going to do before he told anyone at all.

He barely heard the announcement over the public address system.

'British Rail regret to inform passengers . . . the six-fifteen from Cambridge . . . involved in a collision . . . derailment . . . further delays expected . . .'

Patrick Ross took a pinch of furry flesh and sank the needle in an inch. Slowly he released the chlor-diazepoxide into the cat's bloodstream, then laid her on a pad in the small, sterile operating area he'd made ready.

While the tranquillizer took effect, he carefully examined a large-scale map of the mid-brain of the cat. The experiment had taken days to prepare, but it was still really a stab in the dark.

His lab was equipped with the latest optical testing devices and one section was fitted out as a miniature operating theatre. In cages on the floor above, protected by electronic locks and heavily-barred windows, were housed the department's experimental animals: several rabbits, two monkeys, a goat and his own three cats. These cats had all had their striate cortexes ablated. Their eyes still functioned properly, but the visual centre in their brains was absent. They were blind. Brain-blind.

The cat he was working on now, a black and white he'd named Wain, had been specially prepared for this experiment. The previous week, he'd operated to remove a section of her skull, about an inch in diameter. The opening was at present covered with a tamper-proof dressing which could be peeled back to expose the living brain.

The cat was now drowsy and limp. Picking her up carefully, he placed her in a head-frame. He could not fully anaesthetize her, for he needed her to be conscious and keep her eyes open, and he taped her eyelids back to make sure she did. Next, he checked the small strobe was pointing so that it would flash directly into her pupils. Then he inspected the hair-thin recording electrodes, each the size and shape of an ultra-fine acupuncture needle, to see that they were properly connected to the electro-encephalogram. By introducing these into her brain, he'd be able to follow the path stimulated by the strobe; the electrical activity of the cells he passed through would be recorded by the EEG machine on a slowly rolling paper chart. For quick observation, too, the machine had an oscilloscope display, and he'd be watching this carefully for moments when the spikes synchronized with the strobe.

Finally, he swung the microscope head round and angled it over the cat's skull. With the brain map close to hand, he slipped on a pair of surgical gloves and carefully drew back the dressing.

The brain had no sensation, of course, but he

28

always winced at the sight of the pink-grey clots of tissue pulsating gently under their thin membrane.

'Sorry,' he murmured as he introduced the first electrode. 'Nothing *personal*.'

'Where have you been?' asked Lisa when Guy phoned her.

'Staff meeting,' he replied.

'I thought it was half term.'

'For the boys, yes. I've got reports to write tonight, too.'

'I get the message.'

'How did you get on with Sheridan?'

'*He* wouldn't say he'd got plays to write tonight. He fought two duels for his girl.'

'And she had Finals?'

'That's special pleading, and you know it. Actually, I'm dead beat.'

'Don't stay up too late, will you?'

'I wouldn't if you were here.' She laughed. 'See you tomorrow?'

'Let's have lunch. Usual place?'

'Great. Till then, angel.'

'Sleep well. I love you.'

As he put the phone down, his eye caught sight of her photograph propped upon the bookshelves. Even in the space of their conversation, it seemed darkness had fallen and he could no longer make out her smile. Was that how the light would go out in his life?

He went round switching on every lamp in the flat, then sat down with a whisky and began to make plans. He wasn't about to rage, but he wasn't going to go gently into that dark night either. He'd call Patrick Ross in the morning.

CHAPTER THREE

Guy arrived early at the Department of Experimental Biophysics and hung around outside the modular concrete building until the first city clocks chimed eleven. Inside, he was directed to the fourth floor for Dr Patrick Ross.

His subject had been Languages and he had little idea of what a laboratory actually looked like. He'd vaguely expected a room with benches and retorts and flasks of bubbling liquid. Instead, it was more like his old tutor's cramped and cluttered study, only the clutter included computer print-outs and odd bits of electronic equipment. On the desk, among the papers and files, sat a china phrenologist's head, and on the blackboard along the wall opposite was scribbled a mass of equations and the bold question, *Golgi Apparatus = Memory Trace*? Between bookshelves, the walls were lined with softboard, which served as a vast pinboard for print-outs, postcards, reviews, timetables and drug companies' pamphlets. A postcard of Einstein in his laboratory stood as a reminder of the puzzle of genius; *his* desk was noticeably tidy.

Guy was not prepared for the man, either.

Patrick Ross was in his early thirties, slender in build and alert in his movements. His raven hair was swept back and his dark eyes blazed with curiosity and enthusiasm. His face and hands never seemed to rest. He wore a rain-stained suede jerkin over a white tee-shirt and baggy black trousers.

'Come in, come in!' he cried, sweeping a stack of periodicals off a chair onto the floor. 'Sit down.

Coffee? I wouldn't advise it: the stuff's effluent. Have apple juice instead. Better for the adrenal glands, not to mention the stomach lining. Well, what has Berriman been telling you? Brilliant man. Right at the sharp end. Not like us backroom boys . . .'

After ten minutes, Patrick rose to his feet.

'I want you to meet Skinner. I'm afraid you can't come to the labs – they're sticky about security here, with all these break-ins – but I'll bring her to you.'

A few moments later, he came back carrying a sleek black cat. The fur on her crown hadn't yet grown back where it had been shaven, and embedded in the base of her head and held in place by stitches was a tiny microchip socket. Her big, green eyes roamed around, strangely unfocused.

'Skinner, this is Guy,' he said, stroking her lovingly. 'Skinner's my star pupil. She had her striate cortex ablated some weeks ago.'

Guy swallowed. 'You mean, she's blind?'

'Totally brain-blind. I know what you're thinking. It's distressing at first, but one does all one can to minimize the discomfort. I don't think she has such a bad life.'

'Let's not get into a debate over that.'

Patrick acknowledged the point with a nod. He asked him to clear the top of the table, then carefully put the cat down on it.

'Watch,' he said.

Cautiously the creature began prowling around the surface. She walked towards the edge. There was nothing to stop her falling off. Guy started forward to save her. But she put her paw out, gingerly tested the void and pulled back. She continued carefully along the edge until she reached the corner. There she made a turn.

Guy drew in his breath. 'But you said she's blind!'

'She is. She's had the whole of her visual cortex removed.'

'What do you call this, then?'

'Blindsight.'

'Absolutely no way,' repeated Patrick, shaking his head. 'Come back in thirty years and maybe there'll be a way of regenerating brain tissue. But for the present, forget it. If it's dead, it's *dead*.'

'But that cat can *see*!' protested Guy.

'She's not using the dead parts. And her vision is hopelessly defective, anyway. She simply can't detect anything thinner than a pencil.'

'Well? Isn't that better than nothing?'

Having handed him the cat, Patrick went to the blackboard and drew a diagram.

'Look, there are two visual routes in the mammal brain. The normal way you and I are using now goes from the retina, down the optic nerve to the lateral geniculate and ends up at the striate cortex at the back of the skull. Don't ask me who gave them these crazy names. Okay? But before the cortex evolved and took over the higher brain functions, sight was centred in the thalamus, *here*. Now, there's a parallel channel, about a tenth of the capacity of the optic nerve, which runs direct from the retina to a point in the midbrain called the superior colliculus and from there into the posterior association cortex . . .'

'Yes but . . .'

'Hang on. The point is, there's no projection from *there* to the consciousness areas. So, it's not just that Blindsight is a hopelessly rough and ready form of sight, but Skinner doesn't actually *know* she is seeing at all.'

'Do cats know things consciously anyway?'

32

'Fair point. But humans do.' He pointed the chalk towards Guy. 'Put it like this: if *you* were Skinner and I asked you if you could see the table edge, you'd say No. Suppose you didn't fall off either and I asked you why. You'd say you had a hunch. You just guessed.'

'But that is sight of a kind.'

'You have a girlfriend? Okay. Next time you're with her, shut your eyes and try telling yourself you can actually see her, only you're not aware you can.'

Guy handed the cat back. 'Why can't you connect this Blindsight bit up to the consciousness parts? I mean, the brain's only wiring, isn't it?'

Patrick cast him a long, thoughtful look. 'Actually, that's exactly what I'm trying to do. I did an experiment on another cat yesterday to see if I could develop new connections. It's vastly complex. You need a special growth hormone . . .'

'What does it depend on? Money?'

'It needs a breakthrough. I may be on the verge of something, but . . .' He shook his head. 'It's not going to help you, chum. Even if I cracked it, we'd be light-years away from using it on people.'

'So, there's no hope?'

'I would say none at all.'

The two men stood looking at one another in silence. After a long pause, Patrick glanced at the wall-clock and picked up his car-keys.

'Can I drop you somewhere?'

'I envy you scientists,' said Guy as they drove towards the wine bar where he was meeting Lisa for lunch. 'It must be reassuring to feel that ultimately everything can be explained. Even things beyond our present senses.'

'We're still bound by the rules of physics and chemistry,' replied Patrick.

at one level

Guy looked out of the window. The city was packed. Tourists competed with students and cars competed with bicycles for possession of the narrow streets. Somehow there was order in their chaos.

'Strange thing happened a couple of days ago,' he went on. 'Just as I was getting an attack, I had this terrifying nightmare – well, a daydream, I suppose. I saw a train crashing.'

'Hallucinations are quite common with migraines. It's called migraine aura. Ask Berriman. You've probably got some anxiety about train travel.'

'But there *was* a train crash. Yesterday. Didn't you read about it?'

'Synchronicity,' pronounced the scientist. 'Coincidences aren't really as coincidental as we think. Events of a like kind tend to *cluster* together.' He must have seen this didn't satisfy Guy. 'You're not saying you had a premonition?'

'Patrick, I *foresaw* it.'

The other man laughed.

'Let me tell you, there's never been *one single* paranormal event that has stood up to scientific testing! And why not? The cranks' excuse is that *psi* events are lab-shy. The fact is, it can all be accounted for as coincidence or charlatanism.'

'Even so, I wonder.'

Patrick's smile radiated confidence.

'Look, I accept there are things we don't know yet. But the *framework* is unchallengeable. You can't possibly foresee the future because you can't break the rules of time. Now I accept there have been odd cases of remote viewing – people seeing things happening miles away – but at least they're always happening *at the same time*. Think of a television. It never shows you things that haven't happened *yet*. The day you switch on your telly and get *tomorrow's* news, you'll have the men in white coats coming for you.'

'I guess you're right.'

With a laugh, Patrick swerved to the side of the road and pulled up outside the wine bar.

Fifty yards away, Guy could see Lisa coming down the street. She waved.

'That's Lisa,' he said hurriedly to Patrick. 'Don't mention why I came to see you, will you? I'd rather she didn't know.'

'Fine by me.'

Her face as she approached was full of curiosity.

'Hi,' she said, kissing him. 'Who's your friend?'

'Lisa, meet Patrick. I bumped into him in the bookshop. Haven't seen him for years.'

She smiled hello, and then had to step sideways as people from the wine bar spilled out onto the pavement.

'Let's go somewhere else, huh?'

Patrick leaned across and called through the open window. 'It's such a great day, I was going to find a pub in the country. Why don't we all go?'

Guy shot Lisa a glance. 'But you've got work to do.'

'Come on,' urged Patrick, pushing the rear door open, 'give your brain a rest.'

She looked at Guy.

'Shall we? Oh, why not!' she said and climbed in.

'Take love,' said Patrick as they strolled along the river after lunch. 'What does a man *mean* when he says he's in love with a girl?'

'He's crazy about her,' volunteered Lisa.

'She excites him,' offered Guy.

'He loves her company,' she added.

'Right!' Patricks's hands danced. 'We have a state of mind, a hormonal change in the bloodstream and a

35

social interaction. Three different descriptions. But what if I said, Love is such-and-such a cell-firing pattern? Or new synapses in the hypothalamus? Or some special kind of protein synthesis?'

'Frankly, I'd think you were crazy,' said Lisa.

Patrick laughed. He picked up a stick and swiped at a patch of buttercups.

'What is the correct description? Answer: they *all* are. It's a question of levels, that's all.'

'I'd settle for a poem,' she said drily.

'A poem's at one level, high on the scale of abstraction. Below you have psychologists and sociologists giving their accounts, right the way down to atomic physicists. I'm interested in things at cell level. So you see, we're all enquiring about the same thing, just at different levels. No-one has a monopoly of the truth.'

'Why bother with love-cells,' she asked, 'when you've got sonnets?'

Patrick took her seriously. 'Because it's more interesting. The corpus of literature is fixed and finite. It lies behind us. But the brain is like Africa was two centuries ago – a vast, unexplored continent. We can build cars by robot and bio-engineer viruses, but we've no real idea how the brain works. It's the last remaining mystery on this planet. I find that quite thrilling, don't you?'

His question hung unanswered on the hot, still air. Two swans drifted on the meandering river, and between isolated clumps of thorn bush the grass was worn shiny with picnics and courtships.

Guy glanced at Patrick and smiled to himself. The man was extraordinary. They'd only known each other for a few hours and yet he was talking as though they really had been friends for years – and infecting them with his enthusiasm, too.

As they walked back to the car, Patrick asked Lisa

36

about her job at the BBC in London. He went up to town regularly too, he said; through connections of Oliver Brock, his department head, he spent a day a week working with colleagues in the Biochemistry Department at London University, staying overnight in a flat his family owned.

He drove back to town and dropped them off at her flat.

'We must meet up in London,' he said, angling the remark at Lisa.

'Yes, let's,' she replied. 'Guy'll be coming down a lot.'

Guy shook the other man's hand. He couldn't join in the pledge.

'Thanks for the lift and everything,' he said evenly. 'I really appreciate it.'

'Don't mention it. We'll keep in touch.'

Guy stood on the pavement watching the car drive away, empty at heart. He couldn't make plans of any kind. But Lisa could. She had to. She'd be needing new friends.

'Nice bloke,' said Lisa, 'but he never draws breath!'

'Attractive, too,' said Guy.

'What do you mean by that?'

'He certainly took a shine to you.'

She put her arms round him.

'I love you, fool. You're all I want.'

'Lisa.'

He drew her to him so she wouldn't see the pain in his eyes. For a while they clung together in silence.

'I know Jamie's expecting you later, but . . .'

'Come on, darling, you know you've got to work.'

'Stay for coffee. I'll be having some.'

'All right, then.'

'And take your jacket off and be comfortable.'

As she took it off him, a bottle of tablets fell out. She had picked it up and read the label before he could stop her.

'What's Pizotifen?' she demanded.

'Just something for headaches.'

'So you *have* been to a doctor?'

'The school quack. Look, you get down to work. I'll make the coffee.'

Her hand reached for his.

'Guy . . . ?'

'It's all okay.'

He made her sit down and start on her revision notes, then went off to the kitchen. God, it was going to be difficult.

The traffic leaving the city that early Friday afternoon was heavy but before long he found himself on empty country roads. He slowed down, needing the time to think. As the flat fenland gave way to the lusher countryside of Suffolk, he knew what had to be done about Lisa.

He had to break it off.

He'd been a fool to hope that Patrick could help. No-one could. The fact was established: he was going blind. What were Berriman's words? *I can't tell you when, but it will happen. And then, I'm afraid, you'll be completely and irrevocably blind.*

He couldn't visit his blindness on her. It would not be right. She had her whole life ahead of her. She deserved a man with all his faculties intact. She needed someone with whom she could see plays and movies, discuss books, go for walks, play tennis, watch the sunrise and sunset and share all the other visual beauties of life. Blindness was a disablement. If you really loved a person, you couldn't wish a cripple onto them.

38

He had to do it.

But he could not tell her why, either. If she knew, she'd throw up her new career and insist on looking after him. With a blind father, she'd say, now was the time Jamie needed a mother. Was it? Would it ever be? It might take years before the boy would feel comfortable with someone in Sandy's role. Did he really lack a mother? He had Alice, and soon he'd have his father around all the time . . .

And yet, the lad was slightly disturbed: understandable, given the trauma of what happened, but nevertheless a fact. Would he not benefit from a normal family set-up? Surely yes. But at what cost to Lisa? Did he have the right to weigh one person's gain against another's sacrifice? No. She must not be allowed to make the commitment. He had to find a way of ending it before the axe fell. And when it had fallen, after a due lapse of time, maybe then they could come together again and evolve a new form of friendship. Ah, *Christ*.

He'd say nothing to her until she'd finished her Finals. Then he'd find a way of breaking so as to cause her the least hurt.

In the meantime, there was Jamie and Gorselands to consider. The next step was to speak to McVey.

Lisa couldn't work. A thin film of worry kept coming between her and the page. Something was wrong with Guy: she could sense it. He'd denied it, but then he always would.

Eventually, she pushed her books aside and got up. There was only one way of finding out. Jumping on her bicycle, she rode off and in ten minutes she was at the science library. Moments later she was sitting at a cubicle among the rows of students with the smell of formaldehyde and the sweat of study heavy in the air and a copy of Martindale's *Extra Pharmacopoeia* open in front of her at the entry for *Pizotifen*.

After several minutes, she went to the basement and found a pay-phone. She called the Department of Experimental Biophysics and asked to be put through to Dr Patrick Ross.

Patrick was staring out of the pigeon-streaked window at the air-conditioning plants on the flat roofs below when the call came through.

It was Lisa. She sounded anxious.

'Look, I'm really sorry to disturb you,' she began. 'It's just that you're the only person I can think of to ask.'

'What is it?'

'A drug called Pizotifen. Guy's taking it. He says it's for headaches. I read up about it and it said it's specifically for *migraines*. Is that right?'

So Guy hadn't even told her about the attacks.

'Well, it's an antagonist to a particular neurotransmitter.'

'What's that?'

'Five-hydroxy-tryptamine.'

'Don't be dumb, Patrick! I mean what does it *do*?'

'It does as the book says – blocks a brain chemical associated with migraines. But it might not be that,' he added quickly.

'But if it is?'

'Migraines are funny things. Biologically, they're a sort of passive response to a threat. Like feigning death, lying doggo, hibernating. But plenty of people get them.'

'Are you saying there's nothing to worry about?'

'I shouldn't think so.'

'Well, that's a relief.'

The conversation had run its course but he didn't want it to end.

'It was great meeting you,' he said. 'Let's have a drink sometime. After exams, maybe?'

'I really can't see that far ahead, but thanks all the same. And thanks for the reassurance. Guy will be relieved to know he's only feigning death.'

He laughed.

'On one level only, remember. Good luck, Lisa.'

Replacing the phone, he went back to the window and picked up his train of thought.

What had he shown in the three years he'd been working on Blindsight?

He'd shown that a brain-blind cat could distinguish 2-D patterns. Further, he'd traced the actual cluster of cells responsible and located them in the superior colliculus, deep in the mid-brain. He'd shown they fired exactly in synchrony with the strobe flashes, and confirmed this by passing a whole range of objects across the animal's field of vision and recording cell firings.

The next step had been to try to develop this faculty into useful sight by extending the pathways. That was the purpose of the previous night's experiment. And the first computer run-through of the results showed definite signs of neuronal connections. He'd run a good deal more tests first, but eventually he'd ablate the whole brain and examine it histologically to determine exactly where the new axon and dendrite formations were developing.

A mild twinge of excitement shot through him. He had a momentary picture of brain-blind Skinner playing with a ping-pong ball.

Then he thought of Guy.

Poor sod. There'd never be anything he could do for him. Even if he did manage to develop pathways to the motor areas in the cat's brain, perhaps even to certain memory areas, that wouldn't be enough to help Guy. He'd need to have connections made with the uncommitted neurones in his conscious cortex, and cats possessed no comparable area.

What was the point in rolling forward the frontiers of science if in the end you couldn't help people? The fact was inescapable. If you wanted to restore sight to a human being, you had to have a human brain to work on.

? True

CHAPTER FOUR

The boy quietly slid the bolt across his bedroom door and reached under his bed for the shoe-box. From the folds of tissue paper he took out a small wooden crucifix and propped it upright on the the pillow. Kneeling down by the bed, he covered his face with his hands.

Forgive him, he prayed.

After a minute he began to feel the familiar warmth uncurling deep inside his heart, and he knew that he had been heard. The man was still safe.

A few miles from the school, Guy pulled off the road at a deserted picnic area and got out. He wasn't ready yet.

Standing amid the resinous aroma of fir-trees, he looked down a gentle escarpment and out over a patchwork of grass and wheat fields, knotted together by lanes and villages, barns and copses, stretching far into the bluish distance. Shutting his eyes tight, he tried to recreate the view in his mind.

It had gone. Vanished.

He tried again, this time fixating on discarded ice-cream wrappers and ring-pulls lying beside a trash-can, but it was no better. Angrily he kicked the can, sending it clattering away. Then he clenched his fists and held his breath for a count of sixty. This was not the way to deal with it.

He thought back to one early climbing expedition when he'd been stuck on a rock-face, frozen with terror. He'd not dared look up, for the summit rose out of sight into the mists, and he couldn't look down for fear of falling off from vertigo. So he'd tried to imagine that the whole mountain was scarcely bigger than the span of his arms and legs, and all he had to do was shift along to the next hand-hold, the next foot-perch.

Hand, foot, hand, foot. Don't look ahead, don't look behind. That was the trick. That was the way to cope.

He parked in the gravel drive in front of the main school building. He wasn't going up to the McVeys' house just yet. He'd wander round the school first.

He sauntered to the back and sat for a while in the walled kitchen garden. Carrying on, he walked to the tennis courts and gym, beyond which ran the overgrown lane that led to the cottage. Doubling back past the new dormitory wing, he let himself in through the boys' entrance. Inside, the odour of gymshoes, boiled cabbage and floor polish hung indelibly in the air. The corridors were empty, the classrooms silent.

He strolled through the main hall, past the portraits of venerable old boys hanging dustily on the oak-panelled walls, crossed the staff common room with its smell of chalk and pipe-smoke, and went up the back stairs to the music practice rooms. Nothing had changed since he'd been a boy there: still the same battered upright pianos, the same bent old music stands and the same sound-proofing board, all dented and scored.

He opened the lid of a piano and struck a note at random. The B below middle C. Immediately he heard it as the first note of the third *Etude* of Chopin.

This he had to know.

He sat down and shut his eyes tight. Blind tight.

He played the first section reasonably well, for it

was slow and *legato*, and each note could easily be reached without taking the finger off the one before. But the middle part was fast and full of wild leaps, and here he quickly came unstuck, hitting wrong notes and missing others completely. He stopped and began the section again. More mistakes. Then again, more slowly. And yet again, hands together, then hands separately, jabbing each key with savage spite. He missed still more notes. Sweltering with fury, he brought his fist crashing down onto the keyboard.

No, no, *no*!

Keeping his eyes winched tight shut, he slowly removed his hands and spread them over his knees. Then he began his counting. By the count of seventy, he addressed himself to the beginning again.

This time he played the piece through to the end, not faultlessly but at least without faltering. As the final E major chord died away, he heard the creak of a floorboard behind him.

He opened his eyes.

There stood Donald McVey. He must have seen the car and come to look for him. His pale blue eyes showed he was deeply moved.

'That was very fine, Guy.'

'It was bloody awful.'

'Watch out or I'll be adding piano lessons to your timetable when you come.'

Guy stood up and faced his father-in-law. He drew a breath before speaking.

'Mac, I've got to talk to you.'

From McVey's study in his large, comfortable house, Guy looked out at the school spread out below: the rambling stone buildings, the playing-fields and swimming-pool, the surrounding woodland and fields beyond. He was to have been in charge of this one day.

He stood with his back to the headmaster and concentrated on keeping his tone steady.

'I've got something to tell you, Mac,' he said. 'It's bad news. You know those headaches . . .' He took the plunge. 'The fact is, I'm going blind.'

There was a sharp intake of breath.

'My dear boy! What are you saying? Are you *sure*?'

'Yes, yes, quite sure. I've seen the specialists, and there's nothing to be done. Don't worry. I've thought it through. What I need to know is, can I come here earlier? Preferably next term, if that's all right with you. I'd like to settle in before it happens.'

McVey laid a hand on his shoulder and turned him round. His ruddy cheeks were drained of colour and his pale eyes hollow.

'But surely something can be done!'

'No. There's nothing anyone can do – I've *asked*, Mac – so let's accept that. Now, I won't be able to take games, but as for classes . . .'

'Look here . . .'

'There's a blind rehabilitation centre not far away. I'm sure I can work out ways of coping with the teaching. If not, I'll quit. I won't be a burden.'

'For goodness' sake . . .'

'And one more thing.' He held his father-in-law's eye. 'Don't tell people, not yet. Especially not Lisa, if she calls. Now, as for Jamie . . .'

He broke off.

'Spare him,' said the older man gently. 'At least for the time being. He's making such progress.'

'No, it's better he's ready before it happens. The question is . . . I was thinking, maybe . . .'

McVey understood his meaning.

'Yes. I'm sure Alice would tell him, if you wanted her to.'

*

Alice was a quiet, comfortable woman with wispy grey hair and a soft, wise manner. Guy often thought that this was how her daughter Sandy would have looked at fifty. Publicly, Alice had subordinated herself to her more brusque and forthright husband, but there was a quality of silent strength about her, as if she ran off a different, and slightly other-worldly, power supply.

She went white. She took Guy in her arms and held him closely, in silence. When at last she relaxed her embrace and spoke, her tone was practical.

'I'll get Sandy's old room ready upstairs. You'll be just across the landing from Jamie.'

'No. We'll be moving back into the cottage.'

She drew a sharp breath.

'No, you mustn't! You'll be properly looked after up here . . .'

'Alice, I intend to live a normal life. That was our home, and a very happy one. I'll make it so again.'

She bit her lip. Her brow was furrowed and her eyes were wide with anxiety, but she said nothing.

'Alice is right,' said McVey as they walked through the grounds towards the playing fields. 'Don't be stubborn. Think of the lad.'

'I am.'

'Have you any idea what it means to be blind? The things you'll no longer be able to do? Looking after an eleven-year-old boy just isn't on. Especially one like Jamie.'

'Mac, I've thought it through and I've made up my mind.'

They walked on in silence. Guy picked a leaf from a bay tree and rolled it between his fingers. The aroma took him back to his holiday with Lisa last summer, camping in the South of France. This year it was to have been Greece.

'And Lisa,' McVey went on, as if reading his thoughts. 'Shouldn't she be allowed to decide for herself?'

'I'm doing the right thing.'

'By denying her the choice? She might want the challenge.'

'I could never let her make the sacrifice.'

'That's *your* challenge, my boy. It's often harder to receive than to give.'

'Mac, I don't want anyone's help! I don't need looking after! We'll cope on our own, Jamie and me. Please understand.'

McVey shook his head wearily.

'It's your decision.'

They continued past the pavilion and around the edge of the playing fields. A light breeze returned the scent of freshly mown grass. Guy led the way off the perimeter path and took the small track that led through a jungle of overgrown bushes to the cottage that had once been his home.

As he reached the small, broken wooden gate, he drew his breath. It was incredible what three years standing empty had done to the place.

In the early years of the century, the cottage had been a lodge-gate. The main school drive now came in from the other side, leaving the building isolated among a stand of beech-trees at the end of an avenue of rhododendrons and firs. The old wrought-iron gates had been taken down for munitions during the war and the stone pillars once supporting them still lay crumbling among the shrubbery. When Guy and Sandy first married, they'd virtually rebuilt the place, for it had been unoccupied since the resident caretaker died twelve years previously. Now it had once again stood empty, and the garden had gone back to riot and the windows had become a target for boys' catapults. Guy unlocked the front door. As he went in, he was gripped by the feeling that he was stirring up an unfinished past. The place lay eviscerated like a corpse that was still living.

In the sitting-room, he could still see the imprint on the old grey carpet where the sofa and armchair had stood and the stain where a planter had leaked. The wallpaper Sandy had specially chosen showed the marks where pictures had hung, and on the window-sill a diary, three years out of date, lay thick in dust.

In the kitchen, the pebbled linoleum was cut out where the fridge and washing-machine had stood, and in a cupboard he found several jars of preserves and various packets of spices nibbled by mice.

He went up the steep, narrow stairs. Damp had foxed the bathroom walls with mildew and the bath was rust-stained from a leaking tap. He followed the landing round to Jamie's old bedroom at the front, where Star Wars stickers still adorned the walls. The window was cracked; through a gap in the beech-trees he could see the gabled roof of the main school building and, behind it, over the tree-tops, the distant rolling countryside.

'Fine view,' commented McVey drily, joining him at the window.

'That's hardly what I'm after.'

Leaving him staring out of the window, he crossed the landing to the room that had been his and Sandy's bedroom. He opened the door.

'My God,' he breathed.

Over by the window stood the small kidney-shaped table and mirror she'd used as a dressing-table. How had it got left behind? On top, in a neat line, stood several bottles of scent he recognized at once. A makeshift rug lay on the floor where the bed had been and a school chair stood in a corner. He ran his finger over the table top. There was no dust.

He looked in the cupboard where he'd kept his clothes; it was empty. He opened the one next to it. There, hanging on the rail and wrapped in a polythene bag, was a white lacy cotton dress.

He started.

A dress of Sandy's. For a split second he thought it was the one she'd died in.

Had Jamie done this?

He heard McVey's footsteps on the landing. Quickly shutting the cupboard, he left the room and closed the door. Shaken, he led the way slowly downstairs.

He locked up in silence. As he reached the gate at the bottom of the front path, McVey stopped him and laid a hand on his arm.

'You'd both be far better off with us,' he said.

He looked back at the overgrown cottage. 'It'll take a good bit of work,' he said, 'but we'll make a go of it.'

They retraced their steps up the path and along the edge of the playing fields. The sky had filmed over with a thin veil of clouds.

As they climbed through the rockery in the back garden and reached the house, Guy saw a long, drawn, face at a downstairs window. A moment later, Jamie came running out down the gravel path. Slowing as he reached them, he went up to his father and, without a word, wrapped his arms around him.

CHAPTER FIVE

Cambridge was already sloughing off its old skin. Taxis piled with trunks headed for the station and parental estate-cars lined the college entrances. Soon only a skeleton crew of zealous academics would remain to hold back the incursion of tourists and visitors. It made Lisa think of an orchestra hurrying unceremoniously away at the end of a concert while the last notes still lingered in the air, and it reminded her that this was no longer home.

She strolled through the city, wandering along the Backs, through ornamental gardens and across honey-coloured stone quads, finding remembrances of Guy at each turn: the place where they'd hired punts, the wall they'd climbed to crash a May ball, the hidden spot in a meadow where a sudden onrush of lust had overwhelmed them. As she stood on a bridge, staring into the green-brown river, she felt it was right to be leaving. What good were dead memories without the living person?

Back in her flat, she took down the Van Gogh poster and slowly rolled it up. She thought back to the previous summer and the small museum at Arles where they'd bought it. Her eye went to the photos wedged in the sides of the wardrobe mirror: Guy on a park bench, playing drunk; Guy pulling a ghoulish face close to the camera; Guy wearing a battered straw hat and reading Whitman to her with the sun squatting down over the hills of Provence behind. There was one of Jamie, too, wearing the bomber jacket she'd bought him the day he'd come up to

Cambridge. She slipped them hurriedly in among the note-books in her suitcase.

A sabbatical, he'd called it. Twelve months apart.

What had made her agree to such an idea?

It had seemed reasonable, almost an adventure, the way he'd put it to her over lunch two days before. Had the wine turned her head?

He'd taken both her hands in his and looked her full in the eyes. Lisa, darling, he'd said, you're only twenty-one, and a good deal less worldly than you appear. You've had a sheltered upbringing, first in suburban Surrey, now in cloistered Cambridge. You think you know what you want from life, but how can you tell without knowing what else the world has to offer? I'm your first love; you are my second. I've been married, I have a child, I know where I'm going. I want us to be together – God knows I do – but before you decide to settle down you should stretch your wings a bit, get more experience of other people, other life-styles, other circles . . .

'Sleep with other men, you mean?' she'd demanded.

No, he'd insisted, I don't mean we should test our love; we don't need that. Think of it more as a rite of passage, a voyage of discovery, so that when you return at the end you'll be absolutely clear in your heart and mind what you are choosing. All couples inevitably face a crisis at some time or other, however far down the line. Those that survive are the ones that can't be tempted by the unknown. It's a risk, yes. But we have to take it.

'How would we do it?' she'd asked.

We must not see each other, he'd replied. No phone calls, no letters. Total radio silence. And, I'm afraid, no holiday in Greece, either. It's hard but it's the best way. You've got your new job in London – it's the start of a career, for heaven's sake! – and Mac's said he'd take me back at Gorselands next term. I want to spend more time with Jamie; the boy needs me there. So, you see, now is the right moment.

He'd gone on like that and she'd found herself agreeing. More, by the end of lunch she was almost eager to get under way.

Then they'd returned to her flat and spent the afternoon making love. And that evening he'd left her.

Now she sat down on her bed and looked about her. It was hard to imagine she'd ever lived in this room. Clothes, books and ornaments had been packed up in cases and boxes. The carnation she'd worn for Finals was dead in a tumbler on the desk, and propped in the keys of the typewriter stood a sheaf of invitations to celebration parties now long past. Pin-holes and tape-marks betrayed where pictures and posters had once hung, and on the floor lay stacks of books, tied with string and looking strangely insignificant. Her own existence, once resonating from the walls and shelves, now seemed shrunken into a few suitcases and cartons.

She suddenly felt very lonely and confused.

But she had to be strong. She had to tell herself the principle was right, even if she didn't see the reasons so clearly any more. She was plagued with questions. Was she mistaking the real message? Was it Guy's way of saying he wanted *his* freedom? Or had he given up hope that things would work out between Jamie and her? She'd made him admit to having migraines: were the pills doing funny things to his mind? *Trust me*, he'd kept saying. People only resorted to faith and trust when reason failed, and hers was failing fast. Very well then: however hard and unreasonable it seemed, she'd stop asking for explanations and simply *trust*.

53

And she'd get her life together. That afternoon, she'd go round and say goodbye to her friends. If there was no-one she wanted to join on holiday, she'd go with her parents to Cornwall, and then in a few weeks' time she'd come up to London and look for a flat.

Altogether, it was a lame start to a grand voyage.

She took the photos back out of the suitcase and went slowly through them, one after another. A tear fell on one, making a bubble on the emulsion.

How *could* she have agreed to it? Guy, oh Guy, she cried silently to herself, why are you forcing me away? You're all I've ever wanted. What are you doing to us?

Every day after school until the end of term, Guy drove down to Gorselands to work on the cottage. Lisa had left Cambridge and he couldn't bear spending evenings there alone. Besides, he could never be sure how much time he had. Apart from the job of preparing himself mentally, there was so much practical work to be done to make the house ready.

Sandy's things had disappeared from the bedroom; he'd deliberately not mentioned anything about them to Jamie. When it came to working on the cottage, he couldn't make the boy out. At first he seemed reluctant to help. He stood on the sidelines, silent and watchful, while Guy arranged glaziers to fix the windows and builders to repair the roof. When he did lend a hand, he'd spend hours sandpapering a single window-frame, although if Guy tried to take the job over, he'd refuse to let him. He'd go round after the workmen, critically pointing out the defects, and yet when a team of boys were given the job of clearing the garden he insisted on supervising them himself and making sure that everything was done exactly to his specifications.

At the start, Guy thought it was just that, like many children, Jamie didn't like change and he'd now got used to living at his grandparents'. When he tried to talk it through, the boy simply clammed up.

His first understanding came one afternoon when they were choosing colour schemes. They were standing together on the upstairs landing. Guy had a sheaf of colour charts in his hand.

'A fresh start is what we need up here,' he said. 'I vote we have the bathroom blue.'

'Corny,' Jamie responded. 'I liked it when it was yellow.'

'But I thought we'd have the stairway yellow.'

'What's wrong with the beige?'

'It's always been beige. I'm sick of it.'

The boy turned his large, grave eyes on him.

'Dad, can I say something?'

'I know. You want the whole place that dreadful beige.'

'Dad, who's going to be seeing it?'

They stood for a moment in silence, holding each other's eye. Then Guy handed him the colour cards.

'Over to you, Jamie.'

The boy took the cards and laid them aside on a ledge. 'Let's have it how it was,' he said firmly, 'when Mum did it.'

Guy worked hard. He built cupboards and work-tops, ran a rail up the staircase and planned a special kitchen layout so that he could cook meals with his eyes shut. He fitted the sitting-room with shelves for his large record collection and lined the small study with book-cases to house the antiquarian books he'd inherited from his father and hitherto kept in storage. A blind man needing books? Yes, absolutely: books. He was going to make the place as normal as

55

any other home, for he was determined to live as normal a life as any other man.

The boys McVey sent along worked hard. There was Dunn with the asthmatic wheeze, Dixon with the breaking voice and Franklin with the stammer; Guy was already learning how he would have to recognize them. By the end of term, the wilderness around was cut back, flowerbeds were dug and a vegetable patch planted.

His term at the comprehensive ended and he packed up his flat in Cambridge. Jamie helped him load up a van he'd hired; he'd store the things in the McVeys' garage until the cottage was ready to move into. As he drove out of the city, he looked at the spires behind him in the rear-view mirror. This was goodbye to a decade of his life. Goodbye to those spires, too. He'd probably never see them again.

Lisa kept to their arrangement. She did not exchange a word or a note. He read in the papers that she'd been awarded a 2-1 degree and fought the temptation to send her congratulations. He had to force himself to remember that the separation was necessary and that he had to suffer the self-imposed pain in the hope that, starved of its fuel, their love would wither and die and, before long, she would find another to replace it.

He threw himself into the work on the cottage, meaning to silence his mind through exhausting his body. He saw few of his friends, for it was painful to be asked about Lisa and why they'd split up. More and more, he let the walls and woods of Gorselands become the perimeter of his world. But although activity busied his hands, it did not still his heart, and he was no stranger to the quiet cruelties of loneliness and doubt.

His migraines had now settled down to a regular

pattern; they struck every three or four days, usually at dawn. But as July slid into August, the guillotine had still not fallen. Perhaps the pills were containing it, after all?

During an August heat-wave, they moved in to the cottage and threw a small house-warming party.

The art mistress who lived nearby brought a small watercolour. The groundsman presented a kitchen clock. The McVeys, knowing better, gave a canteen of cutlery that had been in Alice's family for generations. And Kathy, the Mobility Officer who was training Guy to cope with his impending disablement, brought him something she told him to open later in private. It was a copy of *Brideshead Revisited*, in Braille.

Jamie had not allowed anyone to set foot in the house until it was finished. Now he proudly took the visitors on a guided tour. He'd rescued their old sofa from the McVeys' staff flat and put it back in its place in the sitting-room. The Russell Flint print once again hung over the fireplace, and on the mantelpiece stood the Peter Pan figurine Sandy had especially loved. Against the wall stood the old upright piano. And so it went on, from room to room.

Guy followed Alice back downstairs.

'Well,' he smiled, 'what do you think?'

She turned. Her plump cheeks were ashen.

'It's like stepping back,' she said.

CHAPTER SIX

Kathy Wilkes ran the rehabilitation centre at the local general hospital. Here, with one assistant, she trained old women with glaucomas and old men with detached retinas to cope with a life of partial sight. She re-taught them how to make tea, boil a kettle, even dress themselves. She gave them lessons in walking down the street, catching a bus, crossing the road and finding the correct money to pay for things. For many the effort was too great and they resigned themselves to a twilight of semi-mobility. But Guy was young, and the years that lay before him depended on how well he mastered blindcraft.

At first he disliked Kathy. She was tall and full-breasted, with a strong, mobile face framed by tumbling red hair. Her voice was deep and penetrating, her movements brisk and assured. He found it unnerving that she looked him straight in the eye, at the right focal length. Later he realized she did it to everyone, sighted or not. From the first moment, she seemed to have decided he was a challenge. Perhaps because he was close to her age – she was thirty-three – or perhaps because he still had his sight, she drove him harder than any of the others.

On Wednesday afternoons she'd take him to the nearby shopping centre. It amused him to imagine how they must look – one chunky, athletic young man wearing a pair of blackened goggles and tapping a white stick along the pavement, followed two yards behind by a commanding redhead calling out instructions.

'What do you do at the kerb? No, you do *not* rely on your ears! Step out now and you'll hit that cyclist . . .'

'Let him get out of my way!' he'd cry in exasperation.

'It's his road.'

'Who's got eyes? Can't he see this white stick?'

'That stick is your antenna, Guy, not your flag.'

There were other times when he'd trip up on a kerb and fall. People would stop to help him up. She'd intervene.

'Leave him, please! He doesn't need help.'

Once, to prove her point, she let a passer-by take him across the road and leave him on the pavement the other side. Suddenly he found he'd completely lost his bearings. He couldn't tell where the noise of the road was coming from and with nothing vertical to touch for reference he soon lost the sense of whether he was upright or tilting over. Gritting his teeth, he struck out and walked straight into a lamppost.

She meant well, but he wished she'd leave him to find his own way.

Yet she was right. Sight was by far the most important faculty. The eyes, she told him, sent the brain more than twice the information of all the other senses put together. It was true that most blind people had some residual sight; only one in seven was totally blind. But for them the impact was overwhelming, as it would be for Guy when his time came. Suddenly, and quite literally, he was going to find himself in the dark. He needed her, and he knew it.

What had he done wrong?

The boy clasped his hands together tighter still and searched the face of Christ for an answer. In the twilight, he could not discern the expression in the eyes that looked down at him from high in the stained glass window.

Every week for the past three years he'd come in secret to this chapel. He'd prayed with all his might. He'd begged for protection for his father. And for these three years he had been heard.

But now no more. God had suddenly withdrawn His grace. Hadn't he prayed hard enough? What had he done to fail him?

The Son of God returned his stare coldly. His half-smile was set grim and inflexible. The boy strained to grasp the message. Gradually he understood.

He'd been wrong; it was God's judgement that his father should be blind. That was why He had withdrawn from him. God's will be done.

Overnight, it seemed to Guy, Jamie's attitude changed and he began taking a positive interest in the practical preparations for the cottage. In the kitchen he built a special knife-rack so there'd be no danger of Guy cutting his fingers. He fitted springs to the overhead cupboards to make sure they kept shut. Kathy had suggested putting rubber bands on jars and bottles to distinguish jam from marmalade and whisky from gin. Jamie devised a better system using a Braille tape-puncher; he'd stick the tape to the glass and adjust it as the levels went down, so that Guy would always know roughly how much there was in a given bottle.

One evening Guy came back earlier than expected and found the boy wearing the goggles, feeling his way round the house. He was just testing how things were, he said, and seeing what else needed to be done.

'You're lucky to have a lad like that,' Kathy said when he told her. 'A wife couldn't be more help to you.'

*

Towards the end of August, Lisa, who was staying with a friend in London while looking for a flat for herself, called Patrick in Cambridge. He was spending the following day in London, and they arranged to meet at his apartment.

Patrick left the Department of Biochemistry early, to be in time to tidy up before she arrived. On the way he bought flowers.

He'd been brought up as a child in this small flat. It lay high up under the eaves of a large white-stuccoed mansion close to Regent's Park. Since his mother had retired to the country a few years before when his father had died, he'd used it as a pied-à-terre. He lived out of a suitcase for he had no desire to move back in properly. With an alcoholic father and no brothers or sisters, he'd suffered as the scapegoat in the family and his studies had become his escape. Intelligent and iconoclastic, he'd shocked the priests at the Catholic school where he went by exploding the Biblical miracles with scientific theories; he'd even come close to being expelled for his explanation of the Virgin Birth, but he stayed on to win the top biology scholarship to Cambridge. Each time he set foot in this flat, however, he was reminded of his bitter, lonely childhood. One day he'd get round to re-painting the walls, re-covering the sofa and getting rid of his mother's collection of Staffordshire figurines. He'd have persuaded her to sell the place long before if they'd been on speaking terms.

Lisa arrived late, flushed from the climb up the stairs. She wore a thin check shirt and loose cotton trousers, for the heat-wave still bore on. He showed her round the fussily-decorated rooms.

'It's convenient for work,' he said apologetically. 'And cheaper than a hotel.'

'Or renting,' she agreed. 'The prices down here are staggering.'

'Guy's doing the right thing, sticking in Cambridge.' He turned towards her. 'How is he?'

She looked away abruptly.

'I wouldn't know.'

'Oh? What about his . . . ?'

'He's gone back to teach at his old school.'

'What's happened?'

'Nothing we haven't made happen.'

'I see.'

'I don't expect you do.'

Puzzled, he went to the kitchen for a corkscrew. He brought the wine and glasses into the main room and led her over to the window. Over the rooftops and television aerials, the tip of Primrose Hill could just be seen; it was a spectacular view.

She was starting her job with BBC television in a few days and he asked her where she was going to live.

'I think I've found a place in Holland Park,' she replied.

'Look, I'm only here one day a week.'

She met his eye.

'It's very kind of you, but . . .'

'Kind?' He laughed. 'You haven't heard the rent yet! No, seriously. You can have the two rooms at the back and I'll fix up the bathroom . . .'

She gave a small, silvery laugh.

'Stop! You don't know me at all. I might have all kinds of anti-social habits.'

'I'm not proposing sharing the toothpaste. It's the obvious thing. What do you say?'

She shook him by the sleeve.

'You're very generous, Patrick, but it's crazy. Anyway, I need to live on my own for a bit.'

'Well, if ever you change your mind.' He heard the disappointment in his own tone and made an effort to brighten. 'Come on, your glass is empty.'

September broke the heat-wave. At Gorselands, the groundsman began marking out the playing-fields for soccer, and decorators set to work to seal the outdoor woodwork against the coming winter. While Guy filled the pot-holes in the old driveway leading from the cottage to the school, McVey worked late into the night drawing up the term's timetables and Alice, as housekeeper for eighty-odd boarders, checked her store-cupboards and linen chests and made up her stock lists.

Guy had a meeting with McVey to agree his own work schedule. The headmaster would only allow him to teach three hours a morning at the start, insisting he kept his afternoons free to attend the Rehab Centre. If he was to be effective as a teacher, he had to develop workable ways of taking lessons and correcting homework. He'd begin by taking French language and Geography, but if all went well, he could add other subjects and work up to having a form of his own. But for taking over when McVey retired, the question was not touched upon. That target had vanished out of sight.

During those weeks, Guy found Lisa constantly in his thoughts. He missed her painfully. Every day something would creep up on him unawares to remind him of her. He'd turn on the radio and her favourite Elgar would be playing. Going through the pockets of a jacket he'd find an old party invitation, or taking up a book he'd come upon a note of hers he'd slipped in as a bookmark. Some weeks before they parted, she'd given him a small bowl of *potpourri*, scented with her own perfume, which he kept in his bedroom where it tormented him by conjuring her up every time he passed. It stood as a daily test of strength, and he often failed the test. If he couldn't cope with that, how was he to handle what was coming?

Fifty yards down the old driveway from the cottage stood a majestic copper beech. Jamie had decided to build a tree-house in it.

He selected two thick boughs a good twenty feet above the ground, and together they built a platform out of planks taken from a derelict shed in the woods. The same shed provided corrugated-iron sheeting for the roof and even a window-frame, which Guy glazed with polythene sheeting. To the west, through the foliage, stretched a fine view over the school playing-fields and away to the far horizon. One evening when the light was failing and Jamie had already gone indoors, he roughly nailed the window-frame in position facing the view. The following morning when he went to help, he found the rope ladder drawn up, forbidding access. And, looking up, he saw that the window had been repositioned to the front.

Jamie spent the next couple of days working on his own. Guy understood and didn't interfere. Then he came down one morning and Jamie told him, with studied casualness, that it was finished.

'Do you want to have a look, Dad? Go ahead.'

He climbed up the rope ladder to a lower platform, where a fixed ladder took him to the tree-house itself. He looked around. Like the boy's bedroom, it was sparsely furnished. In one corner lay a mattress covered in an old car-rug. Boards mounted on bricks formed a low table. Old pillows from the dormitories served as floor-cushions, and by the door stood a camping stove.

There was only one chair and it was placed at the window. He sat down and looked out. It gave a direct line of sight onto the front of the cottage. Jamie was waving at him from the front step.

While Jamie spent the last week of the holidays mostly out of doors – fishing, he said – Guy set out to familiarize himself intimately with the route to the school and the school buildings themselves.

So much of it went by sound. On the concrete of the front path he could snick his metal heel-caps and steer by the resonance from the wooden fence that ran along one side. Thirty-eight paces further on, after the grass, there was a low brick wall from which he could get an echo by snapping his fingers. He was like a bat, operating on sonar. At the bottom of the drive, twenty strides across the gravel took him to the side of the building and a further fifteen to the main entrance.

Inside, he memorized the length of the corridors, the height of light switches, tables, window-sills and lockers, the smells associated with certain rooms, the number of steps in stairways. In the longer flights, he placed tacks on the underside of the bannisters towards the end, in case he lost count.

Finally, one day towards the beginning of term, he tested himself. Without making a single mistake he steered himself the whole route, to the school, round it and home. Back at the cottage, keeping his goggles on, he made himself a congratulatory cup of tea. Filling a teapot or cup was tricky – he had a small wire contraption that hooked over the lip and bleeped when the liquid rose to the top – but this time something went wrong and the teapot overflowed, scalding him with boiling water.

Slowly and deliberately, he took the goggles off and

laid them down on the hard tile floor. Raising his foot, he ground his heel down and went on crushing until the frame was in splinters and the glass pulverized.

He turned away. Squeezing his eyes shut, he began his counting. At one hundred, he went slowly along the corridor into the sitting-room and sat down at the piano. He settled his hands on a chord of C-sharp minor.

It had to be Beethoven. The slow movement of the 'Moonlight' sonata. He forced himself to play slowly and softly, controlling every note of the arpeggios with vicious restraint. Then abruptly, he stopped. He just couldn't go on.

As he looked up, he caught a fleeting glimpse of a face at the window. It was Jamie. The boy stood there, the other side of the glass. He'd been watching. His face was impassive and without expression. After a brief moment, he turned away and vanished. When he reappeared that evening he was full of tales about his day's fishing and made no mention of anything else.

Lisa had found a one-bed basement flat in Holland Park, close enough to the television studios in Wood Lane so that she could walk to work. There she joined in with all the enthusiasm she could muster. She volunteered for extra hours in the videotape department and took part in the canteen gossip with the best of them. But she felt somehow disconnected, as if separated by an invisible sheet from the rest of the world.

It was like a bereavement. At first she hadn't believed it. Then she'd felt rage and resentment, and now there was just a choking emptiness.

In the evenings she often played tennis. Exercise,

Patrick had told her, produced endorphins, the body's own morphine, and she hoped that would somehow counter her numbing pain. At weekends, she went home to her parents in Surrey.

Once a week on a Wednesday, when Patrick was up in town, they had supper together. She began to wonder if it had been Guy's deliberate plan to push her into his arms. To counterbalance this notion, she met up with other friends from Cambridge, too, and went to all the parties she could. She kept herself busy, and soon she was no longer relying on Valium to help her sleep.

One day she looked around her flat at her posters and records, her clothes and shoes, and suddenly she felt their life had ebbed away. They were a skin she'd shed and left lying there, dead and loathsome to the touch. That Saturday she went shopping. She bought a proper bed and a new sofa, a new hi-fi set and a dozen records, a pair of crazy spike-heel shoes and a chic-punk leather jacket. She had her hair streaked, she bought a book on cocktails and for a full week she decided she'd say Yes to any proposition.

But it wasn't quite the same.

Guy had a sense of things impending. He couldn't put his finger on any specific sign, he merely had a feeling that some dark creature within him was stirring from its slumber, some cauldron rising to the boil.

One night, a wind brought down the bole of an elm, long dead and stripped of its bark and upper branches. It fell across the driveway between the cottage and the school. In the morning he and Jamie went to inspect it. It lay like a dead elephant eaten from inside by worm and beetle, its trunk splintered in a thousand fractures.

Jamie grubbed around the rotten pithy core with a stick. But what struck Guy was that in all the perches and hollows there was not a single bird's nest. Then he recalled what the groundsman had said.

'That there tree will be down before the season's up,' he'd prophesied. 'The birds know. They ain't nesting, see.'

The birds could tell when disaster was impending. And now, in just the same intangible way, Guy knew that his time was imminent.

That evening, while Guy was playing the piano in the sitting-room, he had another attack. It came out of the blue, breaking the pattern. The scotoma lasted a full hour and the minor effects lingered on until he went to bed. He increased the dose of Pizotifen still further and managed to get through the night without another until dawn, when he had the worst one he'd known.

In the morning, he called Dr Berriman. Could he fit him in that day? He'd catch a train to London right away. The neurologist offered to see him at two o'clock.

His vision was still corrupted around the edges when he arrived at Harley Street. Berriman checked the back of his head with a stethoscope again and immediately performed another CAT-scan, this time injecting a radio-opaque iodine contrast as a marker. Guy waited in an ante-room until the results came through. Then the doctor brought him in and sat him down in the leather chair, drawing up another for himself. He had the scans in his hand.

He'd had a very heavy bleed during the night, he said. The extravasated blood had been contained, but the angioma was spreading. The process had begun. There was nothing to be done except wait for the inevitable. An operation was too risky; he might end up paralysed as well as blind. There was also the danger that he might not survive at all.

'How long do I have?' Guy asked numbly.

'I can't give you a precise answer.'

'Are we talking weeks?' he demanded. 'Or months?'

Dr Berriman consulted the scans.

'I can't say.'

'*Days?*'

'Hours,' was the reply. 'At the present rate, I'd give you forty-eight hours. Possibly a little more.'

In two days, possibly three, he would be blind. Completely and irrevocably.

CHAPTER SEVEN

That morning Guy watched the dawn rise.

Sitting on a five-bar gate at the edge of the woods and huddled into a duffel-coat against the chill, he stretched his gaze across the wide rolling countryside to where the sky was lightening. Lead gave way to steel, which in turn paled into silver, and gradually the red underlining the tissue of cloud resolved to a soft pink. Then, quite suddenly, heralded by spokes of lemon gold, the rim of the sun appeared above the horizon. It rose fast, changing shape, until it emerged clear of the land, a perfect yellow sphere, and began its ascent into the pale blue sky.

He shut his eyes. A bright cobalt disc lingered as an after-image on the back of his eyelids. Soon that would be the only sun he'd have.

He walked slowly through the grounds. The air was sharp and mist rose like dry ice off the playing fields. Dew etched in silverpoint a million tiny cobwebs on the lawns, and high in the sky the swallows were already feeding.

Today was Friday, and the winter term started on Sunday. Today he could see, and on Sunday he'd be blind.

He turned his steps back towards the cottage and let himself in.

Jamie had coffee ready in the percolator. He followed him with his big, serious eyes as he poured a mug and sat down.

'It's bad, isn't it?' he asked quietly.

'The worst.'

The boy put his hand on his father's shoulder.

'Well, we're ready for it,' he said.

He patted the hand.

'Yes, Jamie. Thank you.'

Guy spent that day going over the school grounds. He went to the river and tracked it back to the pond by the rhododendron shrubbery. He picked up a bird's feather and stared at it for minutes. He examined a snail on a cabbage leaf. A frail butterfly, the tenderest blue. Oak leaves, blotched and rusty, luminescent in the sunlight.

Remember these, he told himself.

He wandered around the school building, the gym and the tennis-court, the out-sheds and the playground. By the swimming-pool he came upon McVey, discussing the new changing-rooms with a carpenter.

He stared into the water. A light wind briefly crazed the surface, then vanished, leaving only winking, dazzling ripples. He felt a sudden dizziness and his mind flashed back to that time by the river . . . the image of a train crashing . . . and he heard Patrick saying, *the day you switch on your telly and get tomorrow's news, you'll have the men in white coats coming for you.* He looked quickly away. Was he losing his sanity?

McVey saw him and came over. As he approached, Guy scrutinized his deep-set, pale blue eyes, his gaunt, apple-red cheeks, his silver, gorse-like hair. Remember this, the voice whispered again.

'Mac,' he said, 'I'll be away tomorrow. Could Jamie come up to you for the day? Would Alice mind?'

The headmaster frowned with concern.

'Of course not. Is everything all right?'

'Fine, fine. Just a few last-minute things to do.'

*

That evening, he walked to the other boundary of the school grounds and watched the sun set.

For a while, the after-glow hung like a backdrop until it slowly furled itself away down behind the sky-line. Above him, a crescent moon shone a degree brighter. As the sky grew darker, he spotted the Pole star and found the Plough. For a while he stared into the infinity of the Milky Way. A meteor briefly flashed across his view, and was gone.

Turning back through the dark woods, he felt the sting of panic. There was too much to see, too much of beauty and wonder to experience, even for the first time, let alone for the last.

That night he didn't go to bed. He sat up, playing old movies on the video in the study: *Some Like It Hot*, the Marx Brothers, the whole of a David Attenborough wildlife series. He didn't touch his record collection; he'd soon have all the time for music he wanted. When the first light of dawn filtered in through the small windows, he switched off the set and went for a walk.

When he returned, Jamie was up, with a hot bath run and bacon and eggs on the stove. He bathed and ate breakfast and by nine a taxi had arrived to take him to the station.

As he was about to leave, he had a second thought.

'Want to come, too?'

The boy shook his head.

'You be alone, Dad. See you tonight.'

Not wanting to waste time in the Underground, he took a cab from Liverpool Street station to the Zoo in Regent's Park.

There he saw birds of paradise with scarlet and blue plumage and quick-blinking eyes. He saw dustymaned lions, nonchalantly copulating. He saw snakes striped green and black and basking among their moultings, and tropical fish that darted in dazzling fluorescent flashes of blue and green.

In the reptile house he watched a small girl staring at a crocodile. Her face was alive with a blend of curiosity and repulsion. The animal suddenly yawned, baring double rows of razor teeth. She drew back in terror, then inched forward again, won over by fascination.

A desperate panic seized him. He wanted, just once, for his last time, to see with eyes as fresh as that child's. He wanted to learn everything all over again, to start the grammar of sight from the beginning.

He strolled through the park. Looking up, he could see sunlight shafting through the branches. The yellowing leaves shone as though the light came from within them. Above, tall white clouds sailed through a perfect blue sky.

He took a taxi to the Tate, to see the Turner collection.

He stood before a painting of a storm, letting the ferocity of the colours and brushwork draw him into the living landscape until he imagined he could hear the wind raging and feel the lash of the rain.

He took a step closer and examined the surface of the painting. In parts, the surface was an impasto of yellows, crimsons and charcoal greys, thrown on as if at random and worked by finger, brush and rag into an effect that was completely truthful, not because of any literal detail but because the impression had captured the essence. Turner could almost have been blind, just as Beethoven was deaf, for he was painting what his *mind* saw.

Would his memory for visual details fade, and was this how he'd see things then? Would he picture storms and stills, landscapes and lakes, people he knew and people he loved, not as photographic likenesses but as the essences of what they were?

Lisa for example.

He turned away abruptly, in a swelter. Bloody stupid question! Who'd ever exchange an actual rose for the concept of one?

Then to the Victoria and Albert museum, to look at illuminated manuscripts and the collection of miniature portraits.

To Kensington Gardens, to see the small bronze statue of Peter Pan, the original of theirs at home, and to watch the children playing with boats on the pond.

To Knightsbridge, where he stared at the flowers in a shop and wondered at the complex beauty of their stamens and pistils – sex organs, as Lisa once bluntly reminded him.

Then to Westminster Pier, to catch a pleasure-boat up to Battersea Park, passing on the right the Houses of Parliament with their lace stonework and, on the left, the great power station with its four Titanic funnels. Gulls followed in their wake, swooping now and then to the water, and on the moss-streaked embankment strollers watched the boat forging up the river and occasionally returned a wave.

Then he walked slowly through the London streets, staring into strangers' faces in the twilight, all the way to Holland Park.

No light showed in the windows of Lisa's basement flat and there was no reply to his ring. He checked the address her mother had given him when he'd phoned the previous day. It was the right place. Half past eight on a Saturday night: could he really have expected her to be home? Hope had over-ridden commonsense.

He sat on the wooden steps and waited. Each time he heard footsteps on the pavement above or a taxi pulling up in the street, his heart quickened a beat, but none brought Lisa.

Half an hour lengthened into an hour. He went back up the steps and leant against the railings. The foliage of the tall gravid chestnuts in the gardens opposite stood out in black silhouette against the glowering city sky, and in the main road beyond he watched the car headlights passing in an endless stream beneath the neon shop-signs.

His digital watch peeped the half hour. Nine-thirty. He couldn't wait any longer. He tore the cover off his cheque-book and began writing a note, but half way through he crumpled it up into his pocket.

Perhaps it was better that way.

Stepping out into the street he hailed a passing cab, climbed in and drove off without a backward glance.

Jamie was asleep when he finally arrived home. He climbed the stairs silently and went into his room.

The bedside light was on and a book lay open on the boy's chest. For a moment, Guy just stood there, transfixed by the beauty and peace of his sleeping face. Bending over him, he left an imperceptible kiss on his forehead, then, turning out the light, backed quietly away and slipped across the landing to his own room.

On Sunday morning the first boarders began to arrive. Estate-cars .olled up the gravel drive like hearses, delivering their cargoes of small boys into the hands of Matron and Alice McVey. The air was full of sharp cries of farewell and the brisk slamming of car doors, while in the dormitories there were the first tears and, among the older boys, tussles over possession of the best beds and lockers.

Guy was exhausted. He'd barely slept all night, rising once again at dawn and prowling the grounds, leaving footprints in the dewy grass and stirring up the low-lying autumnal mists. He paused in the woods, storing the memories, to watch a blackbird dart away angrily at his approach or a squirrel vault between branches and scamper out of view behind a bough.

The waiting was oppressive. When would the blow fall? And how? Had Berriman miscalculated, or was he already on borrowed time? The day passed agonizingly slowly. Perhaps it would come with the nightfall and his light would die with the dying of the day.

At six, the bell tolled for beginning-of-term prayers in the small chapel adjoining the assembly hall. Guy sat down at the back, in the staff pew. Boys in white surplices – among them, Jamie – sang psalms, the congregation knelt in prayer or rose in praise, and as the last hymn rang out, a beam of sunlight shone in directly upon the stained glass halo of Christ at the Last Supper.

Afterwards, he joined the other staff in the common-room for a pre-term sherry. He did not stay long, but left taking several books for his first class the following morning.

The trees resounded with the evensong of birds and the air was rich with the damp mulch of fallen leaves. His heart was light. He had no particular sense of foreboding as he turned the corner and the cottage came into view. Nor did any inner voice prompt him of danger as he continued forward, hugging the books under his arm. A kind of levity had taken hold of him, that feeling of dangerous happiness he should have recognized.

He was twenty yards from home when it struck.

A hammer pounded inside his head. Pain stabbed at the roots of his eyes. A sudden dizziness swung him off balance. The path lurched up towards him, and above his head the trees revolved sickeningly.

He staggered. His hands flew to his temples. The books fell. Inside his skull the swelling grew to a volcano and the roots of his eyes turned to burning pitch.

He sank to his knees and toppled forwards. He could smell leaf-mould and taste earth. He rolled onto his side. Between his fingers, the trees stood out stark against the sky. Their foliage was blackening. The sky was turning to lead and the trees merging with the bushes into a single lifeless monotone.

He crawled a step forward. His hand reached out towards the cottage. There, at his bedroom window, stood Jamie, watching. His face was empty of expression. Already the dull red curtain was drawing itself in from the edges, blotting out trees and roof and walls and drowning everything in an ever-growing pool of darkness, like the iris of a camera being slowly closed, until all he could see was the boy's face in the centre, forever diminishing, and then, quite suddenly . . . nothing.

II

WINTER

LEAR: No eyes in your head? . . .
  yet you see how this world goes.
GLOUCESTER: I see it feelingly.

SHAKESPEARE,
King Lear

CHAPTER EIGHT

It is high summer. The sun is so hot it looks violet. Sandy is lying on a rug. She reaches out and draws him down beside her. The meadow grasses enclose them. He leans forward to kiss her. Gradually her face changes into Lisa's . . .

The alarm went.

No, dear God, no. Give me a while longer in the light.

The alarm went on ringing. He was drowning in darkness. The sightless world was reclaiming him.

He lay frozen rigid, not daring to reach out and turn it off, as the sudden, horrific sensation struck him that he didn't know *where his body began and ended!* Maybe his arm was no more than a stub on his shoulder, or it might at any moment punch through the window-pane. Two months had passed and he was still stricken by this waking terror.

A thousand and one, a thousand and two . . .

As he recited his rosary of numbers, he tried to piece himself together. He drew up his foot and squeezed it. Yes, it was still there, an arm-stretch away. But what *was* an arm-stretch?

Before, when dressing, shaving, eating, drinking, walking, driving or doing anything else, he'd always been able to see his own arms and legs and any number of things to measure his size against. But now he had no proof of his scale or shape, except by touch. No mirror could reassure him he even had a face. His feet only existed when he kicked something.

He thought back to how Jamie, unaware as any

newborn baby that he was distinct from the world about him, gradually learnt by sight and touch that he was separate in a world of separate things. That was how it was for himself now: cut down to infant size, each morning he had to undergo the whole of an infant's struggle and put together the body image that had dissipated during the night.

A thousand and fifty, a thousand and fifty-one . . .

Nearly there, nearly re-established. At sixty, he opened his eyes. Just the familiar dark red blur. He felt the clock. Seven fifteen. Another five minutes before he'd wake Jamie. Five minutes to come to terms with it all over again.

None of his preparations had made him ready for the real thing.

First there was suffocating claustrophobia. He lived in a cube, six foot by six. Its height was marked by door-frames and overhanging branches that clipped him on the forehead, and its width and length were defined by the field he swept ahead of him with his hand or his stick. Skyscrapers and trees might tower above him and fields stretch into the far distance, but they formed no part of his perspective. He was confined to a six-foot fish-bowl.

Scale was one problem. Orientation was quite another.

He had, literally, to keep level-headed or he'd end up leaning or tilting and not even know it. Every few moments he had to touch something horizontal or vertical for reference – the edge of a table, the flat of a wall – and so re-establish his inner horizon. Even so he'd be suddenly seized with an attack of dizziness and then he'd have to stand very still and, by mapping the sounds about him, try and rebuild a picture of where he was. Or that was the theory. In reality, he froze in a blue funk. He'd stand there, paralysed, unable to set a foot forward. If he stepped forward, he might fall off the edge of the world – he might even fall *upwards*.

Had it not been for Jamie . . . But there was no way out. He just bloody well had to get on with it.

Right, he muttered, here goes.

He swung his legs out of bed and stood up. Positioning himself by the edge of the mattress, he reached for his dressing-gown and struck out across the room to the window. Light gusts of rain spattered the panes, bringing the smell of dank, November mulchiness.

It was a new day, and, by God, he was going to make it great.

Jamie scraped his chair as Guy came into the kitchen, a small signal to indicate he was already in the room. Guy trailed his hand along the edge of the table until he found the back of his chair and sat down. He reached for the cornflakes packet. It was, as it should be, centre-left of the table, between the marmalade and the milk-jug.

'Sleep all right?' asked Jamie.

'Yes, fine, thanks. When did you get up?'

'I've been up for ages. I found some mushrooms in the far field. I thought you might like some for breakfast. You fry them, don't you?'

'That'd be great, Jamie. Do you want me to do them?'

'No, honest, Dad, that's all right. I can manage.' His chair scraped again and the cupboard squeaked a little as he took out the pan. 'That was the good news,' he added as he switched on the hob. 'Do you want to hear about the electricity bill?'

'Tell me the worst.'

'Eighty-two pounds. That's a lot, isn't it?'

'Does it say *E*? That means it's estimated. You'll have to read the meter this evening. Did you do your history homework?'

Butter sputtered in the pan.

'Yes, Dad, of course I did. And there's some Christmas cards from the Foot and Mouth Artists.' The tone of the boy's voice changed. 'I thought that's what cows got.'

'People who paint with their feet and mouth, idiot.'

'Paint footprints, you mean?'

Guy laughed.

'We'll give them a fiver and send the cards back. You don't want to overdo those mushrooms, you know. Takes all the taste away.'

'Oh, all right. Do you think they'll be done?'

'Probably. Spoon them out for me up there, and then you can read me your homework.'

'History is stupid,' Jamie muttered. 'Why can't I just do chemistry?'

Guy was aware of an awkward moment when Jamie put knife and fork in his left hand and guided his right to the plate, and a moment later he felt his son's hand light briefly on his shoulder as he passed him on the way to the table.

As Jamie read, Guy stood at the work surface and ate. To the left stood the kettle and the tins – square for tea, round for coffee – then the toaster and, beside it, the bread-bin, with sliced bread for convenience. Further on lay the chopping-board and the nest of knives Jamie had built, and finally the cooker – electric, not gas, for there could be no naked flame in the house. When Guy had finished the mushrooms he put the bread in the toaster. Reaching into the fridge beyond the cooker, he took out the butter-dish from the right side of the second shelf. He could tell by its weight it was nearly empty and he felt around in the upper compartment for a new slab.

'Let me, Dad,' Jamie broke in.

'No, you carry on.'

He cut the slab in two, then returned the other half to the fridge and put the knife in the washing-up bowl. Things left lying around caused spills and cuts. He carried the hot toast to the table and, propping it against the milk jug, sat down and reached out to two o'clock for his cup of tea. It was always a cup, never a mug, for in spite of the bleeper he often overfilled it. He spread butter and marmalade on the toast as best he could, then cut it diagonally in half; it was easier to angle into his mouth that way.

Now and then he interrupted Jamie to correct a point, but he didn't press it. The boy's bent was towards the sciences.

Finally Jamie snapped his exercise book shut.

'Ten out of ten,' he announced ironically.

Guy laughed.

'For originality, yes. Try and stick to interpreting the facts, not inventing them.'

'It's all relative, Dad. My facts aren't your facts. So Mr Reece was saying.'

'But there are some facts which are everybody's. And Columbus sailing on the *Mayflower* isn't one of them.'

'I don't care. Anyway, it's ten past. Shouldn't we be thinking of going?'

As he cleared the plates into the sink where the cleaning lady would wash them up later in the morning, he heard Jamie putting out the milk bottles, just as Sandy used to do at that time. It was almost as if nothing at all had changed in the past three or four years.

He packed his briefcase in his study and called to Jamie to hurry or they'd be late.

*

After Guy had collapsed unconscious outside the cottage, now two months ago, Jamie had rushed to fetch Alice. In turn, she had called an ambulance. He'd prepared for that moment, and the hospital was expecting him. He was kept in for a week, under close observation in case the bleeding spread. It did not, and apart from a few weeks of slurred speech and shaky balance, the only lasting damage was to his sight.

During that week, Alice brought Jamie up to the main house to stay. She remembered how he'd gone into hiding in the woods after his mother Sandy had died and she was determined to keep a close watch on him now. Some nights, she discovered, he sneaked down to the cottage to sleep, creeping back before breakfast, but she felt it wiser not to say anything in case it provoked him. She couldn't predict what he might do, for his reaction to the present crisis puzzled her deeply.

The day after Guy had been taken to hospital, for instance, she'd gone to the school chapel to change the flowers and she noticed a small sheaf of corn, carefully tied with a ribbon and laid at the side of the altar. She knew right away where it had come from – there was only one field of corn on the estate. And she knew who had put it there. But why? At first glance it could have been mistaken for a thanksgiving offering.

Jamie spent every available minute of that week down at the cottage, preparing for his father's return. He meticulously labelled the records with Braille punched tape, made inventories of the household provisions and drew up lists of his own daily duties. If she hadn't know how much he genuinely loved his father, she'd have thought he somehow welcomed the tragedy.

And so, after a week, Guy returned home, a blind man.

The first month was like nothing he'd ever imagined. He fell into a profound depression. No amount of pills could alleviate it. Kathy had warned him, but it was far worse than he could have conceived. Constantly he found himself beleaguered by thoughts of Lisa. He felt her loss more piercingly than ever before. Knowing he could never see her again even if he wanted to filled him with anguish. He ached with hunger for her.

He turned to Jamie for consolation. He found the boy ready, attentive, caring. He grew to rely on him, so much so that at times he had an uncomfortable feeling that he was slipping into the role of the child, with Jamie the parent. But for all Jamie could help in the practicalities of daily life, he couldn't offer support to a man trying to rebuild his shattered life and regain his sense of purpose. What boy of eleven could? What adult, even? Kathy tried: she came round and alternately comforted and chivvied him, but her well-meant therapy was redundant. Only one person had what he needed. Lisa. And the bitterest pill of all was that he'd deliberately denied himself her help.

Lisa jumped out of bed. She'd set her alarm purposely late so that she couldn't linger in bed, thinking.

Though several months had now passed, she still had to fight off the attacks of pain and puzzlement. While the rest of the country was counting shopping days to Christmas, she was counting days to the six-month point of their sabbatical, after which she'd be on the home stretch. There were times, most of all when something funny or beautiful caught her attention, when she wanted so badly to share it with him that she completely lost sight of what on earth they were doing apart. The whole point of the exercise lost its shape and slipped through her fingers, leaving her with nothing to grip onto. Over and over again she replayed that fateful lunch in her mind until she was no longer sure what really had been agreed. For every reason she imagined she remembered, she found twenty reasons against. She quarrelled and argued with him, only to be met by silence, so that she could never be sure if she was far from the mark or which of all the accounts she gave herself, if any, was the true one.

Some nights, when she couldn't face another vapid drinks party or listen to another friend asking after him, she'd stay at home. She'd make herself a meal, telling herself she had to eat, but her stomach would tighten up and refuse the food. She'd drink vodka like medicine. She'd watch television but make nothing of what the faces were mouthing. She'd switch channels and find it was football, Guy's sport, and turn it quickly off.

At other times, though, especially after a hard day's work or a game of tennis, she felt easier. The issue was on hold. Guy was solid, reliable, secure. He'd be there when she came back. And she would.

That day, as she washed and dressed, she went through the whole gamut of her feelings, and by the time she'd put on her pale blue baseball sweater and purple cotton jacket and dabbed a touch of make-up on her face, her mood had swung round to the opposite extreme. She was damned if she'd let it get her down; she had a life to live. It was Wednesday, too, and she was seeing Patrick for supper as usual, and Martin, the editor of a weekly science programme, had invited her to lunch at his home over the weekend. She really couldn't trust her moods.

It was a fine, frosty morning, too. The city was on the move and the crisp air was rich with promise. Locking her front door, she ran quickly up the steps to the street and hurried off towards Television Centre. She was her own person, and she had only to set her mind to it and she could take the lid off the world.

By the evening, Guy was exhausted. Separating the sounds that counted from the myriad that didn't called for incredible mental effort. He was worn out feeling for surfaces and reference-points and translating them into pictures of the world about him. He was only being given the sound-track and he had to invent the film. His inner eyes were tired out from the strain of imagining.

He sat in the kitchen in his old farmhouse chair, a glass of whisky in his hand. It would already be dark: the boy had gone out to the woods to watch badgers.

He sat back and tried to relax. He didn't even have the energy for the piano. The whisky was too strong; he could never get the mix quite right.

After a while he heard footsteps up the front path. It was Hobbs, with the homework. He knew the boy's step, for he had a built-up shoe. The steps came round the side to the kitchen at the back. There was a tap on the door.

'Come in, Hobbs.'

'Evening, sir.'

The boy let himself in and wiped his feet on the mat.

'Clear a space on the table. Something to drink?'

'Wouldn't mind a biscuit, sir.'

'There's some of Mrs McVey's pie still in the oven. Help yourself. How was the grub tonight?'

The boy put a pile of exercise books on the table.

'Dumplings and syrup for pudding. I think Cook has lost her memory, sir.'

'What's the word for that?'

'Am-something.'

'Amnesia. From the Greek. The "mnesia" bit means memory, the "a" means not. Like a-theist and a-gnostic.'

'A-mazingly a-trocious, too.'

The boy scoffed the remains of the pie, then sat down at the other end of the table and began reading out the homework which Guy's form had written during the quiet hour before supper. In theory, they took it in turns to bring it over, but it was invariably Hobbs who came. This unlucky weakling, the runt of a litter of lusty elder brothers, had to endure teasing and torment from the others. Since Guy had put a stop to that, the boy showed his gratitude by fierce loyalty. Guy remembered him as a small lad, with dark hair and moles on his face, but now he was a composite of shuffles and wheezes, a reedy high voice, a thin bony shoulder and faint oil of cloves smell.

'This is Jeffries, sir.'

'Okay,' said Guy wearily. 'Let's hear it.'

'"Depressions. Most cyclones in middle latitudes develop on the polar front where warm air meets cold air. See diagram."'

'Has he got the bobbles and spikes right?'

'I think so, sir. "The cold front overtakes the warm front and then lifts the warm air right off the ground, resulting in a collision."'

'*Occlusion*, the dimwit.'

It was a laborious process. The marking never took less than an hour, but it was the only way.

'"Root crops,"' the boy went on. '"Potatoes were first grown in South America. They were brought over to Europe by the Spanish explorers. They take a long time to grow but they yield more food per acre than any other serial."'

'Cereal with an "s"? Red mark. Too much *Dallas*. On.'

They'd just finished and Hobbs was putting a kettle on for tea when Jamie's footsteps came up the front path and hurried round the back. He burst in, letting a draught of cold, damp air in after him.

'Jeepers, it's cold out there.' Then his voice dulled. 'Hello, Hobbs. You still here?'

'Just going,' replied the boy apologetically. 'We've finished.'

'Good,' said Jamie and disappeared upstairs.

'Okay, Hobbs,' said Guy. 'It's probably time you hopped it. Thanks for your help.'

'See you tomorrow, sir.'

The boy gathered up the exercise books and left. A moment later, Jamie's footsteps came down the corridor.

'Jamie, try and be more decent to that lad, will you?' called Guy.

'We don't need him here, Dad,' the boy replied as he came back in. 'I'll make the tea.'

Jamie had gone to bed. Guy sat listening to a Sibelius symphony with his eyes closed, letting the vast Nordic landscape wash over him and soothe his aching brain. Towards midnight, he rose, turned off the music and went to the kitchen. There he bolted the back door and, running a hand over the cooker plates to see nothing was on, went round the rest of the house making sure the windows were shut and the lights off. He moved around with complete confidence, for every table and chair had its proper place from which it was never allowed to be moved.

Trailing one hand on the bannister, he plodded upstairs, counting the fourteen steps automatically. Ahead on the landing lay a small room Jamie used as his den; Guy never went into it, for the boy was allowed to make all the mess he liked there. On the other side of the bathroom was a small box-room, while at the front of the cottage lay Jamie's bedroom and, opposite, his own.

The faint smell of warm plastic in Jamie's room told him the bedside light was on, and he went over and turned it off. The boy didn't stir, but lay quite still with the sheets drawn high up.

'Sleep tight,' Guy whispered.

At the door he paused, listening for the rise and fall of sleepy breathing, but there was no sound. Suddenly he had the clear impression that the boy was wide awake and watching him.

CHAPTER NINE

Patrick took the stairs two at a time. The Department elevator was too slow for him, especially in his present mood. He felt elated; he'd just received the results of the autopsy on Wain, the black and white cat, which had died two days earlier. Her death was a tragedy in one way but a triumph in another: it proved that the growth hormone had worked! Only it had worked too well. Axons had grown uncontrollably in all directions, causing a tumour on her brain. Still, it showed he was on the right path.

He felt good for another reason, too. He'd phoned Lisa and they were meeting again for supper in London that evening. Reaching his floor, he swung open the fire doors and came face to face with Oliver Brock, his professor. The man beamed at him.

'Ah, Patrick!' he exclaimed. 'Can you spare a moment?'

Oliver led the way into his office. He was a short man with bristly white hair and the habit of constantly picking fluff off his jacket. His pale blue eyes were magnified by thick glasses and he had a dry, acerbic manner. He treated Patrick more critically than others in his department because he expected more of him. In turn, Patrick never wanted to let him down. In some ways he was the father he wished he'd had.

The professor's office was furnished like a consulting room, and even on that dull December morning the green venetian blinds were half closed. A bust of Wagner and a Victorian homily on work woven in needlepoint stood out among the clutter of books and periodicals. He went round the other side of the desk, a sign that this was a formal chat.

'I see we've had another death in the family,' he remarked.

'Yes, uh, the receptors aren't binding properly. I'm getting them to re-work the substrate in London.'

'And it seemed so promising.'

'It is. You saw the tissue slices. One couldn't have expected such a massive rate of RNA synthesis.'

'Science is all about expecting the unexpected. Who said that?'

'You did, Oliver.'

With a faint smile, Oliver pulled out a sheaf of computer print-out. The two men exchanged a knowing glance. These were the departmental accounts, and they both knew he'd been overspending his budget.

'I don't need to remind you,' said the professor quietly, 'the funding review board meets in the New Year. I can't juggle the figures much longer. I can get you more money, but I've got to have results to show.'

Patrick tapped his forehead. Somewhere inside there, among ten thousand million neurones with all their billions of connections, there had to be the answer.

'It's all in here,' he said.

In reply, Oliver tapped the print-out.

'Just get it all in *here*.'

'You'll have it. Give me time.'

The man raised his eyebrows and fixed him with a wry stare.

'You said that before, Patrick. A while ago.'

Screw it, he said to himself as he drove to London that afternoon. Look how far he *had* got in the time. He'd bridged the gap between amphibian and mammal.

94

He'd shown that the same hormone processes that regenerated the axons in a frog's optic nerve could generate new axons in a cat's mid-brain. The only trouble was the growth had gone out of control. Axons had sprouted so thickly in every direction that a tumour developed. He'd got the principle right but the biochemistry wrong.

And now, lying in a small cryostat on the floor of the car and kept frozen in liquid nitrogen, were some twenty slices of Wain's mid-brain. He'd see if the boys in London could re-engineer the molecular structure of the hormone so that it bound differently to the cell membrane. If that could be done, he had his breakthrough.

'The nose or the newt,' said Patrick into his wine over supper that evening. 'That is the question.'

Lisa had never seen him like this. His clockwork had run down; his hands were still and his face set hard and without expression.

'You going to stun me with the answer?'

He frowned, took a breath, thought twice, then launched off on another tack. 'It's like this. If you cut yourself, you heal. The skin cells regenerate. That's true of every organ in your body except the brain. When a brain cell dies, it's dead for ever. Luckily, we've got billions more than we need. But they've got to be encouraged to connect up again. Question: how do you get these new axons to form?'

'Always questions, never answers. Very Socratic.'

A brief smile flitted across his face, then vanished.

'You see, amphibians like frogs and newts can regenerate their central nervous system. Cut the optic nerve behind a frog's eye and it'll grow back, even if you put obstacles in the way. Someone once did the same with a salamander but twisted the eyeball a

95

hundred and eighty degrees; whenever it saw a fly, it darted in the wrong direction. This shows that each cell has its proper address, if you like, and the nerve routes between them recognize this. Destroy one of the two cells of a frog embryo after the first division and you'll end up with half a tadpole. You know that every cell contains the DNA blueprint for the whole body; it may only use a small fraction of the information for itself, but something has to tell it *which* cell it is. You'd look pretty funny with fingers on your chin. Each is like an envelope with its own address. Cancer is a breakdown of the postal system.'

'I'm glad we didn't go for the frog's legs,' she muttered.

'With cats and humans,' he went on, 'there's one big difference. Our central nervous system *doesn't* regenerate. Sever your spinal nerves and you'll be paralysed. A paraplegic is a paraplegic for ever. The only exception is the nose. The olfactory fibres regenerate every ten days or so and find their connections all over again.'

'My money was on the nose.'

He smiled.

'Well, of course, I isolated the hormone responsible for making the axons re-connect in a frog and tried it in a mammal. First on a rat tissue, then in a isolated-brain cat . . .'

'Patrick, I think I've had enough gory details.'

'Sorry, but listen: it worked! But growth has got to be regulated. It would be no good if a child never stopped growing. That's done by a trophic hormone, and the cat's brain, being an adult brain, simply couldn't produce it. You want to know what I did next?'

'Surprise me.'

He poured the wine, savouring the suspense.

96

'Did you know that you were born with almost your full total of brain cells? Your brain is only bigger now because of all the *connections* between them. They are the result of your life, your experience in the world. Roughly speaking, heredity determines the cells you have, environment how they're connected. In fact, in the first year of birth, the brain size trebles! If that happened in the womb, your head would simply be too big to get down the birth canal, and it's already big enough. So, in the foetus, growth is suppressed. What I'm now doing is trying to find the molecule that fits both the growth hormone of the adult frog *and* the suppressor hormone of the mammal foetus. Once I know its biochemistry, I'll be able to synthesize it, and bingo!'

She turned away.

'God, Patrick. The things you do for science.'

'Don't be priggish. Just think: if it works, paraplegics might one day get out of their chairs and walk.'

'One day,' she echoed. 'And what about the suffering in the meantime to defenceless animals? Poking around in their brains . . .'

He looked hard at her. His dark eyes burned into hers.

'The brain is beautiful, Lisa. It's the most perfect work of art you could dream of. A miracle, like the heavens. I'm not poking around for the hell of it. If I didn't believe it could help make life better on this planet, I wouldn't be doing it.'

'What I like about you,' she said, 'is that you seem to have such a sense of purpose.'

Patrick turned to her as he drew up outside his flat. Her own car was parked across the road. He smiled at her.

'A nightcap,' he offered.

'Mustn't,' she replied easily. 'I'm driving.'

'Come on, just a quick one.'

'Stop being purposeful, Patrick.' She took his hand. 'I'd like to come in but I won't. Let's not muddy things. We're friends; don't let's risk that.'

In the light of the street lamp she caught the amusement in his eyes and suddenly felt very affectionate towards him. She leant over and kissed him on the cheek quickly before getting out of the car, then she put her head back in through the open window.

'If I dream about cats,' she said, 'I shall blame you.'

CHAPTER TEN

By early December, Guy was coping as well as he was ever going to, he reckoned. He remembered something Alice McVey had once said to him, exasperated by his surliness, when he was grieving for Sandy in the long aftermath of her death.

'For heaven's sake Guy,' she'd snapped, 'you weren't brought into this world to be happy. Happiness is a by-product. Just get on with it.'

That Calvinist thought had blossomed in his mind like a Spring day. He had laughed at Alice then, but somehow movement had become possible again.

He had not lost Sandy; in her death she had become part of him. In Lisa he had found joy and energy and hope of happiness to come. Blindness had taken that away from him. Like many men, he found it easier to give than to receive, and if the gift was impaired, then it was better not to bestow it at all. Maybe that was pride. Perhaps it was that in coming to terms with his blindness he had to cast aside all earlier aspirations for fulfilment and concentrate on smaller satisfactions.

Which he had. He was blind, but could get about the place quite satisfactorily. He could cope. He was teaching. He played the piano. He could write cheques and address envelopes, and he had a specially modified typewriter for letters and course notes. Exercise was a problem, but he did the Canadian Air Force routine every day. If there were times, especially at night, when he still yearned for Lisa – for those fine sweet pleasures, for the sheer comfort of her arms – well, the denial made him *stronger*.

Of course, none of this would have been possible without Jamie, whose resources seemed unlimited. Alice had remarked on their new-found closeness, yet Guy wondered, sometimes, if he really knew Jamie at all. He had never been a very talkative child, and he seldom spoke his thoughts. Guy constantly found himself wanting to reach out and touch his son's face – literally, to read his expression.

On the last Sunday of term, Jamie sprang a surprise on him: he decorated the sitting-room for Christmas. He led his father round the room, making him touch the decorations – the mistletoe over the door, the tinsel round the pictures, the paper-chains on the walls. He'd even found a Christmas tree from somewhere and hung the old electric lights on it. There was warmth and tenderness in the gesture, and that familiar child's desire to please, and Guy was brought almost to tears by it all. But there was also something else in – well, was it in the tone of the voice? And should Guy have found it disquieting that Jamie had sought to re-create, as he clearly had, an earlier Christmas when Sandy had sprung the same surprise on him? Or only natural that he should want to have things as normal as he remembered them?

They did have a kind of normality, all the same, and one that could be maintained as long as he tempered his ambitions to his abilities.

Then he made the mistake of going to the school play.

He sat in the back row, with Hobbs beside him to tell him what was going on. An enthusiastic roll of thunder on a zinc sheet and a sudden squall from the wind machine heralded the opening tempest. A hush fell over the audience. The storm swallowed the

100

actors' opening lines and raged long after the ship had split apart and sunk.

Miranda made her entrance as a high-treble and there was a heavy crash of water, provoking laughter.

'What's happening?' Guy asks Hobbs.

'It's Smythe, sir. Chucked a bucket of water over Miranda, sir. She's drenched.'

'*The sky, it seems, would pour down stinking pitch . . .*' came the high-pitched voice.

The laughter spread.

'What's going on?' hissed Guy.

'Miranda's speaking to Smythe, but Smythe's in the wings, sir.'

'*O, I have suffered with those that I saw suffer . . .*'

Sporadic clapping from the audience.

'What's that?' snapped Guy.

'It's Miranda again, sir . . .'

'Of course it's Miranda, but what's she doing?'

The boy began to explain, but by then Prospero was in full declamation.

Prospero's wig kept slipping, Hobbs said; the cell door twice fell off its hinges and Ariel tripped on a cardboard rock on his first entry and fell sprawling. The boy gallantly tried describing all this as it happened until Guy found the frustration unbearable. Taking advantage of a lull during a scene change, he slipped away. He collected his duffel-coat from the staff-room and let himself quietly out of the boys' door at the back. He was angry with himself; he should have known better.

He stopped dead on the doorstep. Out there the world was silent, as if muffled in cotton wool. He waited to let his ears adjust, but still nothing. And then he realized.

It was snowing.

Gritting his teeth, he launched off across the yard. Twenty-two steps should take him to the corner, where he'd turn right by the tennis-court. But in the snow, a step was a shuffle and a slide, and twenty-two steps took him to the middle of nowhere. He snicked his heel and snapped his fingers, but no echo returned.

Carrying on gingerly, he found the corner and headed off up the path. Before long the ground became soft and yielding: grass? There should have been gravel. Quite suddenly, he slipped and fell, twisting his ankle.

He struggled to his feet. Where was he? At nine o'clock an owl hooted; at five, distant laughter. That was all. Holding his hands before him like a sleep-walker, he shuffled forwards. After a few paces, he tripped again on a stone and fell forwards into a holly bush. He cursed violently as he extricated himself. He skirted the bush and inched onwards. He recognized none of this. The terrain seemed clumpy, full of tussocks. Then abruptly he collided with a wire mesh fence. At last, the tennis-courts!

He struck off at an angle. Was it his imagination, or had the ground started to fall away? There should be a fence on the right any moment: where was it? He went twenty, thirty paces, and still no fence. He stopped. Silence. Not a sound to help him. Groping with numb, raw hands, he felt around until he found a stone and threw it ahead. It landed with a soft thud among leaves. *Leaves?* There shouldn't be bushes there!

He tripped on a tree-root and fell once again. A tennis-court had got four sides; he'd got the wrong one! Where was the gravel path? Where was the lane leading home? Where *was* home?

And then it dawned on him that he was totally

lost. A blind man at sea in the snow. Snow-blind.

Anger welled up inside him. He clawed his way forward through a tangle of shrubbery, ignoring the thorns lacerating his hands and the branches slashing his face. Swearing foully, using words he'd never used before, he blundered on and on, falling and picking himself up again, crashing into fences and tree-trunks until finally something cracked him on the forehead and he fell, stunned.

He heard the boy's voice from very far off.

'Dad? Dad, where are you?'

He couldn't move. He couldn't call back. He wished he were dead.

Jamie had noticed he'd left the hall. Realizing he'd try and tackle the snow, he'd gone to look for him. The path home was untrodden. Retracing his steps, he'd tracked his father's footprints and falls to the bottom of the shubbery, a hundred and eighty degrees off course.

'For heaven's sake, Dad!' he scolded as he led him home. 'People drown in snow.'

'Only in deep snow.'

'And your hands are covered in cuts.'

Guy had to smile.

'You're beginning to sound like Matron.'

'It's not funny. When we get in you're going to get out of those things or you'll catch cold. I'll make you a hot bath. You must have a medicinal Scotch, too.'

He squeezed the boy's shoulder. 'What a pair we are, eh?'

'Nearly not a pair at all.'

Guy said nothing to that, for he was thinking back three years and how it must have been for Jamie, coming upon his mother lying on the ground exactly like that, only dead.

*

In Cambridge the snow fell slantingly, driven by winds from the east. The sky, a dark bruise, cast the trees and spires in negative relief and kept the lights burning in the Experimental Biophysics labs all through the day.

Two days before the labs closed for the Christmas recess, Patrick received a call from London. The biochemists had got something: they'd engineered an entirely new hormone with a molecular structure common to that of the foetal cat and the frog growth systems. In theory, when introduced into an adult cat's brain, this ought to bind to the proper receptor sites and stimulate axon growth – regulated growth, this time.

His mind raced as he replaced the phone. He'd get down there right away and bring back a sample to Cambridge to test *in vivo*. He was packing his briefcase when the phone rang again. It was Oliver, asking him to look in.

In the professor's office, he broke the news.

'It's promising,' he said with as much restraint as he could.

'Patrick,' Oliver asked quietly, 'what do you think of asking Magnus to cast an eye over it?'

'No-one's muscling in on my work, Oliver.'

'Magnus is the man for myelin. And I suspect Schwann cells are where you'll come a cropper.'

'Come on, Oliver, give me a break. I may be on to something here.'

'We'll take it up after the holiday,' said the professor. He smiled. 'Happy Christmas.'

On Christmas Eve, Guy decided to do something special. He sent Jamie up to Alice and Donald, telling him not to come back down before seven. It was to be a surprise.

He arranged his implements on the work surface: the left-handed tin-opener, the knives for chopping and dicing with their special guards, the small buzzers that indicated when a jug or pan was full. From the cupboard underneath he took out a saucepan with a pouring lip, a colander with handles and a special pan that stopped liquids boiling over. He turned on the cooker. Above, the electric wall-clock bleeped. Six o'clock. An hour to go.

First he turned on the radio. He found a carol service from King's College on Radio Three. Great.

He took the two wild ducks out of the fridge and selected a roasting dish from the bottom drawer of the cooker. He felt for a couple of onions in the vegetable rack. The small knife was on the far left of the work surface, where he'd put it. He peeled the onions over the waste-disposal unit, whipped them back onto the chopping-board and cut them into quarters.

Next, the potatoes. Scrubbing them was good enough. He'd need oranges. He felt in the fruit bowl – where the hell was that knife? – and cut two oranges in half. Squeezing the juice over the ducks and ignoring any pips, he put two halves into each beast, then felt in the drawer for the carving-fork and pricked the skin with the points. He unscrewed the soy sauce bottle and poured some into a cup – reminding himself aloud to put the cap back on this time – and, dipping the pastry brush in, he painted them all over. Reaching for the pepper in the spice rack and checking it by smell, he gave the tray a generous dusting. Last, he added the garlic – the whole unpeeled cloves – and threw them in with the potatoes and onions. Adding a splash of water in the base of the tray, he placed the whole thing in the oven. He set the Braille timer a full three-sixty degrees, got the medicinal Scotch from the bottom cupboard, held a glass under the optic and poured himself a half-time double.

By the time he had finished scrubbing the carrots and chopping the cabbage and putting them in the steamer, he was exhausted. But he still hadn't finished. Hurrying now into the sitting-room, he moved the sofa and chair back to the wall, took everything off the folded table, pulled it out into the centre of the room and opened the flap. The table-cloth and place-mats were in the drawer.

The cupboard by the Christmas tree held the canteen of cutlery the McVeys had given him. He laid five places, aligning the knives and forks properly, and went back for the crystal glasses. He carried them carefully to the table, two at a time, protecting them from knocking into anything. He brought chairs from the study and kitchen and placed them at the table. Sitting down in his own, he positioned all the glasses in a line at two o'clock and practised reaching for them in turn.

Not bad.

Now the candles. The candle-sticks were on the mantelpiece and the new candles he'd bought specially were in a drawer. Matches! God damn it, he'd forgotten to buy *matches*! Did Kathy smoke? Yes. That would mean putting out an ashtray, too.

He heard the sound of a car. He felt his watch. Five to seven: she was early. There was a squeak of brakes. The engine coughed itself to a halt and the car door slammed. Footsteps clattered up the path and a moment later the bell rang.

As he opened the door, the familiar scent blew in on the frosty air. Immediately he saw her: tall, red-haired, looking him straight in the eye.

'Come in, Kathy!'

'Happy Christmas,' she said. 'Here.'

He held out his hand and she gave him a small parcel. Then she let out a small bubbly laugh.

'Mistletoe!' she exclaimed, and in a second he felt her in his arms, lightly against him, her mouth cool on his.

The boy ran ahead of the McVeys. He knew that car. He frowned. What was Kathy doing there? As he reached the top of the path he saw, through the small leaded window in the front door, two figures embracing.

Guy sat at the head of the table during supper, with Jamie at the foot, the end nearest the kitchen. Alice sat on Guy's left, facing Kathy, where she couldn't help noticing the way the young woman kept touching him on the hand whenever she spoke to him. Was that how she drew the attention of her other blind charges? She noticed, too, a warmth in his general manner that she hadn't seen in the past, difficult months. Perhaps it was just merely a justifiable glow of pride that he'd invited friends to his house for supper and he'd shown he could bring it off by himself.

Jamie, on the other hand, looked pale and tired. He was over-excited, constantly jumping to his feet to re-fill plates and glasses. He had developed little pouches under his dark eyes. It was wrong for a boy of eleven, however willing, to have had to shoulder such a responsibility. She'd raised it with Guy often enough, and he'd admitted it worried him, but Jamie would not hear of any change in the way the house was run. What was needed was a woman about the place; she'd always thought so. But not this one.

Shortly before midnight, the gathering broke up. Laughing and joking, they spilled out into the bright, cold night. Cleared of snow, the path prickled with frost. The moon was full, and as they said their goodbyes their breath steamed in the still, frozen air.

Alice led the way.

'Don't come out,' she called to Guy, fearing he might slip on the ice.

She needn't have worried, for Jamie had automatically fallen alongside him. Behind her followed Donald, supporting Kathy by the arm. As they reached her car, Kathy came forward and kissed her goodnight. She couldn't help drawing back. She had nothing against the woman, really. Just so long as Guy didn't get serious about her.

As the car was starting up, Alice's eye was caught by a wavy line running along the passenger side. She took it at first to be a mark made by the frost. But, looking closer, she saw it was a long, savage scratch, gouged deep in the bodywork and running the full length of the car.

Kathy had driven off before she could say anything. She turned to Jamie. The boy held her stare, unblinking.

She had made up her mind. Yes, it was interfering and meddlesome, but she couldn't help herself. As soon as she was inside her own home, she went straight to the sitting-room. From the mantelpiece she took down the Christmas card Lisa had sent. In it she found the phone number of her parents' house. The chances were she'd find her there. Making sure Donald was in his study, she went to the kitchen and picked up the telephone. Things were wrong in that cottage. It needed someone who could see what was going on. A woman. The right woman.

It was time Lisa knew the truth.

CHAPTER ELEVEN

Lisa sat on her bed, her Chinese silk dressing-gown wrapped tightly round her, going over Alice's call the night before for the hundredth time. Voices downstairs reminded her she had to get ready; the neighbours were due in shortly for pre-lunch Christmas cocktails.

You coward, Guy, she thought.

You knew you were going blind back in June. That's why you went to see Patrick. Patrick conspired with you, but he said nothing. All those suppers, asking after you . . .

Guy, oh Guy, why didn't you have the guts to tell me? You rejected me because you were afraid I'd reject you first. Chuck before you get chucked: how adolescent. I thought we had a different kind of love. It's nothing if we can't be honest with each other. Or were you afraid I'd rush to you out of pity? You always had such pride. Yes, you need help, but what's wrong with admitting that? Is it unmanly? Are you afraid it puts you under obligation? God, what a fool I must look! Six months of heartache, wandering around and puzzling it all out, and I got it all wrong. A sabbatical indeed! How cynical, how cowardly. You deserve what you've got.

She bit her lip. She hadn't meant that. She was angry and hurt, but what was that by comparison with what he must feel? Who could imagine what a nightmare it must be to be blind?

She shut her eyes tight.

After about a minute, she had the ugly sensation

that the walls were melting, leaving her like a small child in the middle of a huge stage. She felt about on her bed. Her hand touched a Christmas present. She couldn't find where the wrapping paper had been stuck down and had to rip it open. Inside was a scarf. It felt like wool, perhaps half angora. Red or black, striped or plain? She could always ask. Suppose it was red. Lipstick colour. But as she tried to imagine a pair of painted lips, she realized how hopeless it was: thinking of a thing was not seeing it. Her mother's voice called from downstairs.

'Lisa? Don't be long.'

Keeping her eyes shut, she rose and went over to the wardrobe, stubbing her bare toes on the way. She couldn't find the door catch at first. By feel she chose the cotton blouse with the rounded collar, the pale blue sweatshirt with YALE in rubberized lettering and skin-tight black trousers with loops under the heels. She put on some shoes and took a few steps before realizing they weren't a pair. She sat down at the dressing-table and felt around for her make-up. She lightly rubbed in highlight and shadow and carefully traced the outline of her lips with pencil. She dropped the clip of an ear-ring and spent several minutes on her knees on the carpet, cracking her head on the underside of the table when she got up. Finally, spraying a puff of perfume vaguely behind her ears and running her hands through her short blonde hair, she steadied herself before the mirror and opened her eyes.

Her mouth was smudged with purple lipstick, black eyeshadow stained her cheekbones and bright red blusher ringed her eyes.

As they misted with tears, her mother appeared in the open doorway behind her.

'Darling! Are you all right?'

Lisa put her head in her hands and wept unrestrainedly. For Guy, and for herself. Out of sorrow for him, and out of relief for her fears.

A few days later, Jamie was alone in the cottage, going through the kitchen cupboards and drawing up a shopping list, when he heard the rattle of the letterbox. He went down the corridor and found four envelopes lying on the mat.

Two were New Year cards. The third was a holiday brochure. The last was a letter addressed to Guy Sullivan. He didn't recognize the handwriting. He opened it; he'd have to read it out to his father anyway.

He read it twice. Returning to the kitchen, he slipped it in among a pile of catalogues and circulars at the bottom of a drawer.

January brought a thaw, turning the suburban streets to slush, but it brought no reply from Guy. Perhaps she'd been wrong to write. But the more she'd thought about what Alice had confided to her, the more she realized that he'd broken with her *to spare her*. He hadn't wanted to wish his blindness on her. Go away, he'd really been saying, and in a year's time see if you want to share your life with a blind man and a disturbed kid.

Angel, you poor thing, she said to herself, I don't need a year to know that.

Early that Sunday morning, the first in the new year, she left her parents' house and drove back to London. She had things to do before starting work again the next day, but partly she wondered, too, if he'd got her address and written back to her there. He hadn't. She spent the morning tidying the flat, then around mid-day, with a pale sun wanly shining, she got into her car and, without any specific plan in mind, found herself driving towards Suffolk.

As she drove east, the sun clouded over. Cars began putting on their lights. She turned off the main road and the lanes grew narrow and winding. She felt disembodied, a passenger in her own car. Some outside hand was driving.

Eventually she came to the gates of Gorselands. Momentum carried her in. She forked left down the main drive to the gaunt, silent school buildings, where she took the small track from the car-park that led round the back of the kitchen garden, up the unkempt, beech-lined driveway and finally to the small cottage. Lights burned in the windows. She slowed to a crawl and stopped some yards away. Turning off the engine, she sat without getting out.

What the hell was she doing there?

Guy was plodding through a thriller in Braille when he heard the sound of a car aproaching. It came to a halt, the engine was cut, and then silence. No door slammed, no footsteps came up the path. Puzzled, he returned to the book. A while later he called to Jamie in the kitchen.

'There's somebody outside. See who it is, will you?'

The boy went to the sitting-room window. There was a sharp intake of breath.

'Well?' said Guy.

'I dunno. Never seen the car.'

'Come on, Jamie, who's in it?'

Jamie hesitated.

'It's Lisa.'

Eventually, Guy put on a coat and went out. The path was already thick with frost. At the gate, he stopped.

'Lisa? Where are you?'

A car door opened. He steered towards the sound. He caught her scent on the crisp air and her image flashed before his eyes – her long face, long limbs, short fair hair . . . Suddenly he bumped into her. He drew back sharply.

'What the hell are you doing here?' he demanded.

'Didn't you get my letter?'

'Go away! You're not to come here.'

'Why didn't you *tell* me, Guy? I thought we were worth more than that.'

He felt her hand on his arm. He pulled away.

'Don't,' he said. 'I can't handle it.'

'But don't you understand why I'm here?' she cried in exasperation.

'If *you* understood anything, you wouldn't have come. Please, go away and leave me alone.'

'You can't just order me out of your life!'

'We don't need you, Lisa.'

'You selfish, arrogant shit! What about *me*?'

'Lisa, this is only making it worse for both of us.'

He turned back towards the house.

'Hang on!' she cried. 'I'm coming in. We're going to have this thing out.'

'There's no point. Just go. Please.'

'But can't you *see* . . . ?'

He felt his voice cracking.

'No, Lisa,' he said as he closed the front door. 'That's just what I can't do.'

If Oliver wanted proof, he'd get proof. No isolated tissue slice test, but the full-blooded living thing. Rats. Six subjects, six controls.

Patrick had begun his experiment on Christmas Eve, when the labs were empty and there was no-one to interrupt him. He curtained off one end of his lab so that as little light and sound as possible would filter through, then rigged up sound-proofing partitions in the cages so that each rat was completely insulated from contact with the others. He bedded them deep in cotton-wool and fixed up automatic dispensers to deliver measured doses of food and water. Finally he fixed up a bank of strobe lights and set them to flash at random intervals. Every day he injected the six subjects with a dose of the synthesized hormone and gave saline shots to the six controls. For ten days and nights, with only brief periods of rest, he kept the strobes flashing. And now came the moment of truth. Would he find significant axon growth in the visual cortexes of the subject rats?

On this grey early January Monday, with no-one in the building but the janitor, he began the first test: an iontophoresis on an isolated rat brain. By itself, this would tell him.

He took one of the rats that had received the hormone, anaesthetized it and placed it in a head-frame. Within a minute or two he had cut back the scalp and taken a slice out of the skull. Then, working with great care, using fine scalpels and a microscope, he cut away the nervous connections to the striate cortex at the rear of the brain, though leaving the blood supply intact.

As he worked in under the cortex, he caught his breath involuntarily. Even at a rough glance he could see an inordinate growth in white matter! That suggested massive development of new pathways between the grey cortical cells. And it held out a promise that Oliver's fears were unfounded: much of that white tissue would be myelin, the fatty lipid that insulated the axon pathways. If the Schwann cells there were doing their work, he was home and dry.

Taking a small cluster of electrodes, each supplying a pulsed charge of around a hundred millivolts, he buried it firmly in the base of the striate. That would provide the stimulus in place of the severed nerves. Now he had to trace the pathways by checking for evoked potentials. He took a probe with five fine glass tubes, each no more than half a micron in diameter at the tip, and filled them with recording fluid. He was ready.

For the rest of the day he stood bent over the operating frame, oblivious to time or thirst, barely breathing except to mutter the occasional oath of amazement, as he minutely traced the mass of new pathways that had sprouted in all directions.

In a daze he walked back into his rooms in college that evening. The wind coming off the ice-locked fens moaned through the cloisters and pared living flesh to the quick, but he heard and felt none of this; he was even half way there when he realized he'd left his coat at the labs. As he reached the college gate, the porter signalled to him from his cubicle and raised the small window.

'A young lady left a message for you to call, sir. A Miss Lisa Atkinson.'

He reached into his wallet and took out a fiver.

'Thanks, Harry. Have a drink for the New Year.'

Lisa waited in the reception hall at the Television Centre. One by one she bid goodnight to her colleagues. She gazed about her avidly. Since that afternoon three days before she'd looked at the world differently; she saw things she'd never noticed before. How could one take such a precious gift for granted? The tall foyer, built on a crescent, was aggrandized by fluted columns emblazoned with machine-art symbols and lit by a galaxy of tiny lights suspended in molecular clusters. Modern in its day, it

115

now bore the weary patina of a past generation's taste. She stared down at the floor, carpeted in a utility material that camouflaged coffee-stains. If she had to, would she remember all this?

She looked again at the clock. He was late.

She couldn't free her mind of the sight of Guy: greying, his brow furrowed with the months of strain, his frame stiff and unnaturally erect. The whole sad, painful exchange had lasted only a few moments, but it was enough to tell her he still felt for her as strongly as ever, but he was equally strongly denying it.

Why? Did it have to do with Jamie? She recalled the sight of the boy hovering in the background, watching her with those big, dark, knowing eyes. Was he the one she was up against? Had he somehow given his father a choice – her or him?

The more she strove to understand, the more she became convinced there was a deeper reason. Somehow Guy *needed* to reject her. Perhaps the only way he could cope with being blind was by denying his desire for her. She belonged to his life when he'd had sight, a life he had forfeited. It must take every ounce of his strength to face up to his blindness. To accept her back would be to admit a weakness which, in turn, would undermine that strength. In a way, rejecting her was a measure of his success in coping. But it meant one thing clearly: he would never let her back into his life so long as he was blind.

For ever? She refused to accept that. Patrick knew all about blindness. He must have an answer. She'd tell him everything at last and force him to help.

In the street outside the wine bar, figures huddled into doorways against the sheets of freezing rain and great skirts of spray billowed from the cars and taxis. Inside, the air was hot and sweaty and voices were raised against the heavy rock pumping out from speakers everywhere.

Over her second glass, Lisa came to the point and told Patrick about Guy. He seemed stunned at the news. He questioned her closely, then finally shook his head.

'God, I'm sorry,' he said. 'How awful for you.'

'How awful for *him*, you mean.'

'But at least he saw it coming.'

'So did you, and you didn't tell me. Thanks for nothing.'

'He told me not to.'

'Professional etiquette? How high and moral.'

'But I thought he'd got over it. You said he was better. My God, the poor bastard! It couldn't have happened to a nicer bloke.'

'Come on, don't talk as though he's dead.'

'No, no. He's young enough to adapt. They've got ways of training them these days. In the States they use a thing called facial vision. It's using your ears to detect tiny echoes and changes in air pressure.'

'Why isn't he using that, then?'

'It only works with some people. You've either got it or you haven't.'

'Maybe he has. Why can't anyone do anything? Why can't *you*? You spend your time with blind cats. What about the one you got to see again, what did you call that thing . . . ?'

'Blindsight?' He laughed. 'I told Guy at the beginning, Come back in thirty years. We might have a cure then. Though, actually . . .'

'Actually what?'

'It doesn't matter.'

'Come on, I can see you're bursting to tell me. Here, have some more wine.'

He hesitated. A familiar gleam entered his bright,

dark eyes. His hands grew animated.

'There *have* been interesting developments,' he admitted.

She tried the reverse tack.

'You're not going to bore me with one of your lectures?'

'This couldn't bore you. It's fantastic!'

He'd begun. Once the flow was under way, he couldn't be stopped. She couldn't follow the details but she understood the gist: he'd made a breakthrough. At one point he stopped and reached out his hand.

'Give me your necklace,' he said.

She took it off and handed it to him. He marshalled the salt and pepper pots.

'Basically, it's like this,' he went on. 'The salt cellar is one bank of cells in the rat's brain, and the pepper is another in a different part not normally connected. And this,' he stretched the necklace between them, 'is a bunch of new axons I've made grow. The nerve itself is the string in the middle and the beads are a kind of sheath. Okay? The moment it connects up, you have a new message route. The possibilities are incredible! Just think, I might be able to tell you how much of the rat's brain is wired in and how much develops through experience! I could answer the nature/nurture puzzle. I could solve the whole riddle of memory . . .'

She let him spin off into orbit. When finally he grew speechless, she looked him hard in the eyes.

'Then do something for Guy.'

'Lisa, what we are talking about here are rats and cats. You have to . . .'

'Yes?'

'A hell of a lot more research is needed.'

'You were going to say?'

'That's what I was going to say.'

'You were going to say that you'd have to do it with people.'

'*No*, Lisa. It's not possible.'

'On the contrary, Patrick, from what you've been telling me it's absolutely essential. Why not try Guy, if he's willing?'

CHAPTER TWELVE

For a week Lisa wouldn't leave Patrick alone. She'd forced him that evening to admit that, in theory, the technique could work on a person, but at this stage it would be highly unethical. She couldn't accept that. Anything that could help Guy had to be tried, and screw the ethics. She phoned Patrick time and again over it, but when finally he stopped taking her calls, she realized she had to find another way.

In the canteen at lunch a few days later, she searched for her friend Martin, the editor of the science programme, *State of the Art*. Spotting him across the room, she took her tray over and joined him. He was a tall rake of a man with a forehead and nose in a single straight line, almost horizontal from the way he carried his head tilted back.

'What would you say,' she began, 'if I told you there's a man in Cambridge who has blinded a cat and got it to see again?'

'I'd say tell me more.'

'His name is Patrick Ross and the thing's called Blindsight.'

She told him all she knew and answered his questions as best she could. Skipping coffee, he took her back to his office and called the Department of Experimental Biophysics in Cambridge. He spent a few minutes speaking to the scientist – not mentioning Lisa, at her own request – and fixed an appointment to go up and see him in two days' time.

'Sounds hot,' he said to her as he came off the line. 'I reckon I owe you one.'

She knew how he could settle that.

'Okay, do something for me, will you? I came across this man through my friend Guy . . .'

'The one in Cambridge you mentioned?'

'Yes. I want you to get Patrick to say on camera that this thing would work on a person. If he does, mention Guy Sullivan.' She looked down at her hands. 'I saw Guy for the first time for months a few days ago. He'd had an accident – I didn't know about it – and he's now blind.'

The editor muttered an exclamation.

'Leave it with me,' he said. 'I'll do all I can.'

Three times a week after school, Guy now went jogging round the perimeter of the playing fields. It was already dark, of course, but that didn't worry him. What worried him was the unaccustomed flabbiness he had acquired. Jamie rode a yard or two ahead on his bicycle; he'd rigged up a strip of plastic that clacked against the spokes so that he could follow the noise. The first few times, despite this gadget, he'd gone wildly off course, and so the boy had got hold of two bells of different tones and mounted them on the handlebars, so that by ringing one he could tell him to steer right and ringing the other, left.

Once he got the hang of it and settled into a rhythm, Guy found his mind wandering. He tried to picture Jamie, the small determined figure he remembered, bicycling away ahead of him in the dark, his torchlight stretching forwards onto the track. He wondered what Jamie needed, how much he hindered his son, how harmful, how productive the boy's involvement with his own disabled state might prove.

Was his work suffering? Just the previous day, Jamie had physically taken the homework correction off Hobbs and insisted on doing it himself. It was not right; he had his own to do, and much around the house besides. It had provoked a row out of all proportion to the issue. In future, Guy would go through the homework with Hobbs in a classroom before returning home.

And he thought of Lisa, and ran harder.

Lisa had booked one of the small viewing rooms in the depths of Television Centre. Martin had sent across a videotape of his interview with Patrick, due to go out the following Tuesday.

She set up the tape and scanned it until she came to the item.

Martin opened, speaking to camera.

Martin: *A striking feature of the central nervous system of mammals like you and me is that our nerve fibres, if broken, don't regenerate. Sever your spinal cord and you're paralysed for life. A new development may change all this. It's called* Blindsight, *and it's the discovery of Dr Patrick Ross at Cambridge. His approach is not to regenerate the broken axons but to grow new ones . . .*

Cut to Patrick. He came over well, she had to admit: enthusiastic, engaging, lucid, and handsome, too, though maybe his animated hand movements were excessive for the small screen. He described his experiments with rats and cats, stressing that a lot more work was needed before it was established beyond doubt.

Martin then turned to the applications. When might the technique be ready for clinical trials on humans?

Patrick: *I think we're a good few years away from that.*

Martin: *But can we afford to wait?*

Patrick: *There's a vast amount of work to be done because the prospects are so tremendous. A cure for cortical blindness is only one thing. There's all the other organic brain disorders: strokes, epilepsy, maybe even schizophrenia. Spinal disorders, too, and the lesions that cause paraplegia, as you mentioned.*

Martin: *The blind shall see and the lame shall walk?*

Patrick: *That's the ultimate hope. I'm concentrating on sight to begin with. Partly because it's easy to study in the cat brain.*

Martin: *And partly, am I right, because you have a friend, Guy Sullivan, who is, in fact, cortically blind?*

Patrick (surprised): *Yes, that's so.*

Martin: *Would he benefit from the technique?*

Patrick: *I'd hesitate before suggesting it! You can't jump from rat to human in ten minutes.*

Martin: *But in principle?*

Patrick: *In principle, I'd say yes, he would.*

She let the tape play to the end, but she'd heard what she wanted. She'd get a copy made and pay Guy a visit. In case he'd got rid of his video, she'd take a cassette of the sound track, too. And this time she'd make sure they had some privacy.

She checked the number in her address-book and reached for the phone. She didn't like to involve Alice any more than she had to – she'd already decided she'd have to tell Guy she'd heard about his going blind from a Cambridge friend whose parents lived in Suffolk – but this was essential. It had to be presented properly, and it would be easier if Jamie were not around.

She swapped shifts with a friend and took the Monday afternoon off to drive to Suffolk. Jamie, Alice had assured her, would be in school and Guy should be alone at the cottage. Pockets of freezing fog hampered her journey and it was late and dark when she arrived. She parked up at the McVeys' house and

123

took the path through the rhododendrons down to the cottage. Through a lighted window she could see Guy in his book-lined study, sitting over a typewriter.

As she came up the path, she saw him look up and tilt his head to listen. She rang the door-bell. No answer. Surely he hadn't recognized her step? She rang again, then went round the back and, tapping on the kitchen door, let herself in.

'Guy? It's me, Lisa. Where are you?'

He appeared in the doorway, looking pale in the cold fluorescent light. The lines in his face deepened.

'Lisa, I thought I'd said . . .'

'I won't stay long. I've come to give you something.'

'I don't want anything. Please. You're only making this harder.'

'You'll want *this*. You've still got your video?'

'Lisa,' his tone was softening, 'don't do this.'

'Tell me where the video is.'

He let out an exasperated sigh.

'You're mad, coming all this way for that! I won't be able to see the bloody thing anyway.'

'Just do me a favour. I'll set it up, then go.'

Would he benefit from the technique? In principle, I'd say yes, he would.

She'd left him to play the tape on his own and gone, and now there was only her scent faintly lingering on his cheek to prove she'd been there at all. God, she was a cool one.

He stopped the tape and replayed the last bit.

Benefit? How?

He remembered the blind cat walking round the edge of the table in Patrick's office the first time they'd met. What had he said? *You have a girlfriend? Next time you're with her, shut your eyes and try telling yourself you can actually see her, only you're not aware you*

124

can. What was the benefit if he had to go round working off hunches? Guessing wasn't *seeing*.

No, he wasn't going to be a pawn in some grand play of Patrick's. The man had probably set up the whole interview himself to make a name, get a promotion, secure more funds ... Academia was all politics.

Even if I cracked it, we'd be light years away from using it on people. Quote unquote. Patrick's words, seven months before.

No, it was all fantasy. And dangerous to hope.

The gate slammed and Jamie's footsteps hurried up the front path. He quickly took the tape out of the machine and slipped it into his desk drawer. He didn't want Jamie's hopes raised, too.

The boy went round the back, let himself in, kicked off his shoes and came into the study in stocking feet. He paused for a moment in the doorway.

'Lisa's been here, hasn't she?' he said.

He started.

'Well, yes. She dropped in for a moment.'

'You didn't say she was coming.'

'Come on, old lad! I didn't know.'

'She should stay away.'

'What do you mean by that?'

'She just should. You told her so yourself.'

While the boy went to the kitchen, he put on a record of a Mozart concerto and sat down in the easy chair, drumming his fingers in time to the music. Lisa's visit had opened all the old questions. Was he right to be so hard? What had Mac said at the very beginning, that she had the right to make her own decision? But there was Jamie to think of, too. Perhaps he was so much better these days because he felt secure; it would be wrong to put that at risk. Maybe, as he'd always believed, given

125

time and love, the boy would learn to accept her.

But would he really?

Oliver went through a sheaf of telephone memos, stubbing them down on his desk one by one as he read them. His bristly cheeks were flushed and his eyes were magnified alarmingly behind his glasses.

'The Institute for the Blind. The Spastics Society. The Royal College of Surgeons. Keele University. ABC Television. *The Lancet.* Bethlem Hospital. And at least two members of the board.'

Patrick shrugged.

'They're upset by good publicity?'

'It's *bad* publicity, Patrick, making claims on insufficient evidence.'

'The programme's actually called *State of the Art.*'

The professor shook his head.

'You should make up your mind if you're a scientist or a publicist. If you're a scientist, then observe the traditions. We don't go round blowing our trumpets. Go to the States. They understand that kind of thing better there.'

'Christ, Oliver, what do you want of me?'

'One, a full report. And two, curb your eagerness to expatiate all over the media until your colleagues have given their verdict, and even then, Patrick,' he assumed a pleading tone, 'please remember that science has its codes of behaviour, like any other profession. If we all went round . . .'

Patrick leaned across the desk.

'Oliver,' he said quietly, 'you really don't believe I've made a breakthrough, do you?'

'Science is not a question of belief. I'll be convinced by facts.'

'You're telling me I should stop work on it?'

'Well, now you're already in deep water . . .'

'So it's just that you don't like my table manners?'

The professor teased a fleck off his lapel.

'What did Huxley call the great tragedy of science? "The slaying of a beautiful hypothesis by an ugly fact." Think of me as the ugly fact.'

'No fact is ugly, Oliver. That's the beauty of it. It's just a question of belief.'

Back in his office, Patrick kicked the waste-paper basket across the room. Fuck it! Science was not a gentlemanly game of croquet. It was a jungle in which only the fittest survived. And he knew his own survival was on the line.

The phone rang. He snatched it up irritably.

It was Lisa.

This time he listened.

'Hi, Patrick!' she said. 'You were great. But you didn't tell me!'

'I rather thought you were the inspiration behind it,' he replied.

'Me? I'm just a humble trainee in Current Affairs. Did you know, Guy heard it?' she asked, ignoring the lead. 'I know he'd like you to get in touch.'

'I hope to Christ it didn't raise his hopes.'

'I can't say. He knows I'm in touch with you and he called to see what I knew about it. I told him you'd contact him.'

'He's wasting his time,' he said shortly.

'You've started something there, Patrick. It was you who said it would benefit him. I think you owe him a visit, don't you?'

'Look . . . Well, okay. Give me the address.'

Guy was tidying his desk one evening when a call came through from downstairs: there was a Dr Ross in the main hall asking to see him. Patrick! He made his way along the corridor, over the covered bridge that connected the dormitory block with the main school building and hurried down the central stairway. He heard a heel scrape on the floor and steered towards the sound, holding out his hand.

'Patrick,' he said warmly. 'It's good of you to come.'

A hand clasped his.

'Christ, man, for a moment I thought . . . You're the one who should be on telly, not me.'

'No way! Let's get one thing straight right off. If I do agree to do anything, I'm not going to be wheeled around the country like a circus act. The Man Who Got His Sight Back.'

Patrick cleared his throat.

'Look, I think we're jumping the gun here. I came to tell you it's not on.'

'Not on? That isn't what you told the rest of the world.'

'I think we'd better go somewhere and talk it over.'

Guy took Patrick back to the cottage. He led the way into his study and shut the door. Jamie wouldn't come in. He said he had things to do. Guy could tell from his tone he was deeply suspicious of their visitor.

'Nice lad,' remarked Patrick.

'Don't worry,' responded Guy. 'He's only being protective. Boys are very conservative at that age. You should have heard how he reacted to your tape.'

'My tape?'

'Your interview. Lisa brought a tape of it down.'

'*Lisa?*'

'She dropped in for a second on Monday.' He changed the subject abruptly. Even the mention of her name hurt. 'Right, where do we begin?'

'Now hold on a moment . . .'

'What I want to know about this Blindsight thing,'

128

Guy hurried on, 'is, how can I see things and not realize it?'

'Well, that's the whole trouble. It's just a guessing-game. Not much use to you, I'm afraid.'

'What do you mean, a guessing-game?'

'Do you have a torch? Sorry, I'll ask Jamie.'

He went to the door. From the exchange, Guy could tell the boy had been standing just outside. A minute later, Patrick returned saying he'd found a small pen-light.

'Sit down in that chair,' he ordered. 'Just relax. Don't try and look at anything specific. I'll turn out the table lamp.'

Guy took off his glasses and let his eyes wander around the room. He saw nothing but the perpetual dark red curtain. He'd grown so used to it that he barely noticed it any more. His real sight lay in the pictures he made up in his mind out of what he heard and felt around him.

'I'm shining the light into your eyes now,' Patrick announced. 'Okay, tell me where it is.'

'Come on, man. You know I can't see.'

'Just guess. Point anywhere.'

This was fruitless. With a despairing sigh he reached out his hand. It made contact with the pen-light.

'Good God!'

'Now again.'

Again he touched the light. Each time Patrick asked him to point, he met it unerringly. It was uncanny. How could he be seeing and yet not know he was?

'So how do we do it?' he demanded finally when the demonstration was over.

'Do what?'

'Fiddle with the works inside my head so I *know* I can see the bloody thing.'

'We don't.'

'But you said in the interview . . .'

'Look, I'm looking into something but it's far too early to say if it'd work on a person. You're asking me to jump from mould on a Petri dish to penicillin, all in one go.'

'*That* worked.'

'It took years to develop. Even if the hormone could stimulate growth of new pathways in the brain, I don't know how it could be restricted to the sight areas. For all I know, you'd end up with superfine hearing and still be blind.'

'That would be something. But surely you could fix up something to cut out sound and focus only on sight? A sound-proofed room, for instance. And flashing lights.'

'Well actually . . .' began Patrick in surprise, then stopped. 'Guy, just get this whole idea out of your head. I haven't managed to make it work on a cat yet, let alone on a human being. Do you have any idea of what it takes to get anything new passed? The LD-50 tests alone would take months.'

'What are they?'

'Every new drug is tried out on lab animals to find out what is the lethal dose for fifty per cent of them.'

'But it hasn't killed your cats.'

Patrick hesitated for a second, then went on. 'Scaling up from animal to human isn't that simple, either. For one thing, a cat can't tell you if it's in pain; you can only infer it. For another, you never really know what side-effects there might be, psychological as well as physical. Only a person can tell you that.'

'So you *have* to try it on a person.'

'Well, logically, yes. But you've got to be damn sure first.'

Guy let the silence stretch between them.

'Patrick, answer me a straight question,' he said eventually. 'If I took the risk, what would be the chances?'

The other man paused.

'There are no odds for a thing like this. And besides, *I*'m not going to take the risk.'

'Some friend you'd make.'

'Yes. That's why I won't do it.'

No, said Patrick to himself as he drove back to Cambridge. Absolutely no.

There were labs across the country full of rats recovering from carcinomas, but did they have a cure for cancer yet? How many rabbits was thalidomide tested on and shown to be safe? Even if the tests proved positive, look how long it took to get anything legally passed for human use? Remember Interferon, the magic bullet: they got it to work in hens' eggs back in the Fifties, but only now, thirty years later, had they started using it properly on human patients.

No, he repeated. One swallow did not make a summer; one cat did not make a cure.

His mind turned to Jamie. An extraordinary boy. Certainly very bright, but ... quite normal? At some moments his eyes were dull and introspective, then they'd light up and burn with a frightening intensity. His calm manner seemed to cloak some turbulence boiling away under the surface. There was his funny way of twisting his fingers when he talked. The way he shrank from being touched, too. His unnerving charm. The innocence in his smile, yet the knowingness in his eyes.

'Well?' said Guy as Jamie prepared to go up to bed that night. 'You heard it all. What do you think?'

The boy said nothing.

'I reckon I could twist his arm,' Guy went on.

'You mustn't!' Jamie suddenly blurted out. 'It's wrong! You'll only be punished worse!'

'Come on. There's nothing worse than how I am right now.'

'Something terrible will happen. You'll go mad. Or die.'

'You've got to take risks in life. You think I shouldn't even try?'

The boy's voice fell to a whisper.

'I don't know, I don't know,' he repeated miserably. 'It's just not *right*.'

CHAPTER THIRTEEN

Unethical, improper and probably illegal, but *might it work*? Patrick stood staring into the perspex box in which Tolkien, a sleek grey cat, was going through her paces in a routine vision test, but his mind was fixed on the bigger challenge. *What if*? The question demanded an answer. Science is applied curiosity, Oliver. Of course, he'd be fired on the spot if he was found out. Experimenting with animals was controversial enough and subject to rigorous internal vetting, but with a *human*? Suppose he obtained Guy's consent? They'd say the evidence was insufficient for a man in his right mind to agree to, and Patrick had shamefully exploited his innocent hope. What if he drew up a list of the facts and risks? Wasn't it up to Guy himself, anyway? If Guy insisted on going ahead but signed a disclaimer, would that be irresponsible? Surely he could say he was just helping out a friend?

'I thought Guy was your friend,' Lisa said with bitterness when he'd refused her appeal. 'And I thought I was, too.'

She couldn't understand why he didn't jump at it. Of course, she'd have staked her life, let alone her career. It made him look uncaring and self-centred in her eyes, and the issue was fast turning them into strangers.

On the other hand, if Guy did regain his sight in some form, that would heal *their* split and he himself would be right out of the picture. He'd win back the girl's respect but lose the girl herself – not that he had her now, although there were moments, especially over their weekly suppers, when he still entertained hopes.

He'd face that when, and if, it came. For now, he had to show willing. He'd run a few routine tests and take it to the first stage, then tell Guy there was nothing more to be done. Honour and obligation would be satisfied.

He turned back to the perspex box on the work bench. He'd ablated the cat's striate cortex some days before and he'd started her on the treatment. A thin cluster of wires led from her skull-cap and looped to a lightly-sprung swivelling arm fixed to the roof of the box. At the far end he'd placed a saucer of food and, between the cat and the food, at head-height, a thin electrified rod no thicker than a knitting needle. This produced a mild shock on contact. At that moment she was trying to crawl underneath, but each time she almost made it, she touched the rod and jolted back. He moved the rod to a lower slot. She came forward gingerly again, but this time she stopped, then stepped neatly over it.

She could see the rod and, what was more, she *knew* it!

He looked behind him to the slowly-rolling EEG chart and the oscilloscope mounted on a wheeled trolley beside it. The probe planted in her striate registered just a single, unwaving line, for her visual centre was dead. But the electrode he'd bedded into a tract between the mid-brain and the posterior association cortex was giving an active display of spikes and blips. This was the bundle of axons that had newly sprouted.

First a rat, now a cat. It was working!

But what might the physical risks be? Epileptic seizures were the most likely. If the insulating myelin was not properly laid down around the new axons, that could cause short-circuiting. He had the EEG

134

monitoring the cat's brain day and night and hadn't found evidence of fits yet, but did that mean there couldn't be?

Well, he finally concluded, if Guy was prepared to take responsibility, how could he refuse him the fruits of his discovery? He was, after all, his friend and fellow human being.

Switching off the electrified rod, he crossed the room and picked up the phone.

The phone on the kitchen wall rang. Guy turned down the radio.

'I'll get it,' said Jamie. His tone went flat as he answered it. 'It's Patrick, for you.'

Guy felt his way along the side of the table and Jamie put the receiver into his hand.

'Guy?' began Patrick, 'I've been thinking.'

He spoke for several minutes without drawing breath. Don't expect miracles, he said. There are risks, known and unknown. You'll have to sign a disclaimer. We'll just try a few preliminary tests. Suck it and see.

'When shall I come?' demanded Guy bluntly.

'Sunday morning? We can have the place to ourselves then. How will you get up here?'

'My friend at the Rehab Centre. She's very interested . . .'

'For God's sake, no! You'll have me crucified if this gets out. This is between the two of us, understood?'

'I'll find another way. See you Sunday, around nine?'

He put the phone down and pounded a fist into his palm.

'How about that! He's going to give it a try!'

'Great.'

'Don't sound like that. I'll stop long before anything goes wrong.'

135

'Sure.'

'Just think, you won't have to walk me to school any more! I'll be able to go running on my own, without dragging you out each time! We can have people in and damn the furniture being moved! We won't squabble over homework any more, either! What do you think, Jamie? Jamie?'

But the boy had left the room.

In the early hours of the night, Jamie was sick. Guy put him back to bed, where he lay alternately sweating and shivering. He made him take his temperature; he had a slight fever. He wanted to call Alice down, but the boy refused to hear of it.

'I'll be fine, Dad,' he insisted. 'You go back to bed.'

In the morning, Jamie woke him with a cup of tea.

'Come on, lazybones,' he said. 'Time to get up.'

Guy felt his forehead; it was still very hot. He sent him back to bed at once and phoned Matron. She said she'd come by during the first period.

He went to the bathroom cabinet and felt for the packet marked 'A' for Aspirin and took Jamie in two pills and a toothmug of water. In the kitchen he fumbled around looking for the porridge oats – that was normally Jamie's job – and then dropped the packet on the floor. After a search he found a dustpan and brush in the cupboard under the stairs and swept it up. There was just enough left in the packet to make a weak gruel for the boy. He put it on the stove, but the pan boiled over, trickling scalding lava down the side. He poured it into a bowl, guessing when it was full, and put the bowl on a tray. When he added milk, the bowl overflowed and he had to grope around for a dishcloth to mop it up. Finally, filling a glass with milk, he picked up the tray and headed carefully for the door. He negotiated the corridor by trailing his little finger like a cat's whisker along the wall, and he turned correctly at the bottom of the stairs. He was almost at the top when the edge of the tray caught in the post and slipped sideways, sending glass and bowl onto the floor.

Jamie came running to help.

'I'll do it, Dad,' he said.

'Get back to bed!' he snapped.

Slowly, meticulously, he cleared up the mess. He brought Jamie another glass of milk and a piece of toast on a plate, making two separate journeys. By now he had no time left for his own breakfast. Putting on his jacket and overcoat, he went upstairs to say goodbye.

'I'll come back during break,' he promised.

'Don't make extra trips, Dad. I'll be all right.'

'I'll get one of the boys to take me. Keep tucked up, Jamie.'

He hurried down the front path, which Jamie had cleared of snow, but beyond the gate the going became tough. The snow had been compacted into icy ruts, and several times he slipped. He swore aloud and took to the deeper snow. It was a mistake. He'd gone no more than fifteen steps when he stumbled into a bush and toppled forwards into a drift. He'd veered too far to the left. He struggled to his feet and tried to regain his bearings. Then he heard the padding of feet behind.

'Hang on, Dad, I'm coming!' He felt Jamie's hand on his sleeve, tugging. 'You've got to get back to the path.'

Jamie was shivering with fever.

'What the hell are you doing out here?' he barked. He grabbed the boy's shoulder; he was in his dressing gown. 'Get back inside at once or you'll catch pneumonia!'

'I saw you from my window.'

'You should have been in bed! I don't need helping!'

'But Dad . . .'

'Go back! That's an order!' He spun the boy round and pushed him away. 'Go home. And get into bed.'

He waited until he heard the front door slam, then fumbled his way back until he came upon a tyre-track. God damn it, he needed his eyes.

From his bedroom window, the boy watched the bent figure shuffling through the snow until he was lost from sight. How could his father possibly cope without him?

Matron diagnosed a mild dose of gastric 'flu and recommended he went up to the McVeys' house where Alice could look after him. The boy objected: his father needed his help. Matron told Guy, who put his foot down, and during break he and Alice packed a holdall, wrapped the boy up and took him to the big house, where he was to stay until he was better.

At eight on the Sunday morning, Jake, the young under-gardener, drew up outside the cottage to collect Guy and take him to Cambridge. Guy had been up most of the night, mentally preparing himself, and he was now ready.

As they drove down the winding lanes and into the open countryside, he realized that this was the first time he'd been beyond the school boundaries since he'd gone blind. He'd almost forgotten a world existed outside, and he found it disturbing. Jake said *he'd* only ever been as far as Cambridge twice in his life.

Guy directed him from memory, seeing the city unfold in his mind like a film. They arrived early and the labs were closed, but just as the first clocks were chiming nine, Jake reported a man hurrying towards them, waving anxiously.

'Park around the back,' said Patrick. 'Out of the way.'

Patrick told the young driver to come back at around two o'clock, then steered Guy through the rear entrance and across the foyer to the lifts. Once upstairs in his lab, he sat him down at a table, fetched them both coffee and locked the door from the inside.

'Now,' he began, 'we've got to do this systematically. Step one is a series of visual tests to make sure your eyes and retinas are functioning properly. That'll take an hour or so. I'll be shining lights in your eyes and fitting various contraptions over your head with sliding lenses and prisms. Ready?'

'Fire away.'

He began work, describing what he was doing as he went along.

'First I'm going to check your pupillary reflexes. Do they maintain direct and consensual reactions to light? If so, your lower visual paths are unimpaired.'

After some minutes, he concluded they did.

'Now I'm going to rotate your head, to left and right. See if you can keep your eyes in their original position.' He did this, too. 'Good. Your fixation reflex is fine. I'll just check that with a prism set-up. When you've got it on, your eyes should automatically move outwards, and back again when I take it off.'

They moved as they should.

Patrick finally declared the first stage complete.

'What's the verdict, doc?' asked Guy.

'Well, there's nothing wrong with your eyes

themselves and the pathway through the lateral geniculate is clear up to the lesion in the cortex.'

'Great. What next?'

'That route is the interstate highway, if you like. But as I explained, there's a minor road, too, leading to the superior colliculus in the mid-brain. Now we've got to check that's open for traffic. If so, we can then think about extending it beyond there. More coffee?'

While the Sunday lunch was roasting, Alice packed a basket of provisions, put on her coat and boots and slipped out down to the cottage. Jamie hadn't ordered anything from the shops last time and they'd probably be out of the basics.

She let herself in the front door, but looked about her, stifling a frown. This was no place to raise Jamie in. If she'd had her own way, it would have been pulled down after Sandy died – or, better still, before.

She went to the kitchen and unpacked the basket. On the side lay a pad on which was written 'Milk' and 'Dustbin', each with a tick by it. She felt strangely uneasy, knowing Jamie could write anything he wanted without his father ever seeing.

She was on her way out when an idea struck her. Stopping in the hallway, she turned and went up the stairs.

Jamie's den bore a sign marked 'Private' on the door. The paint had been cleared away round the old mortice lock but the door was open. Feeling slightly ashamed to be snooping, she went in.

Inside, the room was a jumble. On the mantelpiece, among the broken toys and fading postcards, stood a small photo of Sandy, his mother. Above hung a plain wooden crucifix. Hobbies, materials and model aeroplanes, half built and long forgotten, shared the shelves with old paperbacks bought for pennies at bazaars. On a hook behind the door hung the surplice he wore in chapel. On the desk, surrounded by bottles of coloured inks he was experimenting with mixing, was a petty-cash box stuffed with chits, and to the side, on its own table, stood his computer and a pile of cassette programs.

A pin-board on the wall above was covered with lists and notes of every kind. A daily checklist of things to do. Memos scribbled on self-adhesive note-paper with reminders about butter and disinfectant, washing-up liquid and light-bulbs. Two separate week planners, one marked 'Term' and the other 'Hols'. Her eye went to the entry for Sunday afternoon. Between '1.00: Lunch Gran's' and '4.30: Dad's Tea' was the single word, 'Grave'.

She went back up the winding path to her house to see to the family lunch, her step slow and thoughtful.

The first test for Blindsight involved guessing the position of a spot of light.

Patrick set up an Airmark projector at the largest spot size and the brightest setting. He gave Guy a series of three second bursts at a horizontal eccentricity varying from five to thirty-five degrees, in random order, asking him to focus his eyes on where-ever he guessed the light-spot was. He placed silver chloride electrodes in the centre and the canthi of his eyes so as to measure their position exactly. The results were being fed into a computer but, even from visual inspection, he could tell that Guy's guesses correlated almost exactly with the actual position of the light.

Next, he rigged up a white screen a few feet away. Setting up two Leitz 150-watt projectors behind him, he projected a series of patterns of horizontal and vertical lines, crosses and circles onto the

141

screen and asked him to guess what he 'saw'.

His third test was for minimal separable acuity. This time, he seated him in front of an apparatus containing diffraction gratings that produced moiré fringes of varying widths, and asked him to guess when the lines became patterns.

After this, he ran a colour detection test. Using a Keeler projector with Wratten filters designed to let through only red and green light of 700 and 530 nanometres respectively, and varying the intensity and speed of the flashes so that sometimes they were actually below the saccade latency, he asked Guy to guess the colours.

The tests continued into the early afternoon. Finally, he switched off all the apparatus and pulled a packet of stale biscuits from his desk drawer.

'Well?' asked Guy.

'I'd say the correlation factor's pretty damn good,' he replied. 'There's something there we could possibly work on.'

'Let's start. I'm ready.'

Patrick patted him on the shoulder.

'I want to run the results through the computer first. And besides, it'll be a few days before London has built up enough stock of the hormone.'

'Come on, I was expecting to drive home.'

With a laugh, Patrick went over to the cages at the end of the room. In place of the rats in the specially partitioned area, he now had just one cat, Tolkien. He took her out carefully and brought her over to Guy.

'Careful of the head-cap,' he warned. 'This is Tolkien. I want you to make friends. She's going to be like the man that carried the flag in front of the first cars. Everything we do together I'll try out on her first. She's the guinea-pig. It's the best

I can do if you insist on going ahead.'

'I do,' Guy replied, stroking the cat. 'So, what's the plan?'

'I'll give you a programme of hormone injections. They'll have to be made in the carotid artery in the neck, where they'll go straight into the brain. Otherwise the liver will break the stuff down.'

'Painful?'

'Not especially. Then we'll have a series of sessions in front of a strobe flash in a sound-proofed cubicle. That's to stimulate the visual pathways while cutting out other inputs as much as possible. You'll have to *try* and see, as hard as you can. Much will depend on how hard you will it to happen.'

'How many sessions do you think we'll need?'

'Well, extrapolating from the rats I worked with first, I'd say probably eight.'

'And how can we tell how it's going along?'

'I could get you on a scanner from time to time. And I'll keep a chart, of course.'

'A chart? Give me something *I* can see!'

Patrick paused. Eight sessions? An idea occurred to him. He went over to the wall-cabinet and selected a tall glass tube with a standing base and a cap and calibrated on the side. He went to the sink and filled it full. Setting it down on the bench and taking a scalpel, he struck the side sharply. A note rang out as pure as a bell.

'Middle C,' said Guy.

Patrick poured out a small amount of water, and struck the glass again.

'D,' pronounced Guy.

In this way, letting out a larger quantity each time until the tube was empty, he made a complete ascending scale. Axons already budded out into the posterior association cortex; these would have to be developed and extended further into the higher cortical areas, a total distance of about four centimetres. If every note represented half a centimetre's growth, when the octave was complete the connections should have been made and Guy should, in theory, have a glimmering of real sight – seeing-sight, not blindsight.

'When you hit upper C,' he said, 'you'll be there.'

'Let me hear it again.'

Patrick went through the process again. The final upper C rang out, undampened, into the silence.

When Jake dropped Guy at the cottage it was barely four o'clock but the path was already crisp with frost and he could smell the fog hanging like a heavy, damp greatcoat round him. He hurried indoors and went to the kitchen to telephone Jamie. The boy was still feverish but he was up, watching television. Promising to come up shortly, Guy rang off. But his hand lingered on the receiver.

He had Lisa to thank for all of this. What could he say to her? Really very little. Was it in fact necessary to maintain the terms of the sabbatical with her? He'd meant the separation to be for ever, and she must have realized that by now. Would it still have to be, if the treatment worked?

His stomach tautening, he dialled her number in London.

'Lisa?'

'Guy . . .'

'No, don't talk. Listen. I'm very grateful for what you've done, and I'm glad you cared enough to do it. No, wait, don't interrupt; I'm finding this difficult enough as it is. I'm going to go along with what Patrick wants to do, because I'd be a fool not to. If there's the remotest chance . . .'

'Guy, will you . . .'

'Shut up. Sorry. On the other hand, I don't believe in any of it. I can't afford to. Like I can't afford to see you. Or believe in you. So will you please leave me alone? Please?' He was near to weeping. 'Please?'

'I love you, Guy. Call me when you're ready.'

He stood quite still for several minutes until the turbulence inside him grew quieter. Then he went to the living-room and opened the piano. Leaning forward, he felt for the centre and very slowly, with one hand, picked out the scale of C major.

III
SPRING

Any sufficiently advanced technology is
indistinguishable from magic.

ARTHUR C. CLARKE,
Profiles of the Future

CHAPTER FOURTEEN

A cold, grey dawn was breaking over the frost-locked fenlands as Patrick left Cambridge and headed towards Suffolk. Huddled into an overcoat, with the heater full on, he could still feel the icy March wind needling in through the chinks in the old car's bodywork. He blinked hard to fight a wave of sleepiness; he'd been up all night making the final preparations.

Six weeks had passed since he'd agreed to try it out. He'd got off to a disturbing start. Tolkien, the sleek grey cat whom he'd given a scaled-down dose of the first treatment he was giving Guy, had suddenly been striken by terrible seizures, and it looked for a while as if he'd have to abort the whole project. With regular shots of phenobarbitone and careful nursing, however, she'd eventually recovered.

Would the same happen to Guy? He couldn't tell. The best he could do was reduce the initial dosage of the hormone and find him something to dampen the general electrical activity of his brain. He didn't tell Guy about the cat; there was no point in alarming him unnecessarily. He'd already signed the disclaimer and insisted he knew the risks he was taking. But he couldn't understand the delay. Patrick's reply was that since he'd have to be confined to bed after every session and rest in total quiet, it made sense to hold off until the school holidays began.

During those weeks, too, Oliver's attitude had changed. The professor had passed his report around the department and was talking of publishing

149

the inital findings in *Nature*. Scientific discoveries often occurred at the same time in different places around the world, independently and without collusion, and if this was the breakthrough it promised to be, Patrick had to plant his flag on the territory before anyone else could do so. The stakes were high. Very high. Yet here he was, risking it all with an experiment on a human guinea-pig! If that got out he could say goodbye to his career. He talked about the risks to Guy, but what about the risks to *him*?

The treatments would have to be conducted in secret, behind locked doors, on Sundays. And he'd have to invent some cover in case he was seen with Guy coming in and out of the building. He'd take it to two or three sessions, then find some technical excuse to break it off. The whole thing was too dangerous for the both of them.

When Tolkien had developed her *grand mal* seizures, he'd gone to see Guy in a last-ditch effort to try and sell him off the idea. He'd frankly admitted he didn't know what it might do to his brain. Anything could happen. There were bound to be side-effects; some might not show up for years. He was flying by the seat of his pants and Guy was staking his *mind* on it.

But he'd got nowhere. The man was not to be deterred.

On his other flank, Lisa had been waging her own campaign. She'd confessed she'd set him up with Martin; they'd made their peace over that and started having Wednesday night suppers again. Each week he looked forward to their next meeting a little more eagerly: no real conflict of motives there, surely. But she seemed as determined on the treatment as Guy, if not even more so.

Muddled, risky, emotionally tinged though it might

be, it was, he had to admit, an irresistible experiment. When it came down to it, a scientist with an enquiring mind could not turn down such an opportunity. In his heart of hearts, Patrick doubted it would work, but if it did it would be equivalent to having discovered penicillin or the polio vaccine.

As he reached the tumbledown stone wall surrounding the school estate, he felt his pulse rising.

Guy was dressed and ready before Patrick arrived. He sat over a cup of coffee in the kitchen, listening with half an ear to the early Sunday morning farming programme and thinking back to his long talk with Alice the previous night.

They'd spoken of the cycle of misfortunes of the family, of his blindness, of Sandy's illness and of the traumatic incident three years before from which Jamie's troubles sprang. Now it seemed there was a chance to break the mould and make a fresh start.

Alice had urged him to make a life with Lisa. She was a fine girl and he'd be foolish to risk losing her. He wasn't going to do anything, he'd responded, until the treatment was over. If it worked, that would remove one obstacle, but there'd still be Jamie and his jealousy to deal with. And if it didn't work . . .

Pipe-dream or positive cure? It wasn't even as simple as that. There were all kinds of treacherous alternatives in between. Suppose it altered his behaviour in some irremediable way? Suppose he ended up brain-damaged and couldn't teach any more?

'Don't dwell on it,' she'd said.

'If things go wrong,' he'd replied, 'I want you to understand why I did it. And see Jamie does, too.'

She'd squeezed his hand tightly and given him her blessing.

He went to the bottom of the stairs to hear if Jamie

was stirring. He must be still asleep. The boy was exhausted. On top of a term's hard work, he was running the household. He ordered the provisions and paid the milk and cleaning-lady from the petty cash; he'd had the outside pipes lagged during the February freeze and the guttering broken during the thaw repaired. When the snow was too deep for the LPG truck to reach the cottage and they were without hot water or a cooker for a week, he had refused to let them move up to the McVeys' house but filled the house with electric fires and borrowed a camping gas stove on which he cooked their meals. Everyone was impressed. Kathy would come by and take away with her some new tip or trick he'd invented to help a blind person to cope better.

Guy was in the process of filling the percolator, measuring out the water in a small jug, when he heard the crunch of car tyres drawing up on the frosty drive outside.

Simultaneously the phone rang. It was Lisa, her voice thick with a cold.

'Good luck, angel,' she said quickly. 'It can't be worse than Finals.'

'Thanks, Lisa. Look, I . . .'

'Don't. Just good luck.'

The door-bell rang as she put the phone gently down.

As he replaced the receiver, Jamie spoke from the doorway. He'd slipped downstairs, unheard.

'I'll get the door, Dad.'

The building was overheated and airless. The odour of electronic equipment mingled with human perspiration hung in the corridors. Patrick steered him down the back stairs to take the elevator in the basement and made him wait at the top while he checked all was clear. Guy felt his sneakers shouldn't even be squeaking on the linoleum. As soon as they were in the laboratory, Patrick locked the door behind them.

'We'll have to do this at night next time,' he said. 'If there is a next time.'

'There damn well will be,' said Guy. 'How did it go with the cat on its first session?'

'Tolkien? She's fine. When I ran a probe the axons had grown twenty per cent of the way.'

'Twenty per cent? Then I should do it in five!'

'It's exponential, not linear. That's the problem: you need most of the effort to close the small gap. Only a hundred per cent of axon contract is sight. Anything less is still hunch.'

'How will you know how we're doing?'

'We'll need a couple of sessions before we can tell where we are. I'll fix up an appointment on the Addenbrooke's scanner after the second.' He sat him down in the chair he'd used before. 'Okay now, listen while I explain exactly what I'm going to do.'

The cubicle, made of special thick acoustic board, was the size of a small garden shed. Inside, with the door shut, no sound could be heard at all save for a small, almost inaudible hissing piped in through a speaker: white sound, Patrick called it. A cough or a word was instantly absorbed by the soundproofing, and almost at once Guy felt sickeningly disoriented, deprived of his vital echoes and other clues.

The couch he lay on, inclined at a shallow angle, was fitted with a mattress of the kind paraplegics used to prevent bed sores. It was so soft that he could barely sense the weight and position of his own body. And apart from a faintest scent of cat fur and surgical spirit, there was no particular smell there, either.

Glued to his temples and scalp by a special gel with

a numbing agent to deter itching were ten small plastic discs, each housing a tiny electrode. They fed into an EEG machine in the main part of the lab and registered the electrical activity across the surface of his cortex. This indicated his state of relaxation or arousal, but not, of course, the electrical activity going on deep in the mid-brain: that would have required depth electrodes to be implanted surgically, as had been done in the cat. He lay on the couch for a while, trying to acclimatize himself. When the EEG registered alpha waves of around ten cycles per second, suggesting a relaxed, receptive state, Patrick had said, the treatment could begin.

But to his horror, as he lay there, that old familiar panic started creeping over him. He suddenly felt his body melting, dissipating over the edges of the couch, so that he could no longer tell where it began and ended. This was inescapable: the whole point of the chamber was sensory deprivation. Patrick had even given him some little oval pills to dampen out all non-visual input into his brain – that was especially vital for a blind man where the four remaining senses had grown so acute. The whole of the growth hormone was to be concentrated on the Blindsight area in the mid-brain.

Guy felt a real fear. As he strained against the soundproofing to hear something, even his own breathing, he found himself sweltering with panic.

Patrick's voice came quietly over a small speaker somewhere above him.

'Relax. Take it easy. Calm down.'

Guy began counting. *A thousand and one, a thousand and two . . .*

He wanted to close his eyes but they were held open by elasticated tape. He could blink, but unless he consciously moved the lid muscles his eyes stayed open, forced to stare up into the strobe projector mounted in the ceiling just above his head.

'That's better,' Patrick said after a while. 'I'm coming in now.'

The door opened, briefly letting in a shaft of sound.

'Now for the hormone shot,' he said.

He felt his head gently eased to one side and a cotton pad of spirit rubbed over his neck. Fingers pressed down on the artery, then he felt a sharp prick and a thick, blunt needle being fed into the blood vessel. At last it was extracted.

'There. We're on.'

His head was set straight on the soft pillow, he heard a click as the strobe was switched on and, a moment later, the door closed softly, and thereafter there was nothing but the strange hissing of white sound that seemed to come from within his own head.

Patrick looked in through the small window set in the soundproofed door. The figure inside was etched in the searing flicker of the strobe: semi-supine, wearing a sweat-shirt and loose-belted trousers, his mouth clamped in a line of inflexible determination and his eyes, taped wide open, staring straight into the flashing light like an arc-welder without a hood. God knew how he kept himself under control.

He turned and glanced once again over the EEG recorder and the ink-pens scratching out their wave-patterns. An oscilloscope linked to it synthesized these into a single wave-form, and a small LCD display beside it gave a digital reading of the mean frequency. At present they fluctuated between nine and eleven cycles per second, nicely within the alpha-wave band. Guy was in the proper state: relaxed but attentive and receptive.

*

With her good leg half bent in token genuflection, Alice sneaked a glance through her folded hands across at Jamie. The boy was kneeling on the hassock beside her, muttering fervent prayers. She couldn't catch the words, but she knew why he'd been specially keen to go to church that day. She'd been glad to take him – Donald had enough of chapel during term-time – for she wanted to say her own prayers for Guy's healing, too.

The congregation rose for a hymn, but Jamie knelt there a moment longer. She smiled. Whatever else, the boy was strong in faith.

At the end of the service they shook hands with the vicar at the door and headed out into the biting wind towards the car. At the gate, he looked up at her. His dark eyes burned.

'It's *wrong*, Gran,' he said quietly. 'The Lord took Dad's sight away for a purpose.'

'We can't say, Jamie. Perhaps it's a test of some kind.'

The boy looked down, then kicked a stone savagely.

'It was his punishment,' he blurted out. 'And now he's trying to get out of it.'

She grabbed his hand and made him face her.

'How can you speak like that after praying so hard for him?'

The boy pulled away and didn't answer.

And then a terrible thought occurred to her. What exactly *had* he been praying for?

Patrick kept the treatment going without interruption for four hours. Several times during the period the relaxed, drowsy alpha waves slowed down into sleep waves, even once hitting the delta waves of deep sleep, before he'd turned up the volume of the background hiss and managed to pull Guy back up to the surface. Of course, with the reticular-dampening pills he'd given him, he'd be inclined to fall asleep, but if he did his eyeballs would roll upwards and he'd lose the stimulus from the strobe. In fact, it was astonishing that he'd kept alert as he had; it showed remarkable will-power.

Finally, when the time was up, he switched off the strobe and unplugged the EEG recorder. The data now lay in the computer, to be analysed later. Turning off the white-sound tape, he went into the sound-proofed chamber and unhooked the electrode leads. Guy looked grey and haggard. Patrick quickly shone a light-pen into his eyes to check that his pupillary reflexes were unaffected and his retina undamaged, then took his pulse. Everything seemed okay.

'How are you feeling?' he asked.

'Like death,' said Guy in a slurred voice. 'Blistering headache. Dizzy. Sick. For Christ's sake take these damn tapes off.'

Patrick untaped his eyelids. Guy sat up with a groan and pressed his hands to his head.

'If you're going by the theory that it's got to hurt to work, I'd say we just did twenty-five per cent.'

'Just keep quiet. I'm going to put plugs in your ears. You're not to speak till you're home.'

He plugged Guy's ears with cotton-wool and gently steered him back into the lab, where he helped him into his shoes and jacket. He'd give him a drink of water, check his blood pressure and temperature, then get him out of there as quickly as possible. With luck, he'd make it to the car without being spotted. After that he could relax and examine him at leisure.

Guy complained of dizziness and when he spoke he sounded drunk. He'd lost his sense of balance, due to

157

the prolonged sensory deprivation, and he had to be helped to the car like an invalid. Twice on the way his legs gave in under him, and in the car he had to be propped up in his seat like a corpse. Patrick drove the thirty miles to Gorselands carefully, taking the corners gently and steering round the bumps.

As they reached the cottage, Jamie came running down the path to meet them. With the boy's help, he hauled him upstairs to his bedroom, undressed him and put him to bed. Guy had begun shivering with post-operative shock. Jamie brought hot, sweet tea and more blankets, and together they watched over him until he slept.

In the kitchen, Patrick gave his instructions.

'Bed,' he prescribed. 'No noise, no disturbance, just rest and quiet. He's had two of these tablets. Give him two more in the morning and another two tomorrow night.'

He handed the boy four orange tablets.

'What are they?' Jamie asked.

'Oh, it's a compound of scopolamine I made up.'

'What's that?'

'It's an anticholinergic. The idea is to dampen down other messages to the brain. It's the same kind of pill you give for travel sickness. That's why he's groggy.' He rubbed his eyes. He, too, was exhausted; he'd taken a hit of dexamphetamine during the session to keep awake, but that was wearing off. He hadn't slept for forty hours. 'So do you understand what you have to do?'

'Peace and quiet and no visitors. Two pills in the morning, and two at night. Anything else?'

He shook his head.

'You sure you can cope?'

'It's a cinch.' The boy went to the stove. 'You look worse than Dad. Want some coffee?'

'I'd die for some. Jamie, you know something? You're terrific. Oh, I'd better give you my number in case you need me.'

'All right, but I won't.'

Lisa sat crossed-legged on her bed amoung the paper handkerchiefs and the Sunday papers. Her Chinese silk dressing-gown bulged from the jerseys she wore underneath. The central heating was on full and yet she shivered. She made herself a hot brandy and lemon and turned on the television, but she couldn't concentrate on it.

At seven, she called Patrick in his rooms in college. The porter tried his extension but there was no reply. She left a message. Should she call Guy? She had a right to know. But perhaps he really ought not to be disturbed. Come on, she thought; it's not as though he's had a major operation.

She rang the cottage. Jamie answered.

'Hi, Jamie,' she said brightly. 'How did it go with your dad?'

'All right.'

'Can I have a word with him?'

'No.'

'You mean, he's out?'

'He's in bed. Patrick said no-one's to disturb him. And no visitors either.'

'I see. Well, will you say I rang and I'll call to-morrow?'

'He's got to have peace and quiet for two days.'

'But he is okay, isn't he? Jamie?'

'I said he's all right.'

'Is your gran looking after him?'

'I am.'

'Of course you are. Well, you'll be busy, so I won't keep you.'

'Bye, then.'

Wretched little brat, she thought as she put the phone down. Guy's far too indulgent with him. Who does he think he is, telling me I can or can't talk to his dad? If I were his mother I'd give him a piece of my mind.

She'd call Alice after supper. Alice would tell her how the treatment had gone.

'How many fingers, Dad?'

In a blur, Guy located Jamie's voice at the foot of the bed. He opened his eyes; the eyeballs still felt raw and scratchy. His head was splitting and he felt dizzy and nauseous. The worst of his nightmares hadn't been as bad as that afterwards.

'Three,' he guessed.

'Four,' corrected the boy. 'Bad luck. Okay, here's some pills you're to take.'

'Aspirin?'

'Patrick said they're for travel sickness.'

'What's he talking about?'

'Come on, Dad, don't argue. Take them and you can have your tea. I've made you toast and jam, too. You're to stay in bed and not move. I've rigged up a bell that rings downstairs if you want me. Hold out your hand. Here's the bell-push, okay? If you need anything at all, just press it.'

'You think of everything.'

He took the pills and nibbled at some toast, then sank back into the pillows, exhausted.

CHAPTER FIFTEEN

As soon as the brain-dampening pills wore off Guy was on his feet, eager to try anything to speed up his progress. His first words to Jamie on the third morning were to ask if the sun was out. It was, and though it was as pale as a March sun might be, he sat in an old wicker chair in the window of the sitting room, and, with Jamie moving his head from time to time, stared into the incoming rays. As the hours passed, he moved to another room. At dusk, he went to the sitting room and sat in front of the television, with the sound turned down. At night he slept with an Angle-poise lamp shining in his face, hoping to obtain some benefit even through closed lids. Patrick, who visited frequently, didn't think this helped; most of the axon growth, he said, should have occurred during the first few hours after the hormone injection. But Guy was determined not to leave anything to chance.

For days he was beset by vicious headaches. He relinquished to Jamie still more of the mundane jobs about the house. The boy now cooked all their meals, did all the washing up, dealt with the mail and answered the phone.

'I bet you'll be glad when this is over,' Guy said at the end of the first week, 'and we can go back to living a normal life like anyone else.'

'I'm happy. Why do things have to change?'

'You sound like a middle-aged conservative! You can't have progess without change.'

'Who wants progess? That's when things go wrong.'

'Well, okay, technology's a mixed blessing. But it's

not all nuclear bombs and pollution. Nobody dies of polio or TB any more. And look what Patrick's doing. If it works for me, it'll mean all kinds of disabled people could be cured.'

'Some things are right to do, and some aren't.'

'You're a bit young to be such a moralist, Jamie. Who knows which are which? Things aren't inherently good or bad; it's what we do with them that makes them so. Even killing is justified in some circumstances. In war, for example, or in self-defence.'

The boy's voice fell to a shocked whisper.

'Dad! How can you sit there and say that! Killing is *never* right!'

'Tell me one of the Ten Commandments that you'd never break under *any* circumstances. And don't give me, Honour your father and mother.'

'This isn't funny, Dad.'

'I'm being serious. As you get older you'll find the edges get blurred. Often it's a case of the lesser of two evils.'

'The lesser evil is still evil.'

'Jamie, your logic is unfaultable. I can see I'm not going to win this. Come on, get the chess board out and let's see if I can beat you at that.'

The boy got up and went to the cupboard behind the television. There was a rattle as he took out the box of chess pieces.

'I remember you once boasted you could beat me blind-fold,' he said more lightly. 'Well, here's your chance.'

'No problem,' said Guy, knowing he'd be trounced within ten minutes. 'And one hand tied behind my back, too.'

That night, in a dream, he went blind.

He dreamed he was on a boat going up the

Bosphorus. A big party was in progress. All his old friends were there. A firework display lit up a park on the shore. He'd never seen such colours. Lisa appeared. She took him by the hand and led him below deck. She was laughing, a little high. They came to a door marked 'Captain'. He could read the gold lettering. She seemed to have prepared this. She opened the door and drew him in after her. In the centre of the cabin stood a table laid for supper. Cut glass and silver flashed in the candle-light. Through a porthole he could see the fireworks exploding over the shoreline. To one side stood a vase of exotic flowers, in the corner, a large globe on which he could clearly read the names of the continents and great seas. He drank in every shape and colour, for he knew he was dreaming and this was the only world in which he could see.

Lisa was smiling. Her eyes shone and danced. He recognized every line of that face he loved, every angle of that longish nose, every twist of those ironic lips. He was intimately familiar with the way her short fair hair jutted out in a peak over her forehead and swept round flat behind her ear . . .

Her ear? Suddenly he couldn't see it. The rest was there . . . but not her ear! He'd somehow, literally, lost sight of it.

Even as he strained to look, first the side of her neck, then her face and finally her whole head began to disappear. She was still there – he could hear her talking and laughing, he could feel her hand in his – but she no longer filled the space she occupied. The space was blank, filled by something of his own imagining, a complex of sounds and sensations without actual form. He was blind again.

And this was a dream!

He woke with a jolt, bathed in sweat, and spent the

rest of the night tossing and turning, unable to get back to sleep. Dreaming was his only way of seeing. What if he lost even this?

After the second treatment, Guy made a mid-week visit to Addenbrooke's Hospital in Cambridge for the first scan. Everything hung on the results; in the heart of that scanner lay his future. He had to find a way of distancing it, and he began to imagine that this man who was sitting in that seat, wearing those clothes, inhabiting that skin, was someone else.

He met Patrick in the hospital reception area and was led down the labyrinth of overheated corridors to the Radiology department and introduced to the consultant. The two men were clearly old friends.

Patrick had already told him what to expect, but the consultant went through it all again. Guy listened distantly, as though the man was addressing somebody else. This was a PET scan, he was told. It used the new technique of positron emission tomography to scan his brain in slices and show the metabolic rate of various parts. Where it was most active, there'd be the highest uptake of oxygen and glucose. So as to mark this, he'd inhale a gas containing a small dose of a radio-active isotope which the scanner was designed to detect. A strobe would once again stimulate his mid-brain area and any spots of high activity, such as spurs of new axon growth, would then show up brightly. It would be painless and take no more than half an hour and the results, allowing time for analysis, would be through the following day.

He was laid on a narrow couch and a mask was taped over his nose and mouth.

'Eyes wide open,' said the consultant. 'Breathe in.'

He heard the strobe being switched on and the annular hood of the scanner sliding over his head.

'Quite still, now.'

The machine whirred and clicked for five minutes as his proxy lay there on the couch. The real Guy Sullivan was somewhere else, safe and unassailable.

Patrick returned to the hospital at the end of the day. With the consultant watching over his shoulder, he sat at the console and called up the scans. He went through the frames until he located the superior colliculus deep in Guy's mid-brain, then proceeded slice by slice, each taking him a few millimetres at a time deeper into the brain.

The screen began to fill with small coloured flecks, some in clusters, others in diffuse whorls, set against a mottled blue background. He increased the magnification. At once the clusters broke up into tiny sparkling galaxies. Budding out from the top of the colliculus appeared a spur brighter and denser than any of the others. He typed in an instruction to hold on that base and rotate the plane transversely, to simulate a slice taken in a line from the crown of the head to the nose.

It literally sprang off the screen and hit him in the eyes. Behind him, the consultant caught his breath. Patrick adjusted the controls to bring the picture into better focus, then turned up the magnification another factor.

A red line, as fat and firm as a finger, projected from the top of the colliculus in the direction of the posterior association cortex. The density and brightness told him at once these were axons, packed as tightly together as a transatlantic telephone cable. Running along either side, suggesting a laminated covering when viewed in the round, were thicker lines of pale blue, tightly-rolled and convoluted upon themselves. The blue indicated these were areas of low oxygen-glucose take-up, and that suggested these were Schwann cells laying down myelin, the fatty substance vital to insulating the axons. He glanced at the calibration and calculated that the new spur was roughly six-tenths of a centimetre in length.

He stared at the screen. He was witnessing, for the first time in man's history, the creation of a new pathway in the brain. The significance of the constellation before him and its sheer perfection and beauty filled him with wonder. He looked up at his friend and just shook his head, quite speechless.

At nine o'clock the following morning, weary from a sleepness night and tense with the determination to contain his excitement, Patrick presented himself at Oliver's office. The words seemed to fall from his mouth of their own free will as he explained what had been happening. He still could not comprehend the magnitude of the implications. His eyes wandered as he described the parameters he had imposed on the experiment, and he failed to observe the growing horror on the professor's face. When he came to the extraordinary results of the PET scan at Addenbrooke's, however, Oliver could hold his silence no longer.

'For Christ's sake, Patrick,' he exclaimed, 'are you telling me this thing's gone outside the department?'

'This *thing*, as you call it, could be the most exciting scientific breakthrough this century. Come on, Oliver, can't you *see* it?'

'All I can see, you damned young fool, is that you've gone mad. This is a *man* you're operating on, Patrick, and what you are doing is criminal. It could get us all into the most serious trouble. By rights I should suspend you for gross professional misconduct . . .'

'He signed a disclaimer. I have it here. He can't sue.'

'I don't give a damn about the law! I'm talking about ethics. This is not a surgical operation in a hospital. You're conducting an unauthorized experiment on an unauthorized subject. It's quite indefensible and, scientifically, it's in the worst possible taste. The press would jump onto it: a real-life human guinea-pig story. What if your friends in the BBC got hold of it?'

'Maybe I'll give them a call.'

'You'll be out of this department in one minute if you do! Look, Patrick, if you stop what you're doing right this minute, I'll forget this conversation ever happened. But stop you must.'

'Oliver, for God's sake stop being so pompous. Can't you *see* what I'm telling you? Can you *seriously* pass up on an opportunity like this?'

'I have never been more serious in my life when I say that all your activities on this subject must cease as of this moment.' He spread his hands decisively. 'Your choice is perfectly simple: either you stop or you're out. Which is it to be?'

Two days after the scan, Guy was sitting in the living-room when he heard Patrick's car pull up. He'd called to say he was coming; he had the results of the scan but he wasn't going to tell him on the phone.

Jamie was hanging a picture that Sandy had painted in her college days and he'd framed during woodwork classes.

'How does that look, Dad?' he asked.

'Down a bit on the left.'

'Like that?'

'Too much. Up a bit. Stop.'

With a laugh, Guy got up and went to the door as he heard Patrick's footsteps up the path.

He did not get up to see Patrick out. He sat without moving, his hands folded in his lap.

So, the results of the scan were negative. The myelin was breaking up, and ions were leaking across the sheath. There was no point in going on, given all the risks involved. Patrick was calling the whole thing off. Of course, one day, many years down the line, when the hormone was perfected . . .

Goodbye sight. Hello again, sunless prison.

He rose at last and put on a record of a late Beethoven quartet, finding an echo of his own struggle in the composer's rage against deafness. It became too intense and he turned it off. Putting on his duffel-coat, he went for a walk in the chilly late March evening. Without being conscious of it, he found his steps taking him to the field beyond the woods where years before, among the harvest corn, he and Sandy had first made love and where, three summers past, he had carried her emaciated body in his arms and laid her down to die. He listened to the sound of the wind in the bare trees and the rustle of the occasional wild animal among the dead leaves and he thought what he would give just to see her picture again.

Better not to think about it. He'd travelled this road before; there was no point in going through the battle all over again. The thing hadn't worked. If he was disappointed, it was his own fault for having allowed himself to hope. He'd better get back onto the old path again. It didn't mean he couldn't go to Florence in the summer with Jamie. Have cane, will travel. He'd now survived six months of blindness and several more preparing for it. What a waste of all that effort it would be to get his sight back now!

At that thought, he turned and retraced his steps through the wood. When he reached home, he found

Jamie had put on a Noel Coward record and poured him a drink, and from the kitchen came the smell of a roasting chicken.

The following Sunday, Lisa drove to Gorselands for lunch at the McVeys'. She'd received a call from Alice at work on the Friday morning, inviting her down. She knew what was behind it: Patrick had broken the bad news over supper a couple of days before. The scans, he'd said, had come out zero. Since then, all she'd been able to think of was how disappointed Guy must be. And how to get over her own disappointment, too, for the same blow had dashed other promises as well.

On the telephone she'd at first demurred.

'Alice,' she'd said, 'Guy wouldn't want me there.'

'I know all about that,' Alice had briskly replied, 'and I've told Guy not to be so silly.'

At lunch, he was cheerful and animated, but when his face briefly fell into repose she could see that this was only a mask. She was wrung out to witness it. Afterwards, when McVey went to his study and Alice took Jamie upstairs to help her, she suggested they went for a walk. They put on overcoats and wellingtons and stepped out into the damp, overcast afternoon. There his manner changed abruptly and he fell quiet. In silence they walked down the lawn and out across the school playing fields. His arm, slipped through hers, was stiff and unyielding.

She steered them round the back of the school and down the path that led through the wilderness to the river. Neither spoke. From time to time she cast him a sideways glance. His face was like granite. As they reached the tow-path, a pair of moorhens scuttled across the drab brown water and in the willow-trees above the wind stirred uneasily, bringing a hint of rain. The tension rose a degree further.

Fat drops of rain were falling now, pattering on the leaves and plinking in the water. It hadn't occurred to her to bring an umbrella. A hundred yards ahead, by the water's edge, stood a derelict boat-house, its roof half collapsed and its sides gaping open. She urged him forward. The rain began to fall more thickly.

They stopped inside, panting for breath. A smell of mouldering hay filled the air. The rain drummed on the roof and dripped steadily onto an upended rowing-boat. She drew him deeper into the shelter. Suddenly he took her elbows and shook her hard. His face, glistening with rain, was filled with pain and frustration. He opened his mouth but the words seemed too big to come out. After a moment his body relaxed and he allowed her to draw him into her arms.

For a long while they stood there without moving, fused together. Within her, a tide swelled and broke. She took a half-step back and gradually began un-buttoning her cotton check shirt. She took his hand in hers and placed it on her left breast and held it there tightly.

'Don't speak,' she whispered.

Still clasping his hand to her, she unbuckled her jeans and slipped them over her hips and down to the ground, then kicked off her boots. She took both his hands and ran them slowly all over her body, mould-ing every curve and flatness of her naked skin. Then, knotting her fingers into his hair, she drew his head towards her, to crush her lips on his and kiss away the rain and tears.

The boy stood in the shelter of a broad fir-tree and scanned the ground ahead. It was dusk and a light rain fell silently, misting the stone finials on the rear of the main school building. A safety light shone in a corridor and the windows of the ground-floor class-rooms glowed dimly in its faint light.

He felt in his trouser pocket to check he had the ring. Then he slipped round the side to the court-yard. Glancing behind him, he slid up the sash window of the washroom he'd left open and clam-bered in, closing it quickly after him.

Taking off his shoes so as not to leave footprints, he padded hurriedly through the changing-rooms, down the corridor past the staff-room and across the main hall and let himself into the small chapel. Just inside the threshold he stopped and crossed himself, then walked slowly up the aisle. Christ's halo gleamed luminous in the stained glass window above the altar with the fading light behind it, and the Saviour's face bestowed a kindly smile on him. He stood there for a long moment, mesmerized by its beauty, then he reached into his pocket for the ring, his mother's wedding ring, and placed it behind the wooden cross where only Christ would see it.

CHAPTER SIXTEEN

It was three weeks later when Martin changed it all. Lisa had just picked up her tray at the till in the BBC canteen when she saw him waving at her from a table in the far corner. She went over and joined him. Over the meal, they discussed her application to be seconded for a period to *State of the Art*, and this led them onto the programme he'd done on Patrick Ross. Had she seen him, he asked, and was there any follow up?

She was deeply disappointed about Guy's results. The experiment had been a secret, but there seemed no reason any more for that now it had failed. Yes, she said, she had seen Patrick. And what was more, Guy had induced him to try the technique on himself, though, unfortunately it hadn't worked.

Martin's fork dropped to his plate with a clatter.

'You're saying he actually *tried it out* on Guy?'

'Just a couple of times, but he drew a blank. He took him to Addenbrooke's and checked him on some fancy bit of equipment there. Negative.'

'Their PET scanner: I know it. I had it on the programme once. They've got an extraordinary computer imager hooked up to it which lets you see any part of the brain from any angle you want. Twist, revolve, zoom in, zoom out. I'll give the consultant a call. I remember him well.'

'Hang on a minute, Martin. I shouldn't have told you any of this. Do me a favour, leave it alone? It could get Patrick into serious trouble. I mean it.'

'Oh, I wouldn't do that, love.'

*

In the middle of the week, Kathy came round to take Guy to the Rehab Centre where they were holding an Open Day to help raise money for an extension. Gritting his teeth, he went along and let her parade him and show off his blindcraft. He shook hands with a pompous alderman and two reporters from the local paper with never a fumble, he handed round cakes to ladies from the Women's Institute, astonishing them by remembering who was who, and he steered himself round the crowded room without colliding with anyone. He could feel Kathy's pride in him, and he played his party piece at his best for her sake.

Among the patients there was a man who'd lost his sight in an accident at a chemical plant; he'd attempted suicide twice, and Kathy wanted Guy to talk to him. The man had allowed himself to become institutionally dependent, and the more they spoke, the more Guy's anger rose. Better to get on with it and kill yourself, he wanted to say, than whine for pity! But he ended merely mouthing the usual platitudes of encouragement.

The alderman made a florid speech praising the good work of the Centre and applauding the splendid cause it served. Afterwards he came over to Guy and told him the council were giving wholehearted support to the appeal – not financially, though, of course.

Guy leaned towards him.

'I'd close the damn place down,' he said beneath his voice. 'Chuck 'em all out onto the streets. The world is out there, not in here.'

The man laughed, thinking he was joking.

Guy bit his tongue. He counted the minutes until it was over. When finally Kathy took him home, he felt disgusted with himself and somehow tainted. He hadn't wanted to mingle with his tribe, to witness their own daily battles of courage against despair, to be seen to bear the same mark as them.

As they drew up outside the cottage, she took his hand and on the palm she spelled, in Braille, *Bless you*.

That Friday, Lisa was packing up her desk for the weekend when she received a call from Martin.

'I thought you might be interested to know,' he said, 'that the business about your friend Guy's brain scans being negative is, in common scientific parlance, complete and utter crap.'

He went on for a moment before a transatlantic call came through and he had to hang up. She put the phone down in a puzzled daze. What on earth was Patrick up to?

She woke up early and packed a change of clothes in case she had to stay over. She didn't call, for she didn't want to be drawn into a discussion on the phone. It was the first Saturday in April and a sudden blush of Spring had arrived, catching the countryside unawares. Startled hedgerows bristled with tiny buds and the trees she could see from the motorway wore the furriness of a fine mould.

She was in Cambridge by ten. Patrick's car was not in the college car-park nor at the Department. Had she come all this way for nothing? Was he away for the weekend? There was nothing she could do except wait at the labs, knowing that if he was in the city he'd visit them some time during the day. She hung around in the pale, chaste sunshine until, shortly before noon, she saw Patrick's car approach and drive round to the car-park at the back.

She was at the door when he came hurrying up.

'Lisa!' he exclaimed in astonishment. 'What are you doing here?'

'I want a word with you, Patrick. Let's go inside, shall we?'

'I'm sorry, but I had to do it.'

'Why, for God's sake? Give me one decent reason.'

'Lisa, this research is absolutely vital to me . . .'

'And Guy's sight is not absolutely vital to him?'

'Look, if I get thrown out, I'd be no use to Guy anyway. It's in his interest that I stay around to keep work going. Of course I couldn't put it like that to him.'

'I bet not. You knew what he'd say.'

'Look at it from my point of view, just for a second. This thing is *totally unproven*. I've got months of lab tests to do before it's properly validated even on cats. Then maybe I could transfer to the States. Out there it's far easier to get volunteers for experimental work. No reason why Guy shouldn't come over then. If Oliver chucks me out now, and he can, we've lost it, don't you see?'

'There are other universities.'

Patrick gestured around the lab. At the far end, among batteries of scientific equipment, she could see an empty space and a stack of sound-proofing sheets leaning against the wall.

'None with the same equipment, the same facilities.' His manner softened. 'I had to make a snap decision. Oliver was holding a gun to my head. Give it time to settle down, and maybe in a year or so . . .'

'I can't wait a year or so!'

'*You* can't?'

'Guy can't.'

'He'll have to! Okay, I'll admit to you the treatment looks good so far. I've been able to grow axons in a human brain. But you've no idea of the possible dangers. What would actually happen when they all connect up? I don't know, do you? I don't even have a cat to show who's got that far. Christ, Lisa, I'm as blind as Guy in all this. It's so much more *sensible* to hold things until I've got the basics established.'

'If it's so sensible, why did you need to lie to Guy?'

'It was just a small white lie.'

'I call it betrayal. You built up his hopes and then smashed them.'

'All right, Lisa. You want me to give you Guy In Three Months' Time? All right then, listen. He's a mess. He can see you, but what's it like? You're distorted, your arm is sticking out of your nose, your skin is green and your hair is white. Half your face is missing and the rest is a mass of zig-zags and whorls. And Guy himself? He's epileptic. Schizophrenic, too. He has bursts of violence. Terrible hallucinations. You name it!' He paused. 'Do I have the right to risk that for him?'

'We all have a right to decide for ourselves! People must stop deciding for others. Guy decides what's best for me, and you decide what's best for him. We're all responsible adults. Let's make our mistakes if we want. Your job, Patrick, is to tell him the truth, not make his decisions for him.'

'Fine. So let *him* decide for me the risks *I* run?'

'Ah, I see! It's down to that. His sight or your skin.'

'Lisa . . .'

She silenced him with a glare. It was a while before she spoke.

'You're going to do something, Patrick.'

'What?'

'You're coming with me to see Guy right now and we're sorting this thing out.'

Halfway up the rope ladder to the tree-house, the boy

176

saw the car turn up the school drive, sweep round the back of his grandparents' house and finally pull up outside the cottage. No-one got out for a while. Hand gestures he caught through the windows told him the people inside were arguing. Eventually the driver's door opened and Lisa got out. She headed up the front path with Patrick following, his face set and his hands rammed into his pockets. She rang the bell. The door opened and they went in.

Jamie shinned down the knotted rope to the ground, then slipped noiselessly through the budding shrubbery to the side of the house. Through the sitting room window he could see the three of them talking heatedly. Going quickly round the back, he let himself silently into the kitchen, from where he could hear every word of their conversation.

'I don't understand it!' his father was saying angrily. 'You told me the results were no damn good.'

'That's true, I did,' responded Patrick. 'But you see . . .'

Lisa broke in.

'Patrick simply missed the actual spot.'

'*Missed the spot*?' Guy's voice was incredulous.

'We're dealing with microns here,' pleaded Patrick. 'A fraction of a degree off course and you miss the target. It's a needle in a haystack.'

'And now, all of a sudden, the needle turns up.'

'I ran a search program through the computer.'

'You didn't think of doing that before, I suppose?'

Lisa interrupted again. Her tone was conciliatory.

'Look, there's been a slight slip-up, that's all. There's no point in holding an inquest. The fact is the treatment *is* working. So you can get back on track. Patrick's ready to carry on.'

'It's not actually quite that simple . . .' began Patrick.

'Don't listen to him, Guy,' said Lisa brusquely. 'It's prefectly simple. His professor found out about it and hit the roof. He's worried that he'll get the bullet if he's caught doing it again.'

'Wait a minute now . . .' protested Patrick.

'So you'll both have to carry on somewhere else.'

'You're crazy, Lisa. You seem to think specialist labs are two a penny.'

'We went through this in the car. You said equipment was the problem. Okay, what do you need?'

'Well, a strobe, for starters.'

'I'll get the boys in Lighting to fix one.'

'It's far too specialized. Anyway, there's an EEG recorder. Oscilloscopes. Various drugs . . .'

'How big is all that stuff?'

'The units themselves aren't big but that's not the point . . .'

'We'll go to the labs and load up your car.'

'None of that's any use without a proper sound-proofed chamber.'

'Right.' She clapped her hands. 'That's settled, then.'

Guy broke in with a harsh laugh.

'You're hiring a studio at the BBC?'

'No,' she replied decisively. 'We'll use the equipment and the soundproofing panels from the labs and replicate the whole set-up here.'

'*Here*?'

'Right here,' she replied. 'In this house.'

The boy crouched behind the car. It was getting dark and already the lights were on in the downstairs rooms. He could see in but they wouldn't be able to see out.

He unscrewed the petrol cap. With a piece of wire he poked a long strip of rag down the pipe. By capillary action, that would gradually suck up the petrol and serve as a perfect wick.

But he hadn't finished. He darted across the gravel, through a small gate and onto the track that led out through the rhododendron bushes to the playing fields. Breaking into a jog, he skirted the pavilion and, keeping to the trees at the top and cutting through the copse of firs, he finally came to the main school drive. There he turned left and followed it a short way to the wrought-iron gates at the end. He heaved away the boulders on either side and swung the huge, rusty-hinged gates shut.

They'd have to stop to open them. That was where he'd get them.

Guy followed Lisa around the cottage, keeping deliberately in the background as she planned and schemed until finally she forced a solution out. She was amazing. Even Patrick, who'd clearly been reluctant to admit his mistake at first, gradually regained his enthusiasm as the afternoon wore on.

They'd empty the box-room on the upper floor opposite Jamie's den and partition it to form a cubicle using the sound-proofing board from Patrick's lab. Inside, for the couch, they'd use an old door and place the special mattress on top of it. Above, they'd hang a small gantry from the ceiling joists to provide a mounting for the strobe. In the other half of the room, they'd set up a couple of tables to hold the EEG recording and monitoring equipment, the oscilloscope and the desk-top computer, and Patrick would be able to sit and work there while the sessions were in progress.

Guy insisted they stay for supper and sent Jamie up to the McVeys' for some more lamb chops. While the boy was away, he put on his duffel-coat and went into the garden for some potatoes from the shed.

Lisa jumped up.

'Let me do that,' she volunteered.

'No, no. You don't know where they are. Anyway, I don't need a torch – you would, and Jamie's got the only one.'

'Stick as you are,' said Patrick. 'Think of the saving in batteries you're making.'

Guy laughed.

'You know, being disabled I get special allowances for our lighting bills. They're really bright, these bureaucrats. Help yourselves to more drink. I won't be long.'

The evening was mild and a gentle wind blew through the trees all around, and he stood for a moment, savouring its sweet breath. He walked round to the side of the cottage, taking care to avoid the drain that always used to trip him up, and felt for the line of canes that marked the start of the vegetable plot. Opposite stood the small wooden garden shed. He was tracing his fingers along the front to find the door handle when he caught a whiff of something strange. It smelled strongly like petrol.

Jamie's limbs seemed to be in constant motion during supper. Guy, tuning in to him, heard him move his cutlery around, scrape his glass on the table top, shift about on his chair, kick his heels on its legs. He didn't talk much, but when he did his voice was unnaturally tense and flat. He kept jumping up and down to fill the glasses or change the record in the next room. Guy felt himself almost connected to his son by a burning thin wire of tension that cut clean through the atmosphere of celebration.

Eventually Lisa noticed the time.

'Patrick,' she cried, 'we must go! I've got to get you back to Cambridge. I might have to borrow your floor. What about the washing up?'

'Leave that to us,' said Jamie. 'Dad won't let anyone else touch his precious glasses.'

'We're a great team: Jamie washes the plates while I break the glasses,' said Guy. 'Well, if you really must, I'll get your coats.'

Lisa kissed him quickly and led the way out, talking all the while to cover over the awkward moment of leaving. Patrick followed. Guy put his arm on Jamie's shoulder. They stood by the gate, waving. Lisa started her car, reversed and called out goodbye. She gave a blast on her horn and then her tyres slowly crunched away down the drive.

Guy took a deep breath of relief. He felt ashamed. He'd done Jamie an injustice. She'd probably just lost her petrol cap and put that rag in as a bung. He should have left it.

Jamie went into the kitchen. He stacked two plates together, then changed his mind.

'I'll clear up later,' he said. 'I'm going out to watch the badgers.'

'Okay, but don't stay out too long,' said Guy. 'And wrap up well.'

'Sure, Dad.'

He heard the boy put on his anorak and pick up the torch – the torch? it seemed to rattle – and then let himself quickly out of the back door. His ear was automatically following the footsteps as they suddenly broke into a run when he realized with a sickening jolt what that rattle had been.

It was a box of matches.

The footsteps were disappearing away through the rhododendrons, not down the drive the way the car had gone. The boy was taking a short cut! To the cattle grid behind the McVeys' house where the car would have to slow down?

He launched up the path. He'd never taken it at speed before. The bends and twists came to him too quickly. His own noise as he crashed through bushes prevented him hearing the boy ahead, and every few moments he had to stop and listen. He made it to the rockery at the bottom of the McVeys' garden, his face and hands torn and slashed by the branches, before he realized he couldn't hear anything more. The boy must have headed towards the playing field and be running on grass.

Of course, the main gates!

He knew the perimeter track from his jogging, but without Jamie's bicycle clacking ahead he veered off to the left and found himself crashing into the hedge. Trailing one hand along it and holding the other to protect his face, he broke into a trot. Could Jamie hear him? He stopped, but his own panting made it impossible to detect small sounds. Then, some way ahead, he heard a car engine slowing down on its gears and, closer, the crack of a twig. The boy must be in the fir copse! He ploughed on towards the sound of the car. It now came to a halt. A door opened, flooding the night with music. There were voices: Patrick's bewildered; Lisa's, laughing. He was now into the trees. He didn't know this bit. Was there a path? He stumbled into a tree-trunk. Ahead, Patrick was opening the gates. The hinges groaned. He was laughing now, too.

A piercing, high-pitched howl of frustrated rage split the night air.

The voices stopped. The music was hushed. The voices started again, but in a lower register. Lisa called out tentatively, 'Jamie?' Then the engine revved up, gears crashed, a door slammed, tyres spat gravel and the sound of the motor died away down the Suffolk lanes.

Guy clung to the tree, listening. Footfalls, careless of detection, approached. Leaves shuffled, branches cracked. They came closer and paused beside him. When Guy reached out to him, Jamie was shaking uncontrollably.

He drew his son towards him and pressed him tight against his chest, smothering the mute convulsions.

'It's okay, Jamie. Take it easy. It's all right. I understand. I know how you feel. Calm down. Don't think about Lisa. It's just us, you and me, that's all that matters. Don't you see?'

He went on, groping for words to explain it to the boy and to reassure him, while all the time he wanted explanation and reassurance himself.

'Don't you see?' he repeated.

But the boy had gone stiff, allowing his body to be hugged but yielding nothing. And saying nothing.

CHAPTER SEVENTEEN

Love and understanding: that was all the psychotherapy anybody needed, including a boy not far off
his twelfth birthday. Guy sat by Jamie's bed for much
of the night, comforting and reassuring him and trying, too, to coax a reaction out of him.

During those long hours his imagination threw up
every kind of explanation for what underlay Jamie's
problem. Analysis was like pulling a thread on a
jersey: there was no end to the theories you could
advance once you started. Was the boy driven by
some dark jealousy of the mother-substitute, some
fear drawn from the cauldron of the collective unconscious? Did he see Sandy's death as a deliberate
rejection? Indeed, how did he see his own blindness?
His mother dies because she wants to get rid of him,
and his father goes blind so he can't see him any
more? What about the cottage itself, and the powerful
presence of Sandy in every inch of it? Should he send
the boy away to a different school? Or even back up to
the McVeys' house?

No, he repeated firmly: love and understanding,
that was all the psychotherapy the boy needed.

Yet he had tried to *kill* two people.

The next morning, Jamie got up early. He washed
up the previous night's supper, made the breakfast,
drew up a shopping list for the following week and
went round putting the furniture back in its right
place, then he went off outside by himself. During all
this he did not speak a single word. At lunch up at the
McVeys', in front of Donald and Alice, he replied in

monosyllables when Guy addressed him, but back at the cottage he was totally silent. Guy couldn't tell quite where he was in the house or when he entered a room whether Jamie was already there. Also, it was unnerving to be watched.

Why was he doing it? As a reprisal for having been thwarted? Was he inviting punishment, provoking him into taking retributive action? And should he do so? All children needed to be given boundaries beyond which they could not step; it was an essential part of developing a sense of right and wrong. By not punishing him, was he appearing to condone him? No: the boy could not help what he did. In civilized countries a man committing a crime of passion was exonerated. Or a man putting the person he loved out of terminal agony . . .

He stopped there abruptly. He didn't want to pursue that particular train of thought.

Love and understanding meant time and patience, but who could tell how long it might take? If Lisa came down to the cottage in the meantime, mightn't Jamie try to do her violence again? She was clearly in serious danger. For her own sake, she had to be warned off, at least until the treatments were over and he could bring the two of them together and – God damn it – *see* them reconciled.

In the afternoon he sought out Alice. He knew the school grounds so intimately now he hardly needed to think where he was going; once given instructions, the body seemed to find its own way. The crisp, cheerful April wind scattered his uncertainties.

Alice found him before he found her; she called to him from the garden where she was pruning the roses, she said. He sat down on the grass beside her.

'Talk, Guy,' she prompted him gently.

So he told her. He described everything that had happened the previous night. For a few moments after he'd finished, all he heard was the snipping of her secateurs. Then she sighed deeply.

'Guy, don't you think it's time you gave up? Don't you think . . .'

'I am not sending him to a psychiatrist! He was getting along fine until Lisa turned up. He's simply not ready.'

'I think you're making a mistake. Jamie needs a mother.'

'Well, not Lisa, obviously, and certainly not right now. It's Lisa I'm worried about; that's why I came to see you.'

'What can I do?'

'Don't invite her down again. In fact, keep her away. She won't take it from me. Or she'll take it the wrong way.'

'Shall I tell her about Jamie?'

'No, no, you mustn't. I don't know what she might do.' He paused. 'Can you find some other way?'

Early on the Tuesday morning, Patrick turned up at the cottage with a hired van. He'd smuggled the sound-proofing boards and other equipment out of the labs at night. He needn't have worried: in the morning, when Oliver saw they were gone, he approved.

Within moments of Patrick's arrival, Jamie disappeared. There was little Guy could do to help beyond providing tea, beer and moral support, and Patrick couldn't get far without the boy lending a hand. Guy put on his coat and went outside. He reckoned he knew where he'd find Jamie. He went a few yards down the drive and turned sharp left between two clumps of hawthorn. A short way beyond this stood the vast beech-tree in which Jamie had built his house. He stopped at the foot of the tree, listening. Ten, twenty feet above his head, a board creaked.

'Jamie?' he said.

No reply.

'I know you're up there, Jamie. I'm not going to play games. Come and give Patrick a hand, please. It's important.'

He went back indoors. Fifteen minutes later the boy appeared. He acted as though nothing was wrong. In front of Patrick he spoke normally to his father, even volunteering remarks, but behind his back he maintained his stony wall of silence. More than once during the day Guy had to control his anger, but he knew that that would be an admission of failure.

All day, Patrick and Jamie hammered and chiselled away in the small upstairs room, filling the cottage with the shrill whine of the power drill and the resinous tang of sawn wood until, well into the evening, Patrick declared the set-up, though rough and ready, essentially workable.

Guy felt his way round the unfamiliar shapes. The tables of instruments with glass screens and a machine with a chart and strange claw-like pens. A small computer with a typewriter keyboard. A cabinet containing, Patrick said, the scopolamine tablets and disposable hypodermics. The hormone shots, six doses in all, were to be kept in the refrigerator downstairs.

He entered the chamber. The size of a small sauna, it occupied one half of the room. The door was as thick as a fist, with a small double-glazed window set high in it. The walls, lined with perforated softboard, quenched the slightest cough. The couch was inclined at a gentle angle and covered with the special desensitizing mattress and, above it, on a swivelling arm, hung the apparatus housing the strobe. In the background he could hear the low, scrambled hiss of white sound.

'Feels terrific,' he said. 'You think it'll work?'

'As well as it did in the labs.'

'How's Tolkien?'

'Purring away. Okay, when do you want to start?'

'Let's kick off tomorrow morning. Well, Jamie, what do you say? Exciting, eh?'

And Jamie still said nothing.

Lisa sat opposite Alice at a small table in the restaurant on the top floor of the department store. A fine view stretched over the roof-tops to Hyde Park, but she didn't see it; other shoppers were bustling and clamouring around, but she didn't hear them. She listened, unable to touch her plate of salad, as the grey-haired woman told her the reason she'd asked her to lunch.

'I want to talk to you about Guy,' Alice was saying. 'I've known him since he was a boy and I think of him as a son. I don't mean to seem interfering, but I'd like to give you some advice. I'm very fond of you, Lisa, and I want what's best for you, too.'

'I'm listening.'

Alice leaned forward.

'Guy is not ready for you. Not for anybody. No, wait. It was wrong of me to ring you like I did. He's still sick at heart over Sandy. It'll heal, but it'll take some time yet. Do you understand what I am saying?'

Lisa met her eye levelly.

'I know you mean well, Alice,' she said, 'but that's all in the past. The present is what counts. Guy and I have something very special between us. He *needs* me – of course, he's too obstinate to admit it. I understand why. I understand him.'

'I wonder if you really do. Forgive me, Lisa, but I can't believe you know exactly what he went through when Sandy died.' Her voice trailed off. She took a sip of water; she hadn't touched her food, either. Then she looked up abruptly. 'Do you know anything about leukaemia? Sandy was in hospital for three months. They tried every form of chemotherapy. She lost most of her hair. She grew so thin her arms were like match-sticks. For a while she was in intensive care.'

'Alice . . .'

'It's important you appreciate what Guy went through. Listen to me. Eventually she refused to carry on. They were using her as a guinea-pig when there was nothing more they could do. She wanted to come home. She knew it was the end. I helped carry her into the cottage; she was as light as a bird. I kept Jamie away, of course. He came to stay up at our house and I'd bring him down to see her every day. She'd force herself out of bed, put on clothes, make herself up, wear a scarf. What it must have cost her I can't imagine. Afterwards, she'd collapse, and even with the curtains drawn the light would be too bright. Naturally, she felt she was a burden. She wanted to end it. She'd spit out the pills the doctor gave her, but he only gave her injections instead. The drugs were keeping her alive and she wanted to be allowed to go.

'It turned Guy grey, watching her die. The anger, the helplessness, broke him.

'Then she went through a really bad spell and he wouldn't let anyone into the cottage. One night, he sat up with her and they talked it through. And early the next morning – I remember it was one of those misty August days which turn out really hot – he dressed her and carried her out of the house. He took her to a place in a field at the far side of the woods which was very special to them, and laid her down there. That's where she died. He left her and came to find me.

'He was a wreck. A short time after, he had a minor break-down. Then he went to teach in Cambridge, to get away from the house and the memories. Lisa, he may look fine to you, but inside he's still a desperate mess. He has never really got over it.'

'My God,' Lisa breathed. 'Poor Guy.'

Alice nodded gravely.

'With Sandy, he thought he'd found everything he'd dreamed of. Then life dealt him a body-blow like that. It's not even four years ago and he's still off balance. He'd never let on, of course, but he can't escape it. Jamie, too, bears the scars.' She laid her hands on Lisa's. 'Only Guy can sort himself out. So that's why my advice is to keep out of the way for a bit. It's kinder to him and kinder to you.'

Session number three, the first in the cottage, went well. In fact, surprisingly well, in view of the rough-and-ready set-up. Unscientific though it looked, the sensory deprivation chamber seemed to work just as well as back in the labs. Patrick felt pleased with himself and more relaxed, too. Who needed all that ultra-sophisticated back-up when the job could be done in the upstairs room of a private house?

He had a word with his friend the radiologist at Addenbrooke's and took Guy along for a second scan. The results emerged exactly in line with the original projection, and he agreed to continue with the remaining five sessions, doing one a fortnight.

The morning before he was due to give Guy his fourth treatment, he ran Tolkien's own fourth and spent the afternoon running a brain probe to determine the extent of new axon growth. It was well past nightfall before he'd completed his analysis and finished writing up his log. It was extraordinary to see the growth continuing on course.

From the far end of the room a faint miaowing told him that the chlordiazepoxide was wearing off and the cat was coming round. He went on writing, trying to subdue his excitement. He'd got it taped. There was no way Oliver could know what was going on in a cottage thirty miles away. He'd saved his skin and he'd still got a human being to work on. The opportunity without the risk: what could be better?

Slowly he became aware that the plaintive crying from Tolkien's cage had dropped to a low growl, interspersed with a strange, sick coughing. He thought nothing more of it until, suddenly, the cat let out one long drawn-out howl. His blood froze.

She had ripped off the surgical tape holding her skull-cap in place and torn it aside, exposing the pulsing pinky-grey clots of her naked brain. As she saw him, she backed away into the corner of the cage, spitting and snarling. There, crouching on her haunches and howling maniacally, she raised a paw, bared her talons and started to claw her own brains out.

He grabbed a syringe, filled it with chloroform and plunged it in as close to her heart as he could get. Trembling, he scooped up the bits of cerebral matter scattered around onto a ceramic dish and slipped them quickly into the cryostat.

During the long hours of the night he withdrew samples and ran chemical analyses. Throughout the motor cortex he found the cells glutted with enkephalin, a small peptide molecule made by the brain itself as an opiate against pain.

Indescribable agony must have driven the cat to mutilate itself.

Around dawn, he left the labs and went for a walk. The fine fresh Spring air brought the dilemma he faced into sharp focus. Should he, or should he not, go through with Guy's fourth session?

Perhaps you couldn't infer human from cat so easily. Maybe their respective metabolisms differed not only in scale but in other, subtler ways. Maybe as it grew the new pathway had hit an area dense with links to peripheral pain receptors in the cat, but it would bypass this in a human brain. Maybe it was simply a freak event. Maybe this, maybe that . . . All special pleading. When the cat − man analogy worked, he relied on it. Now it gave an unwelcome result, he was ready to scrap it. At least he should be consistent. If he decided to continue with Guy, what was the point of carrying on with the cats in parallel?

As he stared into the silver river at the wake left by a swan, he made up his mind. Science worked by trial and error. You couldn't stop the trial for one single error. He'd be inconsistent. He'd call the event aberrant. He'd work another cat up to the same level and try again. And he'd carry on with Guy. He'd double the dose of scopolamine, give him a strong pain-killer before he started and take all other precautions he could. Guy had accepted there would be risks, so it was on his head.

He *had* to find out. And you could only find out by trying.

'F major, here we come,' said Guy cheerfully as he entered the sound-proofed chamber.

'Just take it easy,' said Patrick, following behind, holding the leads from the electrodes glued to his friend's scalp. 'I don't want you excited. I'm going to give you a double dose of dampeners this time. We may be getting into tricky water here.'

'Seems all plain sailing to me.'

'Don't count your chickens.'

'Don't mix your metaphors.'

He gave him four of the oval orange scopolamine tablets mixed in a solution containing a strong dose of pethidine, a pain-killer that would not constrict his pupils. Then he laid him down on the couch. Connecting up the leads to the EEG recorder outside, he applied the tape to his eyelids and angled the strobe directly overhead. Then he broke open the hormone ampoule and filled the syringe.

'Relax completely,' he said as he dabbed his neck with spirit. 'Let your whole body go. Don't even cross your fingers.'

And gradually he inserted the needle into the bulging artery.

Patrick kept his eye on the oscilloscope. The screen displayed steady alpha waves at eight to ten cycles per second. After an hour without event, he grew relaxed and began chatting to Jamie, who stood quiet and watchful at his elbow. He described the functions of each of the instruments on the panel in front of him: the rheostat controlling the level of white sound, the small flickering lights on the computer showing it was on-line and receiving input from the EEG recorder, and a large milled knob marked *strobe* which controlled the rate of light flicker.

Jamie paid close attention. He was a bright boy and it was good to have him around. Despite first impressions, he seemed perfectly normal. Moody with his father at times, of course, but what boy wasn't? He only had to think of his own childhood to know what it was like being a child brought up among adults. The two of them probably found it equally hard to express their feelings, but he felt that Jamie had, in his own way, rewarded him with his friendship.

Towards the end of the second hour, he went to stretch his legs, leaving Jamie in charge. His night without sleep was catching up with him and he needed a double strong coffee.

The boy listened for the footsteps receding down the stairs. He looked in through the small window at his father, stretched out and staring straight into the searing flashes. He turned back to the panel of instruments.

Slowly he reached his hand forward. Taking hold of the large milled knob marked *strobe*, he turned it forward six full notches.

A crowded shopping mall. A sea of people hurrying in all directions. In the centre, the tall, stooping figure of a man in a pale jacket. He is inching forward against the tide, tapping his way with a white stick.

There's a sudden commotion. A youth in a studded leather jerkin jostles the blind man, knocks him off balance. A second one, his head shaved, dips his hand into the man's pocket and slips out his wallet. He passes it to the first as the blind man sprawls to the ground.

There's a shrill cry from a few yards behind. A young red-haired woman bursts forward. She hurls herself at the shaven headed youth. The other one has vanished. People scream. The crowd parts. The woman won't let go. There's a swift stabbing movement, the flash of a knife. The woman cries out, falls back. The youth breaks free, bolts through the crowd. The woman staggers back, clutching her stomach. Blood spurts from between her fingers. She falls to the ground, writhing. Through the crowd now closing in round her, her face is momentarily in close-up.

It is Kathy.

The boy watched the ink-pens scratching furiously over the chart and the wave patterns jerking wildly on the oscilloscope. Footsteps sounded on the stairs. He switched the knob quickly back. He was sitting reading a book when Patrick came in.

Patrick examined Guy carefully. He inspected the retinas with the ophthalmoscope and checked his pulse and blood pressure. Something was wrong, for he seemed extremely agitated, yet there were none of the signs of physical distress that he'd feared. The pethidine mixed with the dampeners had clearly done its work. With Jamie's help, he steered him down the corridor and put him to bed. All the time, Guy was semi-delirious, rambling on about someone called Kathy and a mugging.

'Call the hospital,' he kept saying in his thick, drugged voice. 'Kathy's been stabbed.'

Patrick turned to Jamie.

'Kathy?'

'The woman from the Centre,' he replied. 'I'll call them.'

A minute later the boy came back.

'Kathy's quite all right, Dad,' he said quickly.

A look of overwhelming relief spread over Guy's face. Patrick gave him a shot of Amytal and in a moment his eyes closed. He had the look, in his sleep, of a man brought back almost too late from the trenches.

*

Every night that week Lisa had been out late, and that evening she'd decided to stay in and go to bed early. She picked at a plate of cheese and, with the television on in the corner, started on a pile of ironing.

Guy would have had his fourth session that day. How had it gone? She'd called Patrick, but there was no reply. Only her conversation with Alice had kept her from phoning Guy direct. She wished she'd never heard all that about Sandy. It hurt her, of course, and it made her feel painfully foolish to think of that wonderful afternoon down in the boat-house. But why listen to Alice? The woman cherished an image of Guy and Sandy as the perfect couple; to keep it intact she was bound to see Guy as traumatized by her death and this as the root of all the trouble.

There was a part of Guy that she knew and Alice could never glimpse. Alice was just a bereaved mother-in-law, living in the past. Sandy was dead, and the dead should not be allowed to poison the happiness of the living.

She put down the iron and reached for the phone.

Jamie answered almost at once.

'Hello, Jamie,' she said pleasantly. 'How are you?'

'What do you want?'

'I was wondering how it went today. Could I speak to your dad?'

'He can't be disturbed.'

'Is he asleep?'

'He can't be disturbed.'

She hesitated for a moment. 'Is everything okay? You don't sound quite right.'

'Everything's fine.'

'Are you sure?' When he didn't reply, she went on, 'What were you up to the other night, trying to spook us out? I jumped out of my skin.'

'Everything's fine, I said.'

'Jamie, I think you're upset with me for some reason. Are you?'

'You don't upset me,' he replied after a moment. 'But you do sometimes Dad. He gets unhappy and muddled.'

'*I* do?'

'I've got to go now. Dad's calling.'

'Hang on, Jamie . . .'

But the boy had hung up, leaving her with a dead line. Slowly she replaced the receiver, then went to the kitchen and poured herself a glass of wine. She turned the television off and sat down in an armchair to think.

Jamie.

She felt sure her hunch had been right all along. Jamie was the obstacle. Not Guy's desire to spare her his blindness, not the denial of her love as a test of his own strength, not even the all-pervasive ghost of Sandy . . . but *Jamie*. Jamie controlled that household. He controlled his father, too: he even decided who should or shouldn't speak to him. Why had he taken this role? And how did he see *her*? He'd clearly taken against her. Why?

The more she reflected on her conversation, the more she realized that Jamie was the key to everything. Perhaps there was no point in approaching Guy until she had come to an understanding with the boy. She'd give it a week or so, maybe until after the next session, and then she'd go down and have it out with him face to face.

Guy was sitting in the front garden in the spring sunshine when Jamie brought him up a mug of tea.

'How're you feeling, Dad?' he asked.

It was the first time he had voluntarily initiated a conversation for a week.

'Pretty good,' replied Guy with deliberate nonchalance. 'My head's still like a volcano, though.' Four days had passed since the last session.

The boy sat down on the lawn beside him. There was a rustle of paper but somehow Guy didn't think Jamie was reading. He didn't want to press him; he was obviously puzzling something out. Eventually the boy spoke again.

'That last time,' he began. 'What really happened?'

'I told you. I had that bad dream. Patrick said things might start going funny around now. Something about the axons growing so fast the insulation can't keep up.'

'Just a dream?'

'A horrible nightmare, like the ones you used to get, remember?'

'They were different.'

This was good. He had to keep the boy talking. 'How can you tell? You can't know my dreams, any more than I can know yours. It's impossible, like knowing another person's pain . . .'

Jamie interrupted him.

'My nightmares were different,' he repeated. 'They didn't come true.'

'Nor mine. You spoke to Kathy yourself, didn't you?'

'She was okay when I called her.'

'Well, then.'

Again that rustle; a newspaper?

'Want to hear something spooky?'

'Try me.'

'Front page of today's *East Anglian Gazette*.' The boy read aloud. '"KNIFE ATTACK VICTIM DIES. Kathy Wilkes, 33, chief Mobility Officer at the County

198

Blind Rehabilitation Centre, died in hospital last night after being attacked and stabbed by an unidentified assailant in the Westway shopping arcade . . .'''

CHAPTER EIGHTEEN

'What the hell is going on, Patrick? And don't fob me off by saying it's coincidence.'

'It could be.'

'I phoned the director at the Rehab Centre and he told me exactly what happened. I *saw* it happening. *Saw* it.'

'All right, I accept that if it's a coincidence, it's a very remote one.'

'Millions to one against.'

'It's still a logical possibility.'

'For God's sake, Patrick! I have a dream in that Frankenstein box of yours, and three days later it happens *exactly as I foresaw it*. I call that a premonition. What I want to know is, what on earth is this treatment doing to me?'

'Hold on. There's no such thing as precognition.'

'You said that before, when I saw that train crash, remember?'

'You certainly weren't having the treatment then.'

'But I was blind. At least, I was having a blinding migraine. It's got to have something to do with that! Think of Tiresias and all the blind seers in history. You know, sometimes I wonder.'

'You wonder what?'

'If by losing my sight I haven't somehow gained *second* sight.'

They walked on for a while until they reached the pavilion. Guy had to sit down. He couldn't think while walking: navigating took up too much of his concentration. They sat on the steps. The smell of fresh creosote on the woodwork reminded him that the summer term was beginning shortly. The sun warmed his knees and shoulders. He wondered with fleeting despair if he'd ever see it before he went mad.

Patrick broke the silence.

'Of course, in theory, if you were looking for some-one with psychic power a blind man would be your best bet.'

'What do you mean?'

'In *psi* events, the brain goes into a state that's indistinguishable from hypnosis. Your psychics prob-ably have a straightforward way of hypnotizing themselves. Take shamans and spirit mediums, for instance. They get themselves into trances by rhythmic dancing, body shaking, fixating on objects. All classic ways of inducing hypnotic states. And all forms of sensory deprivation. In fact, being blind would help. Seventy per cent of the brain's sensory input comes from the eyes. You might say a blind man is living in a perpetual state of sensory depriva-tion.'

'There you are!' cried Guy. 'I'm already half way psychic, and then you put me in that damn chamber which is *designed* to cut out all sound and touch, and you flash lights in my eyes. What do you expect?'

'Tell me,' Patrick said carefully, 'what exactly were you doing when you had that hallucination of the train crashing?'

'Standing by the river, watching Jamie fishing.'

'Was it a bright day? Sunny?'

'Yes, I think it was. I was staring into the water, I remember. I felt sort of . . . mesmerized.'

'Mesmerized: you said it.'

'*You* said it. A blind man under hypnosis can have premonitions.'

'I said he could be psychic. That's different. *If* psychic vision were possible, and there's no evidence for it whatsoever . . .'

'Yes, there is. Me. I'm living proof.'

'I'm talking of evidence that can be scientifically validated. At the very most, psychic vision would only be about things happening at the same time. *Future* vision is out. You can't break the rules of time.'

'Some people think time is serial, not linear.'

'Some people are cranks.'

'Some scientists end up on the scrap-heap of history, Patrick.'

Patrick laughed. 'Then I challenge you. Next session, tell me the winner of the four o'clock at Newmarket. Or any race, anywhere.'

But Guy didn't laugh. This was too big, too frightening to joke about. And he could tell that Patrick, who soon fell silent, knew so, too.

Most of what people called psychic, said Patrick to himself as he drove back to Cambridge, was (a), fakery or (b), delusion or (c), sleight of hand or (d), some highly developed acuity to detect subliminal cues the majority of people missed.

Or (e), coincidence.

One shouldn't discount coincidence so easily. He'd told Guy of the case during the run-up to D-Day when key code-words kept cropping up as clues in the *Daily Telegraph* crossword puzzle. Utah and Omaha, Overlord and Mulberry: code-names for landing beaches, harbours, operations. When it was checked out, it was found that a couple of schoolmasters had compiled the clues in total innocence.

'*Blind* schoolmasters?' Guy had queried with a smile.

But what about all the clues that had not been code-words? In Guy's case, his entire hallucination had been accurate in all its complexity and detail. Nothing was missing, nothing added. Even if you looked at it as a matter of bytes of information passing down a channel, it had to be more than coincidence. It was *communication*.

Pre-vision? No. He resisted that explanation on two counts.

First, while there might be physical models, such as televisions, for psychic vision of events happening at the same time, no machine existed, or could be imagined, that might describe events that hadn't happened *yet*.

Secondly, there were objections of logic: if you could foresee the future, presumably you could do something about it, and if you did, then was *that* the future? That road led rapidly to an infinite regression.

Was it even paranormal? What did that mean, anyway?

Everything that existed could, in principle, be explained. Everything that could be explained was normal. The paranormal was, by definition, that which was not normal. *Ergo*, the paranormal did not exist.

A neat syllogism. But when applied to the present case, he suddenly felt even this simple ground shifting from under him.

This thing *did* exist and it was *not* normal.

The following day, Patrick gave the fifth treatment to Tolstoy, the cat that had replaced the luckless Tolkien and was now Guy's monitor to test the way ahead. During the session, he recorded her brain activity carefully and took regular blood samples in case she had a crisis. But she showed no signs of distress, either before or afterwards. Did this mean the axon path had progressed beyond the danger zone?

He was tiptoeing blindfold through a minefield. He no longer had any idea of what he was doing. At any minute his world of reason and sense might blow apart. Every step brought still more questions. Could he, for instance, presume that Tolkien's self-mutilation had any link with Guy's hullucination? If so, was he saying that the cat had been *psyched out*? What the hell did that mean, in cat's terms? He still had sections of her brain tissue preserved frozen in the cryostat. If he had the time and the tools, would he find there some hitherto unknown brain chemical responsible for firing subcortical cells in some hitherto unknown pattern so as to produce what, in a human brain, constituted a psychic event? What sort of chemical would he be looking for, anyway? An amine? Call it telepathamine? *Televisamine*?

This was science fiction. Modern-day necromancy. Gibberish.

But something *was* happening, and even if he took it right down to the cell level, it still could be any number of things. The Schwann cells could be using the axons as a substrate for migration in a way he didn't understand. Or glial cells acting as substrates for the migration of whole neurones. Even at the molecular level, there could be some alteration in the way sodium and potassium ions were exchanged across the axon membrane, upsetting the way its resting potential was restored.

He simply did not know.

But he must not allow himself to be side-tracked into trying to find out. Not yet. The treatment was the main experiment. So long as it wasn't going positively wrong, he must shelve speculation. Okay, Guy had had a hallucination. That, of itself, was no bad thing.

It could well suggest that the axon path had already begun to form links with the visual processing areas. And, whether called psychic or not, it *had* been simply a hallucination. Certainly not a dream: Rapid Eye Movements would have shown up on the EEG. He'd have found evidence of beta-wave activity on the charts and, as he knew because he was there at the time, he'd only been getting alpha waves. Provided Guy didn't get psyched out like the cat, he'd do better to leave the other questions pending and concentrate on getting the final four sessions right.

'I am the resurrection and the life, saith the Lord. He that believeth in me, though he were dead, yet shall he live . . .'

Guy shifted in his seat. The pew was uncomfortable. His collar and tie were uncomfortable. And, above all, he felt uncomfortable about Kathy. He was to blame. He'd foreseen it, and done nothing. He was the messenger and he hadn't delivered the message.

'We brought nothing into this world,' continued the vicar, 'and it is certain we can carry nothing out. The Lord gave and the Lord hath taken away; blessed be the name of the Lord.'

A blind seer. He'd been given this gift – this curse – of foresight and twice he had failed to act. He could have alerted her beforehand. She needn't have gone in to work that day; she could have taken the man-on-bus drill instead, or stayed in the Centre and given him a Braille lesson. That particular day, that particular place, that time, those people: if she'd avoided just one of those, she'd still be alive today.

Or would she? If it hadn't been then, would it have been the next time she'd gone to that shopping arcade? Or did we all have our hour, the minute when our biological clock just stopped? If she'd been crossing a street at that very second, would a bus have knocked her down instead?

Patrick had rebutted the idea with typical sophistry. If you foresee the future and then you change it, he'd said, *that* becomes the actual future. If so, it wasn't the future you foresaw in the first place. And so on.

No. If humanity had any meaning at all, you had to believe that man had free will. Otherwise we all were clockwork automata, our strings played by some grand invisible puppeteer, and no one of us could ever be held responsible for anything he did. And the world just didn't feel like that.

He could have saved her. He *should* have.

'O death, where is thy sting? O grave, where is thy victory?'

Here, in his heart.

'Step, Dad.'

He put a hand on Jamie's shoulder and followed him out of the cool, musty church and across the bumpy grass to the graveside. The boy had insisted on coming, and he was pleased to have his company. Guy sensed people shifting around him but no-one spoke. Pigeons wooed irreverently in the trees. His dark suit was tight, and in the warm Spring sunlight he began to swelter. He hated funerals.

'Forasmuch as it hath pleased Almighty God of His great mercy,' began the vicar again, 'to take unto Himself the soul of our dear sister here departed . . .'

His mind went back three years. He was standing in the small patch of consecrated ground outside the school chapel, listening to those same words uttered over Sandy's grave. And as he thought back to the last hours of her life, he wondered if these visions had been sent to give him a chance of redeeming himself for the terrible thing he did that morning.

The light had gone out of her eyes. They had turned in on themselves with the effort of coping with the pain. When, in brief moments, he caught a glimpse of her soul through them, he saw exhaustion beyond exhaustion, pain beyond pain. During the days she was back at the cottage, fed with drugs not to cure her – the doctors all agreed she was beyond that – but merely to keep her alive, he watched through the windows of her eyes as hope turned to despair and struggle to defeat.

On that last night he sat up with her, holding her hand, sometimes remaining silent, sometimes reading to her, though he knew she could barely comprehend anything. She was only counting the time before she would be released.

In the early hours she cried out aloud, unable to bear the pain. He tried to give her the analgesic tablets the doctor had left, but she refused them. The look in her eyes blistered his heart.

'Help me,' she whispered.

Towards dawn, she fell asleep. Her breathing grew fainter, her pulse weaker. A deep serenity settled over her features. She was slipping away. Then, quite abruptly, she woke. Her eyes betrayed the terror of finding she was still there, still facing the battle, the rotten husk of her body still refusing to be shed.

They had talked about it when the doctors said she had no chance. He'd agreed he would do what was necessary, if it ever came to it. Of course it wouldn't. But it had.

Some time around nine o'clock, he unhooked the drip from her wrist. He brushed her moulting hair carefully and dressed her in a white cotton dress, now pitifully big for her emaciated body. He put a trace of red on her lips and colouring on her cheeks and dabbed scent on her thin, shrunken neck. Finally, he put her small blue linen sun-hat on her head and held a mirror for her to see herself in. She gave him a smile of such brave reassurance that he had to turn away to hide his tears. At last he lifted her off the bed and, taking a small cushion to support her, took her downstairs in his arms.

The smell of roses and freshly mown grass swam in the August morning air as he carried her down the front path and along the sun-dappled path through the woods. She was as light as though all her substance had fled. From time to time she tried to speak, but he hushed her. At last the path ended and he came to a large field of green-gold corn. He waded in up to his waist until they were some yards from the edge and, flattening a patch just as he had done on that very first day they'd made love, he laid her down. She lay on her back with her eyes half open, full of the yearning for peace. She gave him a smile, her lips puckered in a kiss, then she closed her eyes. After a moment she lost consciousness. With trembling hands and tear-swollen eyes, he took the cushion and, praying for forgiveness, brought it quickly over her face and pressed it down.

'Lord have mercy upon us,' said the vicar.

'Christ, have mercy upon us,' responded the small congregation around the grave.

Christ, have mercy upon me, echoed Guy.

For several days, Jamie was absorbed in his den, working on some project he would not be drawn into revealing. It came to light one morning when Guy came down for breakfast.

'I've got a surprise for you, Dad,' he said. 'It's on your plate.'

Guy smiled. This was the old Jamie. He picked up the small object in its wrapping paper.

'What is it?'

'Open it.'

It was a small plastic disk the size of a penny, with a short tube projecting out of one side and a long thin flex out of the other that ended in a tiny plug.

'It's some kind of electrode,' he guessed. 'I give up.'

'It's an ear-phone.'

'I'm blind, not deaf!'

'Dad, it's a walkie-talkie! You plug it into a receiver in your pocket and I can talk to you from far away. You can go running and I'll direct you by remote control.' The boy must have sensed his reservation. 'Don't you like it?'

'It's very ingenious.'

'Come on, let's try it!'

He hesitated. He wasn't interested in those tricks any more. They were for blind people who were staying blind.

'But Jamie, I'll soon be able to see by myself.'

'You can't be sure.'

'Well, all right. I suppose we could try it out.'

'Left a bit,' said the tiny voice in his ear.

He veered a little to the left. He'd been running for several minutes and already he'd lost all idea of where he was. He knew that Jamie was keeping him to the white line that marked the boundary of the school games field, but where the pavilion or the main school buildings lay he couldn't tell.

'Straighten up. More yet.'

The voice was almost a whisper. It seemed to speak right into his head, insistent and uncannily intimate.

He ran on, going faster or slower, turning to left or to right, just as instructed. It was easier than following the bicycle with its clacking spokes but he wasn't sure he liked being Jamie's model racing car.

'Great. Now slow down. And walk. Count ten and you'll come to the sight-screen. Okay, you got it. Turn ninety degrees to the left and start walking. I'll come down and meet you.'

He took the ear-phone out and after a while he heard Jamie come running up. 'Wasn't that brilliant?' he cried.

'Great.'

'I could talk you all around the place! We can use it going shopping. I can direct you from across the street. When it's too windy, I'll steer you down the school path. You'll never bump into anything again. I can be hundreds of yards away and it'll still work.'

'Where were you just now?'

'In the tree-house.'

'The tree-house? How could you see me?'

'With your binoculars. You don't mind, do you, Dad?'

Certainly not a dream. Rapid Eye Movements would have shown up on the EEG. And so, surely, would a hallucination.

Patrick was in the middle of dinner on High Table when an incredible thought struck him: he hadn't actually physically checked the EEG recordings from that last session. He'd assumed there'd be nothing because he hadn't observed any break in the steady alpha-wave rhythm. But he could have missed a small blip. Some electrical impulses travelled down nerve fibres at a hundred metres a second. Why had he assumed it would take, say, a minute of real time for a one-minute hallucination? Dreams that appeared to last hours to the dreamer might only last a split second of brain-time.

His neighbour, a visiting philosopher, was telling him how he kept a Doberman in his rooms, in spite of strict regulations against dogs in college, and got away with it by naming it Cat . . . But Patrick wasn't listening. He was obsessed by this oversight. Had he missed an important clue?

As soon as the Dean dismissed the table with a mumbled *Benedictus benedicatur*, he hurried off to the labs. A few solitary lights burned in rooms where students were working late for Finals, now only a few weeks away, but otherwise the building was empty and silent. Letting himself into his room with his card-key, he went quickly over to the computer and called up the EEG data file on Session 4.

He ran a search program, looking for unusual spikes or other irregularities in the wave-forms shown on the oscilloscope. Within a moment he had identified a period of some four minutes right in the middle of the session when the mean wave produced by the sensors was just over fifteen cycles per second.

What the hell kind of brain-wave was that?

Hooking up the EEG recorder, he fed the data for those few minutes back into the machine and played it out onto the rolling chart. As he watched, his mouth went dry. There, inscribed quite clearly by the ink-pens, were two quite separate wave-forms. Some showed medium-length alpha waves, but others were almost double the frequency: beta waves.

These signified the Rapid Eye Movement of dream sleep.

Alpha waves and REMs, *simultaneously*!

Guy had been awake and dreaming, both at the same time. This was the hallmark of a hypnotized state. And that, as he knew, was the mode of the brain during a *psi* event.

He pulled a bottle of whisky out from his desk drawer and poured several fingers into a plastic cup. The next step was to pinpoint which piece of equipment had malfunctioned during those crucial four minutes.

Within half an hour he had identified it as the strobe. Somehow the strobe flicker rate had shot up for that period and afterwards reverted to normal.

He walked round the lab, whisky in hand, talking aloud to himself. Just as he reached the cat's cage, his mind went back to his conversation with Guy after that last session and suddenly he made the connection.

Strobe. Flashing light. Flashing *sun*light? Sunlight reflecting off a river? Guy had been standing by the river, staring into the water. It was sunny. And he'd been momentarily blinded by a migraine. Mesmerized, he'd said. *Mesmerized*?

My God.

But what about this time? Four vital minutes, in the middle of the session. How had it happened without his knowing? He'd been there in the room all the time.

Or had he?

Then he remembered. Somewhere in the middle of it all, he'd gone downstairs for some coffee, leaving Jamie in the room.

Jamie had interfered with the strobe setting!

Had the boy fiddled with it for fun? Or deliberately? What the hell was he up to?

Guy picked the last of the lilies of the valley from the patch that had flourished between the rainwater tub and the wall and, filling a can with a little water, took them down to the school. Following the path to the side of the tennis-courts, he came to the small memorial garden lying at the back of the chapel. He went up to the nail-studded wooden door and turned about, then took eight paces diagonally to the right until he could feel the slight rise in the turf that was Sandy's grave.

Lilies of the valley were her favourite flower, and their scent powerfully conjured up her smiling face curtained with long dark hair. Kneeling by the headstone, he reached for the marble vase at the base and drew it towards him. It was heavy, and as he felt for the perforated lid, he realized it was already filled with water and fresh flowers.

That evening, Alice came down to the cottage and he asked her, in passing, what kind of flowers she'd put there. Neither she nor Donald had been to the grave for well over a week, she said.

Guy prepared for the fifth session with a gnawing sense of unease. Patrick was in a cheerful mood and cajoled him like a reluctant child. They were coming into the home straight, he said; only three more to go after this. He set up the apparatus and gave Guy the scopolamine and analgesic tablets.

Guy fingered the pills in the palm of his hand.

'You're sure about these things?' he asked. 'I want vision, not visions.'

'Believe me,' replied Patrick, 'it was aberrant. Tolstoy's been through this next session. It won't happen again.'

'Tolstoy?' queried Jamie from the corner of the small experiment room. 'I thought she was called Tolkien.'

Patrick gave a short laugh.

'Tolkien, Tolstoy, I don't know. You wait till you're grown up, Jamie. You won't always remember their names. Eh, Guy?'

Guy didn't laugh. Four down, four to go. Each time they went further into unknown territory. What if there was a centre of psychic vision in the brain and he was being linked up to that? He'd be a permanent psychic, living through constant premonitions of disasters. Why always disasters, anyway? Perhaps because screams echoed loudest down the corridors of time.

He swallowed the pills in one gulp.

'Come on, then,' he said. 'Let's get on with it.'

Though Jamie was obliging throughout the session, Patrick nevertheless kept a careful eye on him all the time. He wasn't going to tell the boy he knew he'd tampered with the strobe for fear of arousing his hostility. Jamie was trying to wreck the treatment, he'd worked it out, so as to prevent Lisa coming between him and his father. He probably reckoned that if it didn't work and Guy remained blind, she'd ultimately weary of the pursuit and leave the two of them alone in their cosy little household.

Several times Jamie left the room, only to reappear and stand in the shadow, switching his gaze from Patrick to the instruments and back. At one point he offered to take charge if he wanted to go out for a bit, but Patrick knew what was going through his mind. The treatment was throwing up all kinds of side-effects, but the main axon growth did appear to be developing every bit as well as he could have hoped. As he got closer to the finish and the probability of success rose, the stakes rose with it. He'd monitor every minute of what went on in that room. Jamie's mental condition was someone else's problem; to Patrick he was just a poisonous little brat trying to get in his way. And no-one was going to do that.

*

The boy took the hidden path that led in a wide sweep through the undergrowth and came out on the far side of the walled garden. It was already dark and, though he carried a torch, he kept it off. Reaching the courtyard, he climbed through the window into the washroom. Inside, he hurried through the dark passages and up the main stairs. At the landing he turned left and followed the corridor that led over the interconnecting bridge to the dormitory block.

He found the door key to Matron's office hanging on a hook in the sick bay. Inside, he went over to her medicine cabinet. Holding the torch between his teeth so that it shone onto the lock, he worked away with the blade of his pen-knife until he'd slipped the catch. He slid the door open, revealing rows of glass and plastic bottles ranged on the shelves.

He took out the small oval orange tablet he'd brought from home and laid it on the side where he could refer to it for comparison, then started through each bottle and tub in turn. After a minute, he stopped. He'd found what he was looking for.

He held the tablet in the light. It, too, was small, oval and orange.

He took a handful, replaced the bottle, locked the cabinet then turned and retraced his steps, and within a few minutes he was on the path back home.

IV

SUMMER

Time present and time past
Are both perhaps present in time future,
And time future contained in time past.

T. S. ELIOT
Four Quartets

CHAPTER NINETEEN

Summer exploded suddenly upon the Suffolk country-side, catching Guy unawares. A blanket of foliage muffled the school grounds. Quite abruptly, the trees and bushes on the path to the main buildings took a step forward, blotting out the vital echoes, and grass sprang up over the cobble-stones to dampen the snick of his heels. In the space of one week, the whole shape of his world changed: it had closed in on him, confusing him with its babel of birdsong and disorientating him with its newly burgeoned forms.

The summer term had started and he began taking a stick to walk to school, though he hid it behind a gutter once there. On the pretext of having work to prepare before school began, he'd leave the cottage early each morning, often before Jamie. He was uncomfortable with the ear-phone, which the boy insisted was the perfect answer, but he didn't want to upset him by saying so. Anyway, God willing, he soon wouldn't be needing any of that.

He was teaching three afternoons a week as well as mornings now, and he added to his timetable by helping out in the music department and giving after-hours coaching in French and Geography to boys sitting entrance exams to higher schools. He would come home late and exhausted to find Jamie doing his homework on the kitchen table, the whisky out, ice in the bucket and their supper cooking in the oven.

He'd agreed with Patrick they'd run the sixth session a week after the following Sunday – Jamie turned twelve on the Saturday – but as it was a long exeat weekend he'd have time to recover before school began again. They'd continue with the seventh a fortnight later, on the Saturday before half-term week, and the eighth and final one as soon after that as they could, depending on the results. And then? He thought back to May of the previous year – Cambridge with Lisa, carefree and in love, with no notion of the black clouds on the horizon. Had he looked over his shoulder then, would he have seen them looming there? He shuddered to think. But now he had a chance to break the chain and prove that nobody's fate was irreversible.

And Jamie seemed to have turned the corner with the flowering of the season. At school, he kept himself less aloof from the other boys and even turned up for cricket practice in the nets. At home, he became more talkative. Perhaps time was healing him after all. This was not the disturbed Jamie, capable of wilful acts of violence. This was a different boy: keen, questioning, and far more sure of himself. Guy wasn't at all clear where this had come from, but he was glad about it.

The following evening, he was letting himself in the front door when Jamie called out from the study.

'Watch out, Dad! Boxes in the hall.'

Guy's hand touched a pile of cartons stacked against the wall. The boy came out into the corridor.

'Kathy's books: her parents sent them to you. I'm putting them in order. "S" has three dots and "T" four, right?'

'You mean they're Braille?'

''Course. Do you want them by title or author?'

'I don't want them at all. Leave them in their boxes. They can go to the Centre.'

'But, Dad, you like reading.'

'With my own eyes, I do.'

'But suppose . . .'

'Just let's think positively. Anyway, I couldn't accept them. I feel too bad about her.'

'You've no need to.'

'You saw what happened. I did nothing to save her.'

'You couldn't have anyway. It was meant to happen.'

'Why was it meant?'

'Because.'

He led the way into the kitchen and poured himself a beer. The boy had such unswerving belief; his faith had always been unshakable.

'Come on, Jamie, that's no answer. Is everything meant? Are wars meant? Old Joss dying of cancer: was that meant? Were you meant to come twentieth in History last term? What if you'd worked a bit harder?'

'Some things are, some aren't. It's up to God.'

'Suppose I'd warned the police beforehand and they'd caught those muggers. Then what?'

'God would have got her some other way. And he'd have punished you for interfering.'

'If I make you do your homework and stop you coming bottom in History, do I incur divine wrath? Should I *prevent* you doing your homework?'

'Dad, you always reduce things to a joke.'

'It's not a joke, it's a practical instance. A general proposition can only be tested out in particular cases. It only takes one case to refute it. Does this?'

'I don't know. I'm not God. I just know there's right and there's wrong.'

'Is it meant,' he went on, unable to stop worrying at it, 'when a person does wrong? It would be pretty rough if God punished people for things He'd made them do in the first place. If I told you to break a school rule and then gave you a detention for it, you wouldn't be too happy.'

Jamie sighed impatiently.

'It doesn't start off like that, Dad. You can do anything you like to begin with. But if you do something wrong, you get punished. *That*'s what's meant. Okay?'

'I see.'

He sipped his beer. It was subtle, for all its apparent simplicity. You had free will to determine your actions, but if they infringed the rules, what followed was inevitable, destined. But it provoked all sorts of questions. Where did you start from? Last week? Some age at which you could be held responsible for your actions? Your own birth? People brought up in a lapsarian tradition thought it was too late anyway; we were already fallen creatures. No wonder fatalism abounded, no wonder astrology flourished and there was such widespread belief in predetermination. Taking Jamie's model to its logical conclusion, the rules had already been broken and everything that we did or that happened to us was predestined. What a bleak scenario! Where was redemption? Forgiveness? What did it mean to talk of free will if it was denied you before you had a chance to exercise it?

And then, what about the innocents, caught up in someone else's punishment? Kathy, for instance. What had she done wrong?

'But that doesn't explain how Kathy's death was meant,' he went on. 'She hadn't done any wrong. Or interfered in the grand design.'

Jamie said nothing.

'Well, had she?' persisted Guy.

'Think about it, Dad.'

Friday was sunny and bright. Inside the BBC building it was hot and airless. Lisa, feeling restless, spent her lunch hour strolling in Holland Park. A warm,

222

scented wind stirred the young leaves, bringing back memories of that time the previous year when she was with Guy in Cambridge. She recalled the times they'd gone punting, the parties and the films they'd enjoyed together. She pictured their special place in the fields where on hot afternoons they'd take a picnic and lie in the grass, talking and reading and sometimes making love, and she thought with a trembling pulse of that afternoon in the boat-house. Why couldn't it be like that always?

Because of Jamie.

Jamie stood in their way. There could be no future in their relationship while he blocked it.

It was time she came to terms with the boy.

A few days before, over supper at a friend's house, she'd met a child psychiatrist. She'd told her all about the situation and asked her how she could win Jamie over.

'A child,' the woman had told her, 'invariably sees the death of a parent as a rejection. At his age, Jamie knows intellectually that his mother is dead, but emotionally he's too young to cope with it. He wants to believe she is still there. But clearly she isn't. So, rather than adjust himself to suit the reality, he adjusts the reality to suit him. He *becomes* his missing mother. He takes over her role as mother of the family.'

'He certainly runs that household,' she'd agreed.

'He'll *mother* his father, too. He'll look after him, cook for him, nurse him. This gets reinforced each time a person says how wonderful he is to cope so well, how grown-up and responsible he is. Of course, the boy himself has no experience of what running a household really entails, and so he's apt to become obsessive about his role. That means two important things. First, deep down, he *wants his father blind*. In

223

that way his father is dependent on him. If Guy regained his sight, Jamie would lose him.'

She'd reflected on this for a moment. Was it really in Jamie's interest to keep Guy blind? The thought was horrifying.

'The second thing,' the psychiatrist had gone on to say, 'is that he feels threatened by you. As his father's girlfriend and potentially his step-mother, you deny him his mother role. That's why he can't allow you near.'

'But what do I do?' she'd protested in despair. 'Try to make him mother *me*? Become *his* child?'

The woman had shaken her head and picked her words.

'What a lonely mother needs is another lonely mother to talk to. Talk to him about affairs of the house. Treat him like another woman, burdened with domestic chores. Make him feel he's your equal and you don't threaten him. Above all, never mention Guy in your conversations.'

Lisa had reached the small formal garden behind the Orangery and she slowed her pace to help herself think better. Her plan had been to go down to Gorselands and have it out with Jamie face to face, but that approach now seemed wrong. But how could she follow the psychiatrist's advice? She couldn't exactly drop in now and then for a domestic heart-to-heart. For one thing, how would she avoid Guy? It seemed there was no way she could communicate with the boy at all.

What a lonely mother needs is another lonely mother to talk to.

She stopped abruptly in her tracks. She had the answer. If she couldn't actually talk to him, she'd write.

*

It startled Patrick when Jamie turned up with Guy at Addenbrooke's for the scan following the fifth treatment, but it did not exactly surprise him.

There was an unmistakable challenge in the boy's eyes, as if he expected Patrick to turn him away. What's he up to now? Patrick wondered as he led father and son down the corridors. Jamie's incessant questions about the signs and the technical paraphernalia lying around attracted the amused attention of passing nurses. That's all we need, he thought savagely as he hurried them into Radiology. He introduced him to the consultant, and in the boy's immediate attentive charm he saw for the first time the elements that linked the boy and the man; what Jamie might become, or could conceal.

Describing for Jamie's benefit what he was doing as he went along, the consultant laid Guy on the couch and slipped the mask over his mouth for the radioactive gas.

'Doesn't radiation cause cancer?' asked Jamie.

The man raised his eyebrows.

'That's an intelligent question,' he said. 'But the answer is No, not this particular isotope at this dosage.'

'Why not give Dad an X-ray instead?'

'We mainly use X-rays these days just to look at bones. Over there we have a CAT scanner, and that X-rays the brain and shows up strokes and tumours. But in your dad's case we want to see what the brain looks like when it's actually working, which bits are more active than others. We need this beast, the PET scanner, for that.'

He switched on the strobe above Guy's head and the scanner whirred and clicked.

'They're always right?' asked the boy after a moment.

'They're always accurate, but what you get may not be the whole story. That's where interpretation comes in.'

'So they can be wrong?'

'*I* can be wrong.'

When the scan was over, they waited in the ante-room for an hour while the results were processed by the computer to produce a three-dimensional image of the central section of Guy's brain. Finally, the consultant called them in again.

Patrick sat down at the terminal.

'Mind if I do it?' he asked. Without waiting for a reply he keyed in instructions. 'We'll go to the previous base and lock on to that.'

'What can you see?' demanded Guy.

'It's coming up now. Look! Just look at that red spur! Hang on while I get a calibration.'

'Logarithmic,' advised the consultant.

'What does it *show*?' persisted Guy.

'Hang on a bit . . . Yes, it's right there. It's absolutely on target. Three more sessions and you should be home.'

'Unless you're wrong,' murmured Jamie.

'Just look at it, Jamie! Can you see the gap? Look how far the pathway's grown and measure it for yourself. Isn't that the most exciting thing you've seen in your life?'

Guy reached out and put an arm round the boy. His body was stiff and unyielding.

'What do you say about miracles, eh, Jamie? *They* must be meant, mustn't they? Well, I call this a modern-day miracle.'

Lisa sat cross-legged on the bed in her basement flat. Several small objects lay scattered on the bedspread, and on her lap she held a pad of writing paper. She chewed her pen in thought. It was vital to get the tone right.

Dear Jamie,

she began carefully,

Just a quick note to wish you a very happy birthday and send you a few things.

Those sweatshirts seem to be all the rage in London. I think dark blue suits you, but they come in many other colours. Let me know if you want to change it. I've put my address at the top of this letter.

An electric can opener – don't laugh – seems a pretty daft gadget, I know, but you might find it useful. I moved to a new flat a while ago and I'm finding mine extraordinarily handy.

It's getting hot and stuffy in London, and I'm madly jealous of you being in the country. I'm sure you're keeping cool!

Once again, many happy returns.

Much love,
Lisa.

P.S. The football's only a bit of nonsense. You might have fun with it, though. It's got a special rattle built in!

She wrote it out again with a few small changes. Deciding her handwriting looked deliberately simplified, she copied it out again normally. Then she packed up the parcel and addressed it to *James Sullivan, The Cottage, Gorselands School*. He was sure to open the mail himself, so there was no reason for Guy

227

to know. Unless he told him, of course, and she reckoned he wouldn't.

She waited until late that Thursday before posting it. That way, Jamie would receive it on his birthday.

As Guy came downstairs the school bell tolled the half hour in the distance. Eight-thirty: late for a Saturday, but then school had gone down for the long exeat weekend. He knew Jamie was up, for he'd heard him answer the postman's ring and the smell of coffee was filtering up from the kitchen. He stole silently along to the sitting-room and opened the piano. He began a soft roll in the bass and, raising it to a *fortissimo*, he broke loudly into song: *Happy Birthday To You* . . .

Slow hand-clapping from the kitchen greeted him.

'I thought you'd been in the choir,' called Jamie.

Guy shut the piano and followed the aroma of coffee down the corridor.

'That was before my voice broke.' He felt for the boy and gave him a hug. 'Happy birthday, Jamie.'

'Thanks, Dad. Now sit down. Boiled egg, or fried?'

Guy sat down and reached for the cornflakes, then stopped.

'I feel like something different today,' he said. 'Fetch the Shredded Wheat, will you?'

The boy went to the cupboard. 'What's this inside the packet?'

'What's what?'

There was a rustle of paper.

'It's a diver's watch! Great!'

'On second thoughts,' said Guy with a frown, 'I think I'd prefer porridge.'

'Porridge? In summer? Well, all right.'

The porridge packet turned out to contain an

228

envelope with a book token. In among the Shreddies were rolls of film, for a camera hidden in the Weetabix.

'I've got you something, too, Dad.'

Jamie crossed the room and a moment later put a package on the table in front of him.

'It's supposed to be *your* birthday!' protested Guy.

'Go on, open it.'

It was too big for a shoe-box. It rattled when he shook it. A large tin of sweets? He opened it carefully. It took him a second before he realized it was a football.

'It rattles,' explained the boy, 'so you can hear it. The instructions say you can dribble, shoot, pass – everything. We can go up and down the pitch, passing it. Far better than jogging.'

A rattling football. A blind man's football. Was the miracle to be a mirage?

'It's great,' he said tightly. 'You shouldn't have.'

'It's only a bit of nonsense. Right, what about your egg?'

That afternoon, they took the football onto the playing fields and ran up and down, passing it between them. Guy found it almost impossible. He'd hear the rattle but he could never trap the ball properly; he'd snick it with his boot or miss it entirely, and then, as it slowed down, the rattle would die away and Jamie would have to run and fetch it. He played on, however, until he was tired out. He leaned against a goal-post while he caught his breath.

'Let's do something less strenuous,' he suggested. 'How about a walk down by the river? We could play the describing game.'

This was a game Jamie had invented in the early blind days. He'd lead him on long rambles all over the estate, describing everything he saw in fine detail: trees, plants, birds, rabbits, foxes, the ground, the sky. He remembered the shock when one mid-winter day Jamie described the grass as green; somehow he'd developed the idea that grass, like leaves, went brown in winter.

'I'm fed up with that,' replied Jamie. 'It's puerile.'

'But you used to love it!' Guy was puzzled: for no reason he could fathom, the boy had recently taken a sudden dislike to that game. But it was his birthday and he didn't want to upset him. 'What shall we play, then?'

'Genius.'

Genius of Gorselands was a quiz game. Jamie invariably won, for the odds were heavily stacked in his favour.

'Come along, then.'

They strolled across the playing fields and down towards the river. The warm air was heady and scented. Guy knew his way perfectly well, but Jamie insisted on taking his arm and conducting him along with great solicitude.

When they reached the river he could smell the hot, reedy odour of the water. As they turned down the tow-path, Jamie pressed something into his hand.

'Yours for two,' he said. 'Give you a clue. It's drab brown.'

'Pigeon feather,' guessed Guy.

'I said, *brown*! Give up. It's the tail feather of a hen pheasant. Dad, I sometimes wonder.' He put a flower into his palm. 'Now a really difficult one. What's this?'

'Feels like a Michaelmas daisy, but it's the wrong time of year. I'd say . . . a cornflower.'

'No, no, Dad,' said Jamie exasperatedly. 'Feel the

230

leaves. They're ovate. And there aren't any ray florets. A clue: it's yellow.'

'Pass.'

'*Pulicaria dysenterica*. Common fleabane. I lead by eight points to three. You owe me fifty pee.'

'This is getting expensive.'

'That's private education, Dad.'

They walked on slowly, continuing to play the game. His inner eyes were growing tired. It was strenuous, struggling to make pictures in his head of the world as it really was. At last, as they reached the boat-house, he suggested they stopped and sat down. He wanted a quiet moment to savour memories. He felt the ground for a soft patch of grass.

'Hey, mind that *trifolium ochroleucon*!' cried Jamie. 'Yours for two.'

'Sulphur clover. That's twenty pee back to me.'

Jamie laughed.

'It's a good thing I'm in charge of the house-keeping.'

Late that night, after checking the doors and windows were locked and the lights turned off, Guy went upstairs. He took his shoes off on the landing and stood just inside Jamie's bedroom, listening to the rise and fall of his breathing. A slight breeze through the open window blew a curtain against his hand, and he started. The boy stirred, turned over and instantly fell back to sleep.

He stood there for a while. Patrick was coming down the following day to give him the sixth session. Of course, Jamie was right to sound notes of caution. He obviously wanted to protect him in case there was a disappointment, and so he was carrying on as if nothing was likely to happen. Naturally, if the treatment did work, the boy would be the first to rejoice. If not, then the football and the ear-phone, the Braille books and the describing games would all have been to the point. He'd do well to follow suit and make no assumptions. Hope was traitor to the heart.

CHAPTER TWENTY

Guy led the way up the narrow stairs. Behind came Patrick, with the lop-sided step of a man carrying a heavy case. Jamie followed. As soon as he entered the small experiment room, Guy began loosening his shirt and cuffs.

'Calm down, Guy,' said Patrick. 'I don't want you over-excited.'

He sat impatiently while Patrick switched on the equipment and ran a number of tests to check its functioning. Then the electrodes were glued in place with the special conductive gel and he was led into the sound-proofed compartment where he was helped onto the couch.

Patrick angled the strobe above him and announced all was ready.

'Jamie,' he called quietly, 'would you fetch me the scopolamine?'

'The orange ones?' queried the boy.

'That's right. I've got the pethidine here.'

Guy took the pills and lay back. He heard the door shut, and the insidious white sound began hissing in his ear. Almost at once the familiar, nauseous panic seized him. Where did his body begin and end? Were the walls closing in on him, or was he inflating out towards them?

'Relax,' came Patrick's whisper.

He began counting. At fifty he could still feel the dread. At sixty, it was no better. By eighty, he was sweating.

'Come on, calm down.'

There was an edge in the voice.

Patrick frowned. The brain-dampening pills were taking a hell of a long time to act. Was Guy developing an immunity? He'd already had to wait ten minutes before he'd got alpha waves and could give him the hormone shot, but when he'd switched on the strobe the EEG waves had gone berserk. For a while he kept the lumen level turned down, but would a lower brightness have the same effect? Gradually he built it back up again, keeping his eye fixed on the oscilloscope. There were periods when the waves settled down to a steady ten to twelve cycles per second, but then there'd be a sudden surge and they'd race up to twenty or more. By alternately juggling with the brightness level and slowing the white-sound tape so that the component sounds unscrambled and became audible, he managed to keep the waves down to the necessary rhythmic, relaxed levels. But something wasn't right.

For two hours he operated like this. For a while after that it seemed he'd got it under control, and he began to relax.

The first sign of things going actually wrong was an abrupt change in the rhythmic scratching of the inkpens. A second later, a low groan issued from the chamber. An alarm message began flashing up on the computer screen.

He flung the door open. Guy was on his feet, staggering about clutching his head, with a look of ferocious anguish on his ashen face. He broke out of the chamber and blundered around the room, feeling for the door. Patrick was unable to stop him as he burst out onto the landing, but he managed to corner him before he reached the stairs.

'Get my bag!' he shouted to Jamie.

The boy came running with the case. Patrick fumbled for a vial of chlorpromazine. Filling a syringe, he grabbed at Guy's arm but the man tore away, sank to the floor and curled up like a foetus, shaking in agony. Patrick knelt down beside him and rammed the needle into his buttock. Using his full weight, he pinned him firmly until he'd expelled the tranquillizer into his flesh and it had begun to take effect.

'The scope!' he called.

The boy handed him the ophthalmoscope. He peered into each eye in turn. The retinas looked fine. He tore off the tapes holding the lids open and laid him on his back. He was already shivering; hypothermia could be a danger.

He called for blankets.

He covered him and took his blood pressure. It had dropped severely. He took it again a few moments later. If it fell any lower, he'd have to give him a shot of atropine.

Guy looked terrible. His face was grey and blotched, his eyes rolled and squinted, his tongue was swollen and he was having difficulty breathing. Patrick kept his finger on his pulse. At what point should he call a doctor? He swallowed. If what he'd been doing got out . . .

First thing was to get him to bed and then he'd sit down and think it through. He'd already formed one conclusion: this damn business had to end.

He checked Guy's pulse and blood pressure regularly over the next hours. They gradually improved. He kept him warm, quiet and sedated. He decided to stay over that night. Jamie said that the McVeys would give him a bed, but he wanted to be there, on hand. Together they heated up a steak and kidney pie from the freezer. They didn't speak much;

the atmosphere was tense and anxious.

'He will be okay, won't he?' asked Jamie.

'We're over the worst,' he replied.

'Looks like you got it wrong after all.'

'Well,' he admitted, 'I hadn't bargained for that.'

'So, you're going to stop?'

'I'll stop until I know what went wrong.'

'You'll never find that out.'

'Oh?'

'It's not going to work.'

'Not at this rate,' he agreed. 'He'd pack it in, if he's got any sense.'

A frown crossed the boy's pale, oval face.

'You think Dad's got *any* sense?'

By Monday afternoon, Patrick felt happy to leave Guy in Jamie's hands. The sedatives had worn off and he was talking quite lucidly now. He'd been through hell. What had happened? What did it mean? Was the treatment breaking down? Would he have to go through the same torture during the next two sessions?

Patrick tried to suggest a delay while he tested the programme on a wider sample of lab subjects, but Guy wouldn't hear of it. He'd set his sights, he said with emphasis, on the half-term holiday two weeks away and, pain or no pain, he wasn't going to let that opportunity slip. All he wanted was to know that they were still on course.

Patrick returned to Cambridge, full of anxiety and doubt. He took with him the computer data diskette and the bottle of scopolamine tablets, planning to re-formulate them at a higher strength. As he drove slowly through the winding country lanes, with the sun dying away over his left shoulder, all he could see was the look on Guy's face as he'd opened the chamber door, intercut with the image of Tolkien the cat as she bared her claws and razored into her own brain.

He ran a search program through the computer, but nothing showed up except what he already knew: Guy had suffered something akin to a brainstorm. What could he do? He only had his cats to work with, and their evidence was unreliable. Tolkien had freaked out on the fourth session; on his fourth, Guy had merely had disturbing hallucinations. He had freaked out on his sixth, however, while Tolstoy had suffered nothing at all on hers. The analogy was patently flawed, but it was all he had to go on, short of unzipping Guy's skull and taking a look inside.

There was only one thing to do: take a cat right through to the end of the treatment.

Seated at the foot of a lighting gantry during a break in the recording, Lisa took out her pad and wrote Jamie a letter.

Dear Jamie,

she wrote,

I'm in the studio right now. Things are pretty hectic. I'm snatching a moment to get away from it all and write a note. Current Affairs programmes are always frantic, full of last-minute crises. I've put in for a secondment to that science programme . . .

'Secondment?' she wondered; he could look the word up.

. . . but I won't know for a month or so.

Oh yes. I saw this key-ring in a shop. I've got one myself and I'd be lost without it. I'm always forgetting where I've put my keys down. It's called "Bleep 'n' Keep" because if you lose it, you just clap your hands four times and it makes a loud bleep. You don't even have to be in the same room. Neat, isn't it?

I'm sure you're coping brilliantly down there. Running a house is quite a business. Or so I find, and I've only got one person to cater for!

There goes my call. Got to fly now.

Lots of love,
Lisa.

On Tuesday morning Patrick gave Tolstoy the cat her eighth dose. He kept rigorously to the pattern of the last four: the same dose of scopolamine, the same concentration of growth hormone, the same length of time under a strobe of the same intensity and flicker-rate. Afterwards he put her in her cage, the depth electrodes in her mid-brain still wired up to the EEG recorder, but with small mittens on her paws in case she was driven to mimic Tolkien's act when the tranquillizer wore off.

She was fine, however, and he judged that by nightfall she would be ready for the real test: had she, or had she not, regained some actual, conscious vision?

Throughout the day, he stalked around, unable to contain his excitement. To avoid the temptation to test her before the treatment had had a proper chance to work, he left the labs and walked around the city, staring sightlessly in bookshop windows. Sauntering through the park, he'd stop abruptly in mid-track, causing oarsmen on training runs or mothers wheeling strollers to collide into him.

It was a two-edged sword. If the answer was No and the cat was still effectively blind, then the work he was doing for Oliver was a waste of time. Why perform a minutely painstaking analysis of the effect of the growth hormone on a single, carefully standardized tissue slice when he knew the end result was negative? What would he say to the professor? And how would he cope with knowing that his whole work to date had taken him up a *cul de sac*?

But if it was Yes, how the hell would he *prove* it? If he wheeled Guy out on stage, he'd stir up such muck in the scientific establishment that he'd be instantly dismissed for unethical practices – never mind if his patient could *see* or not – and his work would never be given serious examination. If he wheeled the cat out as evidence, they'd immediately discount the statistical significance of a sample of one.

He'd go to America. Attitudes were positive there; if they liked an idea, they'd run with it. Here, in Cambridge, they were anti-success; they carped and back-stabbed and brought out the knives at the least hint of it. Yes, he'd go where the soil was more expansive, more amenable. If you could grow new pathways in the brain, what couldn't you do? Repairing paraplegics and healing the blind and deaf were only the beginning.

The brain was both plastic and specific. Some things, like memory, seemed to be located all over it, perhaps in many places simultaneously. But other functions did relate to particular parts. Broca's and Wernicke's areas in the left hemisphere, for instance, controlled speech. Just above, in the strip relating to motor functions, distinct areas controlled the lips and jaw, the tongue and throat. If you could grow axons and develop neuronal connections between these, could you not create new kinds of abilities, new powers, new faculties, new *people*? Night vision could be developed for soldiers by growing new connections from the rods in their retinas. Organic mental diseases could be cured. Schizophrenia would be eradicated.

Yet all these were merely extensions of what existed at present. What about the faculties that we did not *yet* possess? What could you create if you could wire up some of the billions of unused cells in the human brain?

Patrick returned to the labs feeling like a volcano about to burst. He was standing on the leading edge of mankind's evolution! Man differed from chimpanzee and gorilla by just *one per cent* of his genetic make-up. That one per cent of his DNA accounted for speech, self-awareness, the ability to count, to generalize and form concepts . . . What would the *next* one per cent give man? And who would give it to him?

The instant he saw the cat, he knew something was wrong.

She sat in her cage, twitching oddly. She kept rubbing her head with her paw, and for a moment he thought she had some irritation in her eye. When she saw him, she took a step forward and fell. Her forelegs had lost all muscle tone. He picked her up and examined her carefully. Her whole body trembled with small, convulsive *tics*. Alarmed, he set her down on the bench. Bent and twisted, her legs folded under her again. Her head lolled slack, then would jerk round at an awkward angle. Her eyeballs rolled about without focusing and then would suddenly judder from side to side. She could not control her head or her limbs. She was spastic.

But could she *see*?

He examined her retinas, pressing his thumb on the side of her eyeballs to hold them steady. At a superficial glance, they looked undamaged. He wiggled his fingers to the side to check her peripheral vision; sometimes she'd turn her head, other times not. If she couldn't control her gaze, how could he test her for sight at all?

By now he was sweating profusely and his hands were trembling. He put her in a frame to keep her head steady and passed objects in front of her eyes: a pencil, a toy mouse, the tangle of cassette tape she liked to play with. He shone lights in her eyes. He made as if to hit her in the face, to check her menace reflex. He rotated her head while getting her to fixate on a point, and tried to see if her eyes stayed still. He drew the blinds and tested her eye movements with a prism and he rotated drums with striped lines before her eyes. When they were steady enough to let him perform the tests, he was amazed and excited by the results.

She really had regained some degree of sight. Real sight.

But what was wrong? Had he forced the axon growth too fast and not given time for the myelin to be properly laid down? But then his sweat turned cold. Her problem was mechanical, he realized, not visual. She couldn't control or co-ordinate her body movements. The trouble lay in the motor areas of her cortex. Not in the sight areas he'd been working on, but elsewhere altogether.

Alarm bells began ringing in his head. Had he concentrated so single-mindedly on her mid-brain that he'd ignored the side-effects on other parts of her brain? He'd assumed that, with the enforced sensory deprivation, all the growth hormone would attach itself to binding sites in the Blindsight area. What if some stray hormone material had begun building connections elsewhere? What if it had provoked a dangerous build-up in glial cells?

The more he examined the cat, the more this initial guess took on the horrific proportions of certainty. The result could not have been more bitter. On the credit side, she had gained, however dimly, a new ability to see. On the debit side, she had contracted exactly what Wain had before her, the cat with which he'd started it all.

A tumour on the brain.

Patrick spent that Wednesday morning performing an angiogram on the cat. He had the results through by mid-day. They showed a distorted pattern of blood vessels in the motor area at the front of her brain. A scan proved beyond doubt that she had a rapidly-growing cancerous tumour. At the rate it was spreading, he gave her no more than a few days to live.

There was only one thing to do: take out her brain and examine it directly. This meant destroying the living evidence of his success, but it had to be done. He'd make damn sure he came out with a comprehensive histological analysis, showing irrefutably the new visual pathway, or else his claims would only be met with derision.

He spent the rest of the day carefully preparing for the 2-DG operation. The cat was his entire proof. His career hung on the quality of the evidence he produced now.

At dawn on Thursday morning, while the labs were empty, he began the operation to ablate her brain. He injected the radio-active [14 C]-2-oxyglucose through a catheter in her femoral vein. Fixing her in a restraining frame and connecting up the electrodes bedded in her skull-cap, he switched on the strobe.

When he was satisfied the marker had reached the brain and was registering activity in the new visual pathway, he anaesthetized her, then injected formalin in through her neck artery, using her own circulation to pump the fixing agent into her brain.

Within moments, the cat was dead.

Using a scalpel and miniature electric saw, he carefully removed the top of her skull and eased the tiny lump of pink-grey porridge-like matter free of its connective tissues, then slipped it quickly into the cryostat where it would be frozen rock hard. Shortly he'd slice it into micron-thin wafers and place them on photo-sensitive emulsion, where the radioactive particles would leave a clear impression of the areas of high activity at the moment of death. He'd increased the specific activity of the carbon marker to speed up the process, but even so the results would take twenty-four hours to come through. On Friday morning he'd know the answer.

Dear Jamie,

Another wonderful sunny morning! The thought of being cooped up in a hot studio is awful. Still, we weren't put on this earth to laze about.

I must tell you: I found the most delicious strawberries in a street market yesterday. English, and only 60p a pound! I bought so much I was up half the night, making jam. The only thing was, I forgot to shut the window. There's a bees' nest just outside the back door, and this morning I found a whole swarm had got in! Still, they can't have liked my jam that much since they were all at the window, trying to get out.

I got them out one by one with a cup and a postcard. It's an old trick. Works with spiders, too. The brutes keep coming up the overflow pipe

into the bath and I hate having to deal with them.
I heard on the radio the other day that it takes a thousand bees to make one teaspoon of honey. Were *they* put on this earth for that? All part of the Grand Design, I suppose.
Hope the hot weather isn't causing you problems. The milk goes off, the bread goes stale – you know how it is.

Much love,
Lisa.

Patrick began the histological analysis of the brain tissue slices around mid-day on the Friday. By late in the afternoon he had his answer. It was both the most he'd hoped for and the worst he'd dreaded.

The good news was very good. The cross-sections of the cat's mid-brain took his breath away. Where the glucose had been taken up, the grains had turned black, giving the impression of a comet in negative, surging in a single spur from the superior colliculus through to the cortical association areas. Under a microscope, the pattern broke up into individual constellations, dense clusters of black dots, each giving off a myriad of fine, wispy branches, but all connected, all leading in one direction.

Yes, the cat *had* regained her sight, and here was the proof.

But the bad news was very bad.

Just below the frontal lobe a massive tumour had developed, solid with glial cells. These cells normally clustered around neurones to provide the nutrients they could not synthesize themselves and fabricated the myelin sheaths in which the long-distance axons were wrapped. Unlike neurones, these cells could divide. And here they had been dividing in swarms.

244

The culprit was the hormone compound. Mammals were born with a low glial count, which rapidly increased in the period immediately after birth. The hormone had been deliberately engineered to mimic foetal growth. Had it therefore fooled the brain into switching back on its neonatal chemistry? Or was it the sudden spurt of axon growth in the mid-brain that had provoked an uncontrolled production of myelin-fabricating cells in another part of the brain simultaneously?

He could determine the exact cause later. Right now, the effect was what mattered. It was plain. As a direct result of the treatment, the cat had developed cancer of the brain.

And he was due to go down to Gorselands the next morning and give Guy his seventh session.

That night, he slept restlessly, prey to terrible anxieties. It was no longer a question, as Lisa had put it, of his skin versus Guy's sight. Guy's *life* was at stake. He thought back to the previous session at the cottage: the muscular slackness, the shaking, the pain – were these the first signs of a tumour developing? He'd managed to book an appointment with the consultant at Addenbrooke's for late the following afternoon, and he'd drag Guy along, willing or unwilling. True, they hadn't picked up anything serious in previous scans. Was that because there *was* nothing serious? Or because they simply hadn't been looking for it? To carry on with the treatment was now, of course, unthinkable. He could only pray it was not already too late to stop the rot and save his friend.

In the morning, he went to the labs and packed his briefcase. Guy wouldn't be able actually to see the histological plates, but Jamie could witness the story they told. It was all over. Maybe, in some years, when he'd learned how to localize the growth . . .

How could he break it to Guy, after all he'd been through?

He rang Lisa. She was appalled.

'You *can't* stop now!' she cried.

'Lisa, I'm going down this afternoon to tell him the whole thing is off. Once and for all. Definitively. It may already be too late.'

'What do you mean?'

'There could be complications. I can't say more than that.'

'Don't give me that all over again! Guy knows the risks. He won't take No for an answer now. Not when he's almost there.'

'He will after I've seen him! Anyway, it's out of his hands. I've made my decision.'

'Screw you, Patrick. He doesn't need you to do it. Anyone can. *I* will.'

'You'll do no such thing!'

'I damn well will!'

'For Christ's sake, keep out of this! The experiment's over. Get it?'

'Want to bet?'

'Lisa . . . !'

'See you, Patrick.'

The line went dead. He stormed around the lab, putting his things together. The stupid girl, why couldn't she leave things she didn't understand alone? People thought science was a toy: pick it up when you want fun, drop it when you're bored. Science was a deadly serious business. He'd better tell her about the cat. He'd call her back and explain. He reached for the receiver.

The phone rang for half a minute. He dialled again. There was still no reply. Was she deliberately not answering? Or was she being typically impetuous?

He'd bet his life she was already in her car, heading out of London. God damn the interfering bitch! *Screw you, Patrick. He doesn't need you to do it. Anyone can. I will.* He'd better get to Guy first, or she would. Should he phone him? No, better to tackle it face to face. If he left now, he'd arrive well ahead of her.

He drove fast. Anger added its own fuel to his disappointment. A light drizzle blurred his windscreen. He was blocked behind a stream of caravans heading for the coast. Though he leapfrogged them one by one, there was always another ahead. The countryside grew flatter. The road widened into three lanes, and he accelerated. He overtook an estate car, a builders' van, a horse box, slipping back into the nearside lane each time. He drew up behind a caravan and pulled out. Ahead, coming in the opposite direction, throwing up a cloud of spray, was a cattle truck. The central lane was clear. He put his foot down.

A silver car suddenly appeared out of the spray, overtaking the truck. In the same lane, heading full at him. He stamped on his brakes. The caravan beside him stupidly braked, too. The truck flashed its lights. Too late. There was no room. The silver car was just feet away. He could see every line in the driver's face.

Everything slowed. He was going to die, and there was no hurry. He hit the silver car on his offside wing and began a gentle, balletic clockwise spin down the centre lane. One moment he was pointing ahead, the next he could see the rear of the truck, skidding as it braked. The leading edge of the caravan caught him and kicked him into a tighter spin. He slid across the road, where he hit the kerb broadsides and toppled into a somersault, over and over, sky and earth, sky and earth.

CHAPTER TWENTY-ONE

The boy took the letters out of his desk and read them through once again. He frowned. They made him feel strange, as if they were addressed to somebody else. He knew they were trying to throw him off course. Just like the presents – the sweatshirt and the can opener, the football and the key-ring. Sent to make it harder for him.

He re-read the last letter. *All part of the Grand Design, I suppose.* If she knew anything about that, she'd never have meddled with the treatments in the first place.

He sat for several minutes with his arms wrapped round his head, swaying back and forth and fighting down the anger.

Finally, uncoiling himself, he turned back to the desk and took out a pad. For a moment he sat over the paper, his hands shaking, then slowly he reached for his pen and began to write a reply.

Guy stood at the back door, listening. Sometimes it was hard to tell if it was raining or it was just the wind stirring the trees. He took a step forward and held out his hand. A fine drizzle was falling. Jamie had told him the spinach was going to seed, and he wanted to put in another row. Was it worth starting on it?

He heard a car drive up at the front and went round the side of the house. On the path he could hear Alice's distinctive footsteps. She was taking Jamie into Cambridge that morning to help her carry her shopping. It was odd of her to drive down, he thought, rather than phone for the boy to run up. They had to leave right away, she explained; she'd forgotten she had an early appointment.

Guy went upstairs and tapped on Jamie's door.

'You can't come in!' cried the boy.

'Gran's here,' he called through the door. 'She's got to leave straight away.'

'I'm not ready.'

'Then get ready.'

'Can't she do it on her own?'

'Come on, Jamie, she's away next week, you know that. She's stocking up the pantry.'

'I'll miss Patrick.'

'We won't begin without you, Jamie. Come along, now.'

The boy sealed the envelope. If he posted it in town, no-one would know. Downstairs, his father was calling him again. He opened the door. On the landing he paused. Facing him across the top of the stairway lay the treatment room.

The voices were in the kitchen. There was no-one to see. He stepped quickly across the landing and slipped into the room. Once inside, he went swiftly over to the instrument panel and turned the aluminium knob marked *strobe* six notches to the right. Then he left the room, shutting the door carefully and with a whistle went to his bedroom to put on a jacket.

If he didn't get back in time, they could start without him.

Lisa slowed down as she came to the stone perimeter wall of the school. Turning in through the main gates, she headed to the right, up the steep track that led to the McVeys' large Victorian house. There was no-one anywhere about.

She drove cautiously round the back of the house, in case Alice hadn't done her job and Jamie was still there. In the garage at the back she saw Alice's Metro had gone and began to feel easier.

On the way down, she'd stopped at a motorway service station and phoned her. She'd told her Patrick was refusing to go on with the treatment and she had to see Guy urgently about it – but she just felt it might be better without Jamie around. Alice had understood immediately and promised to take the boy off for the day to give her a clear run. In the rest room she'd washed her face and hands to remove her scent. If Jamie discovered she'd come to see Guy, it would destroy the even tempo of the relationship she was creating through the letters. Worse, too, if he found she'd been giving him his next treatment: then she'd have an enemy for life. But she wasn't telling Alice that. No-one knew her stratagem with the boy.

She turned the car about and drove back down to the school, parking behind the main buildings where she felt it was less exposed. She went on foot up the drive to the cottage among the trees. The light rain had stopped, but the ground was soft and her heels kept sinking in. She looked about her nervously. She felt sure there were eyes watching her from the beech-trees, from the rhododendron bushes, from behind the dark-reflecting window-panes.

Taking a deep breath, she opened the gate and went up the path, conscious of the sound of her heels on the concrete. She had barely reached the top when a voice called out her name.

'Lisa!'

Guy appeared round the side. He stood there, in old gardening trousers and a collarless workman's shirt, trying to locate her, his head moving from side to side like a deer following scent.

Guy put the phone down. There was no reply from Patrick's rooms in college or from the labs. Lisa must be right: he was on his way. The coward! On, off, on, off: he was playing cat and mouse. One moment he was thrilled it was going so well, the next he was jittering about his job. *There could be complications*: he'd heard that before! *He* was the one taking the risks and suffering the agonies. It was his choice. Patrick would be arriving any minute; he'd remove the equipment and that would be the end of it. He had to be forestalled. Somehow they had to go ahead with the session there and then. But how? Jamie wasn't even around.

'Tell me what has to be done,' said Lisa practically.

'It's too complicated! There's the electrodes to glue on . . .'

'They don't *do* anything, do they? They just record things. We can do without them.'

'But the strobe . . .'

'I can turn a switch on, Guy.'

'And that white sound.'

'He said that was just a tape. I'm in the BBC, don't forget.'

'Have you ever given an injection?'

She hesitated.

'Sure.'

'No, you haven't.'

'I've seen enough done in my time. Stop raising obstacles. You want to do it, or you don't. If you do, then get yourself together. Okay?'

He paused. His hand touched hers.

'Look,' she added, 'let's get one thing straight before we start. I'm not doing this with any motive about *us*. I have no preconceptions about the future.

Even if it does work and you wanted me back in your life, I'm not sure if I'd want to come. We couldn't pick up the threads just where we'd left off. Too much water has passed under too many bridges. We'd have to find a new way. Become strangers again. Rediscover each other from scratch. Maybe we'd find we had both moved on.'

He smiled, though the words stung. Wasn't this just what he'd encouraged her to say when, almost a year ago, he'd suggested they split?

Guy sat on the couch in the padded chamber, waiting. Lisa had found everything except the orange scopolamine tablets. The bottle was not on the shelf, nor in the fridge with the ampoules. He suggested the bathroom, but she drew a blank there too. Had Patrick taken them already? This was really serious; they were crucial to dampen out extraneous sensory inputs and focus the full force of the stimulus on the new visual pathways.

After a while he heard a cry from across the landing.

'They were in Jamie's den,' she said as she came back in.

'God knows what they're doing in there.'

'I have my theories.'

'You've got him wrong. He's just a little disturbed.'

'We won't go into that now. How many do you take?'

'Four.'

'Here. Now lie back and I'll do your eyelids.'

She fixed the tape carefully to pin the lids open. She tested out the strobe and switched on the white sound, then left him for a few minutes with the door shut, as he'd instructed. Once again the tentacles of panic slithered over his body and he began his counting. But this time, by fifty, he felt quite calm. Distantly, he heard the door open and cool hands eased his head to the side. There was pressure on his neck, a moment's pause, then the sharp, hard pain of the needle. He forced himself to relax. A moment later he felt it being withdrawn, his head set straight and the lightest of kisses brushing his forehead.

'That hurt you more than it hurt me,' she whispered.

He heard the click as the strobe was switched on and a muffled thud as the door closed. Then all sensation was blotted out except for the low, insidious hiss that seemed to come from within his own head.

Something white. Dark white, as white goes in moonlight. White against black. No, against dark green. It's all scratchy. Flecked. Grainy. Comes and goes. Gaps appear, then fill again. It's a two-tone jigsaw, with pieces coming in and out all the time.

It's gone.

It comes back again. This time it's closer. A *sleeve*! A sleeve of a woman's dress. I don't know how I know. The stitching, the dart in the side of the dress. It fades. A sponge wipes black over it, and it's gone again. Inked out.

A flash, dazzlingly bright! A complete dress. A woman wearing a white dress. She lies face down. Lying in a tangle of something. A tangle of grass. Corn.

A woman in a white dress lying among dark green corn.

Vanishes again. This time it leaves an after-image like a television just turned off. Glows grey on grey. Now it brightens briefly. Flickers, off and on, pulsing with the strobe. Pumping the image in.

Suddenly something different. It's a spike. Two spikes. Jutting out of something. Fingers holding this thing. It fades in and out of focus, drunkenly. Now it fills out, adding more bits. The fingers grow into hands, hands into wrists, wrists into arms. Arms meet chest. On the chest is a head. With dark hair. Ferocious eyes. A pale, oval face.

Jamie's face.

The hands come closer. The thing jabs the air. The spikes glint. He's going to stab the woman in the white dress. Jab and stab and spike the woman in the white dress.

I must . . .

Lisa sat beside the bed, holding Guy's hand. His breathing had returned to normal and his pulse was steady. She was still shaking. He was two hours into the session when he'd let out a cry of such awful terror she'd thought he was dying. She'd hauled him out at once; nothing could be worth suffering that kind of distress. He now lay in bed, drowsy from two more orange tablets he'd told her to give him at the end, his eyes still taped open, at his own insistence, and staring into the Anglepoise lamp on the bedside table. That infernal chamber would send the sanest man mad. So long as light shone in his eyes, why wouldn't this do instead?

She waited at his side as the hours passed. By three o'clock, she was growing nervous. Jamie would soon be back. Alice wouldn't see her car outside and might think she'd gone. Where was Patrick? Her plan had been to get rid of him before Jamie returned; that way, Guy could say that he had come early and given him the treatment. But suppose he arrived *after* Jamie? How would Guy explain it then? There was nothing she could do except hope he'd turned back, unable to face Guy with the news.

She looked at her watch: she had to leave right away. Each minute increased the risk of coming face to face with Jamie. She went quickly round the cottage, checking she had left no traces: no lipstick on cups, no blonde hairs on the chair, no belongings anywhere. If Patrick did come, he'd be certain to confiscate the drugs to stop the final session going ahead. So she hid the last remaining hormone ampoule in the Thermos flask, slipping an ice cube in to keep it chilled, and put the small pile of orange tablets she'd found in Jamie's room in an envelope in the dressing-table drawer.

She was ready. She checked Guy's pulse one last time, tucked him up and went downstairs, then she collected her bag from by the front door and left. Pausing only to make sure she was alone, she hurried down the path and followed her own footsteps back down the drive to the car-park at the back of the main school buildings.

'Dad? Dad, where are you?'

'Upstairs,' he croaked.

Feet hurried up the stairs, first to the treatment room, then along the landing to his bedroom. He heard the boy catch his breath.

'He did you!'

'Couldn't wait.'

Jamie felt his forehead, then took his pulse.

'He had no business! Are you okay?'

'Pretty much,' he groaned, struggling to sit up. 'Wasn't as bad as last time. Some funny dreams, though. What's the time?'

'Half past three. You had your tablets?'

'Yes. What were they doing in your room?'

'In my room?'

'We looked everywhere.' His head throbbed and he hardly recognized his own voice, slurred with the drugs. 'Forget it. Did you have a good time?'

'Lie back. Don't talk. I'll turn this stupid light out. He said it wouldn't help. And for goodness' sake let's get those tapes off your eyes. You're crazy.'

'I'm dying for some tea.'

'Just wait. You shouldn't be in such a hurry. You'll have to learn.'

He lay back without protest as the boy ripped off the tapes and pulled up the sheets higher. Sounds came in and out of focus. How long had Lisa been gone? What an amazing girl she was.

The footsteps stomped over to the door.

'Jamie,' he called. 'Play me a B, will you?'

The boy looked at his submariner's watch: it was nearly six. Time to finish camouflaging the tree-house before Gran came down and went fussing about the place. He put on his wellingtons at the back door and went round to the front. The sky had cleared and he could see a tinge of crimson through the trees as he slipped through the gate.

He had gone a few paces when he stopped. There, clearly visible in the soft earth, were footprints. A woman's footprints. Small heels coming up the drive, small heels going back down. And not a tyre-mark of a car, Patrick's or any other, in evidence anywhere.

Guy woke and felt his watch. Five to eleven. Night or morning? The crows were bickering in the elms behind the cottage: it was morning. The distant tolling of the chapel bell confirmed it. He'd slept eighteen hours. His head ached and he felt drugged.

What had happened yesterday? Lisa had come. She'd given him the seventh treatment. He'd had a terrible dream. A woman in white, lying sprawled among the green corn.

Sandy. Sandy, in her white dress, sprawled among the corn, exactly as he'd left her. The image of that terrible morning still haunted his memory.

Overcome with grief, he'd left her lying there and stumbled away to tell Alice.

And Jamie had found her.

The boy had disappeared for two days. On the third he turned up, dirty, dishevelled and mute. He'd been living in the woods. For a week he didn't speak to Guy. And then, slowly, Alice got it out of him. He'd gone for a walk and come upon his mother lying in the field. He'd thought she was asleep and tried to wake her.

If only Guy hadn't left her there.

The horrific image in his dream of Jamie hovering over Sandy with that look in his eyes was directly born out of this guilt. But what were those spikes the boy seemed to be jabbing at her? Presumably his subconscious mind had put them there; *he* was the murderer, but he'd symbolically transferred the instrument of murder into innocent hands.

He felt sick. That field often recurred in his nightmares. But at least it *was* a nightmare, not a vision of the future like the train crash and Kathy's murder. He recognized that white dress and that field from his memory. The fifth and sixth sessions had gone ahead without dreams of any kind. It looked as if he was in the clear on that. He was heading for normal vision, not psychic vision. Normal sight, not second sight.

He lay back, exhausted by the effort of thinking. But he felt relieved. That ugly memory had already happened; he wasn't being called on to live it again. And his sight was going to be normal.

He sat in a cane chair in the front garden, staring into the sun and blinking rapidly in an attempt to give the effect of a strobe. Patrick had explained that the brain sends its messages in small parcels; giving it a single, unchanging stream of stimuli made it hebetate and lose interest until ultimately the circuits shut off. The brain was like a child, he'd said, responding only to change and novelty. People could live by a main road or on an aircraft flight-path and end up not hearing the noise. His mind began to wander. Did this, he wondered, explain why Beethoven made so much use of trills in his later piano music? A man going deaf might only *hear* a piano note when trilled. A violin played *vibrato* was the same. Was that why strings often sounded more alive than a percussion instrument like a piano? He was idly pursuing this line of thought when he heard footsteps coming round the back of the cottage. He recognized them at once, and the urgency in the gait.

'Alice!' he said. 'What's the matter?'

'Don't get up,' she said. 'I'll bring a chair.'

'Something's wrong, isn't it?'

'We've had a call; it's your friend Patrick. He's had a car accident.'

'My God! Is he bad?'

'It's his spine. They can't say yet. He went through the windscreen.'

'Where is he? When did it happen? My God, he was probably on the way here: that's why he never turned up yesterday.'

'He's in Addenbrooke's. They're operating this morning. You could call the hospital tonight.'

Jesus Christ, he thought. What a bitterly savage irony.

'And now Patrick.' He shook his head. 'It's almost as if there's a curse . . .'

'Now, Guy, enough of that.'

They lapsed briefly into silence.

'I've been thinking Donald and I shouldn't go away tomorrow,' she went on after a while. 'Not just at this moment.'

'Of course you must!'

'I don't feel happy. There's Jamie, too . . .'

'Don't worry about Jamie. He's got everything under control. I'm living in the Ritz here. Breakfast in bed, a bell for room service . . . Really, Alice, stop fretting. It'll be all right. Next week I'll go and see Patrick in hospital. And I mean, *see* him.'

'Something tells me . . .'

'Alice, it's going to be all right.'

Jamie brought a picnic lunch into the garden and spread a rug on the grass. He had made cheese and cucumber sandwiches, his own no doubt thickly laced with mayonnaise spread, and a jug of lemon barley water with a sprig of mint. The sun beat down pitilessly and barely a breath of wind stirred the trees. The air was heady with the scent of roses and loud with the buzz of foraging bees. Guy got down onto the rug.

'Point me, will you?' he asked, losing the direction of the sun.

'You're wasting your time, Dad.'

'The world goes round on hope,' responded Guy. 'Faith, hope and charity.'

'And common-sense. Didn't Patrick tell you that yesterday?'

'He, uh . . .'

'Didn't he leave any message for me either?'

'No, nothing. Nothing special. Just the usual. Give

your dad plenty of rest. Don't let him lift a finger.
Wait on him hand and foot. Put in for double pocket-
money . . .'

There was a moment's silence, then the boy got
up.

'I'm not hungry,' he said in a tight voice.

'Jamie, what's the matter? Jamie?'

The reply came from down by the gate.

'You forget, Dad. I'm not blind.'

Guy closed the study door. He picked up the phone,
dialled Directory Enquiries and asked the number of
the Addenbrooke Hospital. A few moments later he
was speaking to the sister in charge of the spinal
injuries ward.

'I'm a friend of Patrick Ross,' he said. 'I heard
about the accident. How is he? What happened?'

'It's a C-5 fracture,' replied the sister. 'We've done
X-rays but it's too early to say.'

'Can I speak to him?'

'He's still sedated.'

'Would you tell him Guy Sullivan called?'

'Your name is Guy?' Her tone changed. 'He's been
asking for you urgently. There's a message for you. It
didn't make much sense to me, but he seemed so insistent. I wrote it down. Hold on a second.' A moment
later she came back on the line. 'Here it is. "Cat died
after the eighth. Brain tumour. Tell Guy." Does that
mean anything to you? Hello? Mr Sullivan? Are you
there?'

He hardly recognized his own voice when he spoke.

'Yes. I understand. Thank you, sister.'

Cat died after the eighth. Brain tumour. Tell Guy.

Yes, he understood very well.

Back to Beethoven. The Fourth Piano Concerto.

Major tenths doing battle with the powers of darkness. Struggle and triumph, trial and victory. Guy sat in his leather chair long after the record had ended, with the needle tracing an endless groove. All that struggle and no triumph, all that trial and no victory.

In his pocket, his hand touched the key-ring bleeper Jamie had given him. So, he was back to blindcraft and gimmickry. Possibly worse: had the seeds of a tumour already been sown? Still blind and now brain-damaged, was that the outcome? Where was the justice in that?

Slowly, aching from fighting the disappointment, he rose to his feet and turned off the record-player. Outside, an owl hooted. What was the time? It didn't matter. Nothing mattered any more.

He opened the door. He was worn out but he knew he couldn't sleep. He'd drink himself into a stupor. Why bother to spare the liver when the brain was rotten?

He went down the corridor to the kitchen. As he opened the door, he tripped and fell forwards. His outstretched hand caught the oil-cloth on the table and plates crashed to the floor. What the hell was going on? Chairs were never left in the way! And the table should be over to the left. He clambered to his feet and took a step towards the sink, colliding with his tall-backed farmhouse chair. Jesus Christ, had they had burglars? He fumbled his way to the side-board. In the cabinet above the percolator, he'd find the drink. The kettle was where the percolator should have been. The bread-bin was where the kettle should have been. The knife-rack was in the toaster's place, the sugar-bowl in the tea-tin's. He felt in the cupboard. Jam, not whisky. He flew into a rage. He flung open each cupboard in turn. He bent to grope in the cabinets under the sink, cracking his head on a door he'd left open as he rose. The wound was wet and tasted of blood.

'Jamie!' he roared upstairs. 'What the hell is this about?'

No reply.

He went round the room. Nothing was in its proper place. He felt dizzy, disorientated. Suddenly this was not the kitchen he knew. It was enemy territory, a threatening, alien land. What was a coal scuttle doing in the gangway? Empty milk bottles *inside* the back door? Glasses perched on the edge of surfaces?

He retraced his steps down the corridor and went into the sitting-room, remembering there'd once been a bottle on the shelf behind the television. The moment he walked into the room, he could tell it was all changed about. The echoes were different. He stopped dead, gripped by the fear of the unknown and unsafe. Gingerly he put out a hand. He felt the back of an armchair. An armchair in the doorway? As he skirted it, something fluttered against his face. He let out a sharp cry and recoiled. The house had become a ghost tunnel. He fell on all fours. The sofa stood where the television should be. Or did it? Slowly he realized he was losing his bearings *in his own home*! Which way was the window? He listened, but there was no sound, not even the cry of an owl, to tell him. Was he facing the wall or the door, the fireplace or the corner? He located the table and sat on the floor against a leg, shivering with rage and frustration and the bitter disappointment of it all.

He guessed why Jamie had done this. The boy must have realized he'd lied to him. Patrick had not come by and given him the treatment. He must have somehow discovered who had. His father had betrayed him, and this was his punishment.

Jamie, Jamie, he cried to himself, all that's over now. There'll be no more madness. I'm staying blind forever. I need you. Don't forsake me now.

CHAPTER TWENTY-TWO

Guy stood on the landing, listening. Not a sound came from the kitchen. Wrapping his towelling dressing-gown around him, he put his head round the boy's bedroom door.

'Morning, Jamie. Rise and shine.'

There was no reply. He went in. Almost at once he barked his shins on a low table, sending a tub of pencils rolling onto the floor. That table wasn't supposed to be there.

'Come on, I know you're there,' he laughed.

Still no reply. No sound of breathing, either. He felt his way round the edge until he came to the bed; it lay across the room from where it should be, and it was made. He felt his watch. Eight-twenty. Not especially late; it was a holiday week, after all.

He went to the bathroom. Knowing what to expect, he found his razor was on a different shelf, but the toothpaste was in the usual mug. He'd begun brushing his teeth with it when he realized it was hair gel. He smiled tightly. Well, if it was to be a game . . .

He took off his watch and stepped into the shower cabinet. He wasn't going to be caught again. But no, the shampoo was proper shampoo and the soap, as far as he could tell, wasn't that trick black stuff. He whistled. He had every reason to be depressed, but today he felt surprisingly good. The die was cast; it was almost a relief to know there was nothing he could do about it.

A sound outside. A creak.

He started. He turned off the shower and listened.

Complete silence. This was crazy. He resumed his showering, whistling more loudly.

After he'd dried himself, he slipped on his dressing-gown and reached for his watch by the basin. It wasn't there. Had he put it in his pocket? Or on the shelf?

He frowned. Stealing a blind man's watch was taking the joke a bit far.

He dressed, almost surprised to find his trousers and track-shoes in their proper place. At least the boy observed some rules of the game and kept his bedroom off bounds. He went downstairs more gingerly than usual. Was the bannister rail slightly loose? He was imagining it. He swept each stair with his foot before he stepped on it, in case there was something to slip on.

The kitchen had been re-arranged yet again. The table was butted against the far window, chairs were scattered haphazardly everywhere, the kettle was in a cupboard and the radio straddled the top corner of the fridge so that he brushed it as he passed and sent it crashing to the ground. As he bent to pick up the pieces, a broom-handle jabbed him in the chest, narrowly missing his throat.

He felt his way to the table. No cornflakes, no milk, no plates or spoons. The sugar-bowl was upside down. As he lifted it, a small creature darted out, scrabbled over his wrist and ran away down the table-leg. He leapt back. This was no longer funny. He'd damn well go and have breakfast with Alice and Donald if this was how the boy wanted to play it.

And then he remembered that Alice and Donald weren't there. They'd left at dawn for a few days' break by the sea.

He had to think this out. In Jamie's mind, this was punishment for betraying his trust. He mustn't get angry; that would only drive the boy to escalate the issue. No, he had to rely on the old weapons: love, understanding and time.

From the cupboard under the stairs he took the rattling football and went outside. He bounced it a few times on the concrete path, half expecting Jamie to come forward, then with a shrug he carried it up the winding path that led through the shrubbery at the bottom of Alice's garden and out onto the school playing-fields. There he set it down and began to dribble it up and down.

He kept count of his steps. A hundred forward; turn about, and a hundred back. Down behind the school buildings, a motor mower was at work on the lawns, and this gave him orientation. Where was Jamie? Surely this would bring him out. He loved the game. He only needed a few minutes with the boy and it could all be sorted out. He'd explain the misunderstanding and tell him what Patrick had said. No more treatments: that was a promise. They'd make it up, and life would return to normal.

On the tenth stretch, the mower stopped. He carried on for another two lengths. Then slowly he grew to realize he was lost. The grounds were silent. There was not even a distant car to tell him where the road lay. He stood there for a while, feeling utterly dejected. Then he did the only thing possible in that situation: he began walking ahead, very slowly, in a straight line, keeping his hand out, until he hit something.

The boy watched from his tree-house. After a while he put the binoculars away and climbed down to the platform below, using the rope ladder to let himself down to the ground. Moving fast through the thick green undergrowth, he skirted the cottage in a wide arc and slipped in through the kitchen door. He went straight upstairs to the treatment room.

First he ripped the wires out of the back of the oscilloscope and with a chair-leg he smashed the grey glass screen. Then he flung the broken instrument on the floor and stamped on the metal casing until it burst apart, spewing microchips and circuit boards. Next he attacked the EEG recorder and hurled it bodily across the room. Taking hold of the table by its front edge, he upended it, sending the control panel crashing to the floor.

Then he set upon the chamber. He wrenched out the cables of fine wires that led out to the EEG recorder. He kicked over the couch and slashed the mattress with his penknife. Grabbing the strobe in both hands, he tore it off its mounting and flung it into the corner. With his heel he hacked away at the joints where the sound-proofing panels were nailed together until the supports began to give, the boards splintered and, one by one, the sides came apart and collapsed in a tangled mass on the floor.

Towelling her hair dry as she went, Lisa picked up the mail off the doormat and hurried down the corridor to the kitchen. She was going to be late for work on Monday morning again. She scanned the letters as she waited for the kettle to boil. One was written in a child's hand and bore a Cambridge postmark. She tore it open at once. She read the short note four or five times, then put it down and stared out of the window into the overgrown garden. A strip of tinsel strung on a cane to scare away birds fluttered and flashed in the wind, but she barely noticed it.

Stop it! the note read. *You don't understand! He's got to take his punishment. You can't change that. Don't interfere.*

There was no mention of the presents, no response

to her careful familiarities. Only this strange, manic command. *His punishment*: what could it possibly mean?

She looked at the postmark. He'd posted it in the town while she'd been at the cottage, giving Guy his treatment. What had happened when Patrick turned up? Had Jamie returned by then? Had Patrick noticed anything odd about the boy? She'd phoned him constantly over the weekend but hadn't been able to reach him. She looked at her watch. Ten to nine. He might just conceivably be in the labs now.

She called, and was put through to Oliver Brock.

She waited in the accident ward while nurses attended to Patrick behind a curtain. She'd taken the day off work and driven fast up to Cambridge. After a few minutes the screen was drawn aside and the nurse indicated the patient was ready to be seen. Oliver had told her he'd been in an accident, but he hadn't prepared her for this.

Patrick lay on his back, rigid and unmoving, staring at the ceiling. His head was shaved bald. The points of a pair of calipers were set into his skull just above each temple and connected at the back of his head to a cable that ran over a pulley at the end of the bed to a set of metal weights designed to keep his spine under constant tension. His face was swollen and covered in stitches and both arms were encased in plaster up to the shoulders.

She stood over him so that he could see her. The sight of her filled him with great agitation and distress. He tried to raise his head, but the steel pincers restrained him, and when he attempted to speak, the words came out thick and incoherent.

'Lie still,' she urged.

She reached for the fingers projecting out of the

plaster and gave them a comforting squeeze, but she could see he was desperate to get something across to her.

'The cat's dead,' he slurred. 'Tumour on the brain. The last one did it. No more treatments.'

A wave of horror hit her. What the hell had she done, forcing that session on Guy?

'The seventh . . .' she faltered. 'That was okay?'

'The seventh was okay.'

'Thank Christ.'

His eyes widened in alarm.

'You didn't . . . ?'

'No, Patrick. I didn't.'

A look of relief flooded his face. What else could she say? The first thing she'd do was rush Guy into hospital for a scan. Patrick was beginning to ramble now. She couldn't make out all he was saying and tried to hush him, but he still wouldn't be quieted.

'I should have stopped it before,' he kept saying. 'I saw the side-effects. The pain. And those nightmares.'

'Nightmares?' She was thinking back to the last session.

'Precognitions. Like his premonition before Kathy died.'

'Patrick,' she laughed uneasily, 'you don't believe in that psychic nonsense!'

'I do now. I know: I was there. He foresaw everything, exactly as it happened. I know how, too. It was Jamie's doing.'

'Jamie?' she snapped.

'Fiddled with the strobe. Turned up the setting. Wanted to sabotage the thing.'

And his voice began to degenerate until she could understand no more.

*

269

Jamie didn't appear all morning. When the battery clock on the kitchen wall said it was time for lunch, Guy found the bread, cheese and fruit and laid it out, but the boy didn't turn up. This was taking it too far. The place was in a shambles. He was damned if he was going to live surrounded by chaos for a moment longer.

He stormed into the sitting-room and set about restoring the furniture to its place. The sofa went lengthwise across the room, but in order to get it there he had to move the low table and the television. This in turn meant finding temporary places for the two armchairs and shifting the writing-desk. He kept tripping over the standard lamp and twice he knocked the phone off the window-ledge. The map grew muddled in his mind. Where was the sofa now? And the second armchair? Was he facing the fireplace or the door? Every minute he'd have to feel his way back to the window and regain his bearings before starting again. His fury rose and, with his fury, his unease. It took so little to throw his entire world out of balance. At a stroke, he'd been rendered helpless.

The phone rang. He let it ring. Jamie usually answered it; perhaps it would draw him out from hiding. It rang ceaselessly. Finally he went to pick it up and fell headlong over the low table.

It was Lisa, calling from Cambridge.

She'd been to see Patrick in hospital; he was in bad shape. Patrick had told her two things it was vital he knew. One was about the cat.

'I know about the cat,' he said tersely. 'It's no longer relevant. I've given the treatment up. That's all over and done with now.'

'Maybe the damage is done,' she said. 'We've got to get you a scan . . .'

'Then it's too late anyway.'

'And there's Jamie,' she went on after a moment's icy silence. 'You'd better know the boy's been trying to wreck the whole treatment. He's been sabotaging it all along.'

He interrupted her bluntly.

'None of that matters now. I told you, I've given it all up.'

'It matters that he's been fiddling with the strobe. Patrick said he turned up the setting. He also said you had a premonition of Kathy's death. That's what sparked it off. I wouldn't mind betting he did the same last time, too, the brat.'

'Don't be absurd,' he snapped, then controlled himself. 'I'm sorry. Don't let Patrick unnerve you. I had some bad dreams last time, okay. But not premonitions. I *know*. I dreamed about things that happened years ago.'

'Have you checked the strobe?'

'I don't need to check the strobe. I'll never be using it again.'

She hesitated.

'Look, I think I should come over.'

'No, don't do that. Jamie's playing up a bit. Leave it for a while, till things settle down. Then we'll sit down and talk it all through.'

She seemed about to protest, but contained herself.

'Sure,' she said easily. 'Make it next year. Suits me fine. Meantime, just remember what I said about that boy of yours.'

He put the phone down and stood for a while with his eyes shut, holding onto the edge of the window-sill to keep his balance. That was the trouble with letting people in. However well-meaning, they always knew better. Jamie was *his son* and he was going to see to him in his own way.

After a few minutes, he took a Braille book from his study and went out of the house. He'd find a spot under a tree and read for a while until he'd calmed his mind.

The boy crouched in the bushes as the man came down the garden path carrying a book. Holding his breath, he watched him open the gate and head directly towards him. He passed so close he could have reached out and touched him.

Without the least twig snapping, he slipped across the drive and up the path into the cottage. Running upstairs, he grabbed a holdall and packed it with sweaters, shoes and the torch. In the kitchen he threw in pork pies, cheese, apples and cans of Coke. Stuffing a cold sausage into his mouth, he sneaked along the corridor into the sitting-room. With the screwdriver blade on his pen-knife he removed the wires from the back of the telephone, putting the set back where it was. Then he went upstairs and disabled the set there in the same way.

On the way out he stopped. He switched the hall light on. He took out his pen-knife again and unscrewed the protective plastic cover, exposing the bare terminals.

Then he picked up his holdall and vanished.

On the phone Guy's tone had alarmed Lisa: he'd sounded on the verge of cracking up. She should be there, with him.

But she couldn't, because of Jamie. Yet the boy was a danger to his father – all the more so as his father refused to see it. He was cracking up under the strain of the responsibility, too, as his garbled note showed. No, there was only one thing to do: meet him face to face.

She went to a Post Office and bought a first-class letter-card.

Dear Jamie,

she wrote,

> I'm in Cambridge for a day or two and I'll be passing your way tomorrow, Tuesday. Let's meet, shall we? How about one o'clock, down by the river near the bridge? That way we shan't be disturbed. See you then.
>
> As always,
> Lisa.

She posted it to catch the three-fifty collection. Barring strikes, it would be on his doormat the following morning. Then she called the BBC and arranged to take a second day's leave of absence. She'd stay overnight with friends in Cambridge and visit Patrick again in the morning before driving down to Gorselands for the rendezvous. In the meantime, she'd better plan her angle very carefully. She'd only have one shot at it.

Guy slammed the book shut in frustration. Where the hell *was* Jamie? How long could this go on? What could he *do*? Perhaps he should have asked Lisa to come.

He sat for a moment in the sunshine. The school was deserted; apart from a hedge-trimmer buzzing far away down by the drive, there was no sound but the bees foraging in the foliage above him and a skylark warbling high in the sky. He got up and walked slowly back to the cottage. There was work to be done to prepare for the second half of term. He'd put it off, half hoping he might have the use of his eyes by then.

The house was still empty. He went to the kitchen and made a cup of tea. Feeling around for the milk, he found that cheese, cold sausages and pork pies had gone. The boy had raided the fridge. At least he was eating.

He went upstairs to the bathroom, and as he reached the top of the landing, he stopped. Lisa's words came back to him: *Have you checked the strobe?* Why should he? There again, why shouldn't he?

He went over to the treatment room.

The door would only open an inch; something was wedged behind it. He pushed. There was the sound of wood sliding on boards. He stepped in, his foot crunching glass. The air hung heavy with resin and dust. He reached out for the edge of the table, but met a void. He took another step forward and tripped. He flung his hand out to save himself and stabbed it on a row of sharp tacks sticking up out of a splintered board. Gingerly, he felt his way round the room, an inch at a time.

The place was wrecked. Bits of equipment lay all over the floor, some completely shattered, others broken up into components, only held together by their wires. The chamber itself was reduced to rubble, the boards smashed and the sheets of sound-proofing hacked to pieces. Upside-down among the debris he found the table. Working his fingers round the back, he located the small Dymotape label marked, *strobe*. He reached for the milled metal knob. His hands were trembling now. He already knew what he would find.

The knob had been turned way up to the limit.

*

He sat on the topmost stair, his head in his hands.

This was Jamie. This was *his own son*!

But that was not all.

So, the strobe *had* been turned up during the last session. If Patrick was right . . .

'Dreams,' he'd blithely said, 'not premonitions.'

How could he be so sure?

Of course it was his memory, fuelled by guilt and grief, throwing up the nightmare! It had been Sandy. Sandy in her white dress, sprawled in the dark green corn.

Why, then, was it twilight? She had died in the full brightness of the morning. And now he came to think of it, it had been late August and the corn was ripe. Golden, not green.

For God's sake, how could he tell one green from another? He'd forgotten what the colour green *was*.

But the dream had been in two distinct parts. He'd glibly assumed the first sprang from his memory and the second from his fantasy. Certainly, they weren't both memories: he hadn't seen Jamie on that day. But what if they were both fantasies?

He went very cold.

He'd foreseen Jamie killing someone. And it wasn't Sandy.

'Oh my God,' he gasped.

It was Lisa.

The boy had tried it before. This time he was actually going to go through with it.

Frantically he thought back to the train crash and to Kathy's death. How long had it been between the premonition and the event? The same in both cases: three days. If that was the pattern, where would it take him? Tuesday afternoon. The scene had been dark, in twilight. So, Tuesday evening. It was now Monday afternoon. How long did that give him? A little over twenty-four hours.

Twenty-four hours. He had to find Jamie. So long as he kept the boy within his reach every hour of the forthcoming day, everything would be all right. He'd call Lisa and check she was in London, well out of the way. Destiny had had the edge on him up until now. This time he was going to outwit it. He'd face it and forestall it by the sheer force of his human will.

CHAPTER TWENTY-THREE

Guy left the cottage and went to the foot of the large beech where Jamie had his tree-house.

'Jamie?' he called. 'Come down. We need to talk.'

There was no reply.

'Come down! That's an order.'

In response, a pigeon took flight, crashing its way through the foliage. Was the boy not there after all?

'I'm counting. One . . .'

Silence.

'Two . . .'

A twig snapped close behind him. He started, a thick welt of sweat breaking over his skin. A second later, the same twig snapped again. No, it was a bird cracking a snail on a stone. Still no sound came from the tree above him.

'Three! Right, Jamie. I'll see you in my study!'

He turned about and stormed back towards the house. That would be the rest of the term's pocket-money and no outings for a month. As he reached the small wooden gate, he paused in his tracks. He was sure he'd left it open. Had it swung shut by itself? There was scarcely a breath of wind.

Every house has its own peculiar noises, and as the heat of the day died away, the floorboards in the old cottage eased their shoulders. Standing at the foot of the stairs, Guy fancied he heard a step on the landing above, and a moment later another in the study beside him. He was beleaguered by false clues.

He went upstairs and checked the bathroom, probing with his hands. It was empty. As he shut the door, he wondered if the boy was crouching behind the bath, or maybe hiding flat against the wall behind the door, and he had to go back in to make sure. He tried the den. Not knowing the lay-out, he walked straight into a jutting shelf and jabbed his forehead. He listened, honing his ears. There was a faint pattering sound. Just a butterfly caught at the window. He opened the window, and a moment later the fluttering stopped. But the room was empty.

He went from room to room, convinced that Jamie was somewhere there. He checked the cupboard under the stairs that housed the mains electricity switches. He felt behind the sofa and chairs in the sitting-room ... Then *tap*! *Tap-tap*! The boy was outside, knocking on the window-pane, taunting him.

In a flash he was out of the front door.

'Right! Come here!'

But there was no sound of scurrying feet, not even footsteps tiptoeing away down the path, only silence, and the tap-tapping on the window went on. Unnerved, he stepped forward and reached out towards the source of the sound. It was the television aerial. One end hung free; it had been cut.

Shaking, he went back indoors. He was overreacting. The boy had probably gone fishing; he always said they rose best in the evening. He'd be back by nightfall.

He found the bottle of Scotch and poured a drink, early though it was. He put on a record: an Offenbach overture, to raise his spirits. But his thoughts kept coming between him and the music. Eventually he turned it down and went to the telephone. These fears were stupid, but at least phoning Lisa would allay them once and for all. He'd call her at her flat in London. He could imagine her reply when he asked the absurd question what she was doing tomorrow. 'Working, of course!' 'At the BBC?' 'Where else?'

He lifted the receiver. The line was dead. He tapped the cradle up and down. Still no joy. He picked up the set to shake it. The cable fell out of the back. The wires had been unscrewed from the terminals.

He went upstairs to his bedroom. That was out of bounds, according to the rules of Jamie's game. He sat on his bed, lifted the receiver and started to dial Lisa's number. As he put it to his ear, he knew the rules had changed. And it was no longer a game.

A wind was rising. It breathed in through the open windows of his study, flinging summer evening scents into the room. He'd been sitting there for a while, forcing himself to concentrate on his French syllabus for the rest of term, when he realized it had grown cool. A dank chill now filled the air. He felt for the time, but remembered his watch was missing. With a spurt of annoyance, he went to the kitchen and felt the hands of the wall-clock. Ten past four. Impossible! He listened. It had stopped. He unhooked the clock and checked the back. The battery was missing.

A reference-point: Jamie had paid a visit at ten past four. Where had he himself been then? Out in the drive, yelling up into the tree like an idiot?

He was damned if he was going to be made a fool of.

Putting on a jersey, he slipped out of the back door and followed the path, overgrown with rhododendrons, up to the McVeys' house. He felt for the key to their front door on his new key-ring and let himself in.

The house was silent but for the stately ticking of the grandfather clock in the hall. He fiddled with the catch on the glass face to open it and brushed his fingertips lightly over the hands. Eight twenty-five.

He trailed his hand along the dado-rail until he came to Donald's study. The door was open, but he tripped over the door-stop and fell, bringing a coffee-table and a heavy glass ashtray crashing to the floor. Picking himself up, he groped for the desk he knew to be in the centre of the room and felt around the leather-covered top until he lit upon the telephone. He picked up the receiver. At least this one was working.

He dialled Lisa's flat in London. There was no reply. He let it ring on and on. He tried again in case it was a wrong connection. But she was obviously out. Half past eight on a Monday night? Out to supper, a movie, the theatre? Wherever she was, she wouldn't be back for a few hours. He'd try later.

Growing increasingly troubled, he retraced his steps back home to the cottage. He let himself back into the kitchen, turned on the light and went to the fridge, but he had no stomach for food. Instead, he poured a glass of whisky and perched on the edge of the table, thinking. Jamie could be anywhere out there. His bet was he was holed up in his tree-house, but there was no way he could climb up and flush him out. The boy could equally well be anywhere in the grounds. He knew every inch of them, and he knew his way about at night perfectly from his badger-watching. He could survive in the woods for days. He'd done it before, after Sandy's death. This time he was well provisioned, too. He'd probably stocked up again on his raid at four.

There was nothing he could do but turn all the house lights on as a beacon in the night and hope that the welcoming sight would entice him back. If that didn't work after a few hours, he'd have to think again.

His drink in one hand, he went down the corridor. At the foot of the stairs he felt for the light-switch. Just as his fingers brushed the switch and he noted fleetingly that it was already on, a sudden, violent bolt of electricity knocked him off his feet and flung him backwards across the hall. Cracking the side of his head on the stone window-sill, he crumpled to the ground. Inside his skull rose a haze of shooting-stars that exploded briefly, hung in the black sky and then went out.

The boy put the binoculars down. He was satisfied. With the hall light on, he could see everything that went on in the house. He reached into the holdall and felt around for a pork pie. His fingers lit upon the small envelope containing the oval orange pills the woman had hidden.

So, he had the pills. He'd smashed the equipment. But he hadn't been able to find the final hormone ampoule. If she'd hidden the pills from him, she'd have hidden that, too. But where? It wasn't in the fridge. It wasn't anywhere. And until he'd found and destroyed it, he couldn't be absolutely certain.

But there was time. He wasn't sleepy. He had cans of Coke full of caffeine to keep him awake anyway. That was no worry. He'd watch and wait. Sooner or later the man would lead him to it.

Guy came to in a blur of pain. He touched the side of his head; the blood was already dry. What had happened? He remembered he'd been going to turn the lights on . . . He eased himself upright, every joint in his body crying out. What was the time? How long had he been there? He felt automatically for his watch. He listened for clues, but there was silence. Only the inky cool draught filtering in through the door-frame told him it was well into the night.

He had to speak to Lisa.

He fumbled his way into the kitchen and stood on the back doorstep listening to the sounds of the night. For the first time he felt a stab of real fear. What was that rustling in the undergrowth? That slithering in the bushes over there? Was that a fox coughing or . . . ?

Bracing his nerves, he stepped forward. Nothing tripped him, nothing pounced. Leaves brushed his arms and face as he hastened up the steep path that led to the McVeys' house. He let himself in and made his way carefully across the hall, stopping to tell the time. One fifteen. It was too bad if he woke her.

He dialled, but there was still no answer. He broke into a sweat. What if he couldn't get hold of her in the morning either?

He couldn't take that chance. He had to do something about Jamie. The boy had to be caught and trapped. But how? He couldn't go after him out there. He had to lure him back into the house.

He went to the dining-room and poured himself another drink, then sat down at the table and put his head in his hands. There *had* to be a way.

Slowly an idea formed as he reasoned out Jamie's behaviour. Why had he smashed the equipment? To prevent him carrying on with the treatment; of course, he wasn't to know that he'd decided to stop it anyway. Okay. That was the angle. Right now, Jamie would be assuming that he'd succeeded in putting the machinery out of action. What if he could be led to think he'd *failed*? What if he actually saw, from his vantage point in the trees, the final treatment going ahead? Wouldn't he be forced back in to finish off his work? And couldn't he then be snared?

In the summer before Sandy died, they'd all three

282

gone to Spain. He'd taken an eight-millimetre movie and he remembered taking it up to the McVeys' house one evening when they'd returned back home and showing it on Donald's screen. The projector had been kept in a cupboard in the living-room. Was it still there? And the film?

Back in the cottage, he took a broom from the cupboard under the stairs and very carefully angled it up against the light-switch in the hall until he heard the click as it went off. The house was now in darkness. He could move about undetected.

The first step was to set the trap.

To keep a control on the boy's movements, there could only be one channel of entry and exit. He locked both the front and back doors and removed the keys. Then he went round securing all the bolts on the downstairs windows, with the exception of the window in his study, which he left deliberately open. He made sure the key to the study door was on the corridor side, so that he could lock it once the boy was indoors and block off his most obvious escape route.

The next step was to set up the decoy.

Carrying the projector upstairs to his bedroom, he drew the curtains shut to form a screen and placed it on a table immediately in front. He plugged it in, rewound the film and made sure it was pointing directly at the curtains. Then, removing the lens so that it would just produce a bright flicker as the film went through, he switched the lamp on and set it rolling.

All he could do now was wait.

Shortly before two o'clock, a sudden snarl and a violent tussle in the undergrowth beneath the tree jolted the boy awake from his doze. He peered out at the cottage through the gap in the thick foliage. Something funny was going on. He grabbed the binoculars.

Only one room was lit. The curtains were drawn, but from the bright flicker coming through them he could clearly see what was going on inside.

He'd got the strobe going again!

In fury, he slipped down to the ground. There he hesitated, all his senses alert. The clouds parted for a brief moment, letting through the light of a thin crescent moon. From the fur and claw-marks in the earth he could see a fox had made a kill.

He crossed the driveway quickly and, stealing up the side of the cottage fence, let himself into the back garden. Picking up the brick that kept the back gate open, he went up to the kitchen door. It was locked. He carried on round, finding all the windows shut until he came to the study.

Within seconds he was inside. He crept to the foot of the stairs. There were clicking sounds coming from the bedroom above. He tightened his grip on the brick. Step by step he began ascending the stairs. Halfway up, he stopped. A cleverer idea had occurred to him.

Tiptoeing down to the bottom, he slipped along the corridor. After a few paces he came to the small door to the cupboard under the stairs. He'd pull out the mains fuses and that would put paid to any tricks.

He opened the door and stepped inside. The musty smell of furniture polish and dusters met him. He fumbled around for the light-switch but he couldn't find it. He traced his fingers along the wall inside the door until he came to . . .

A hand!

He let out a scream.

At once a second hand whiplashed onto his wrist and locked it fast.

'Got you!'

As he sprang back, the vice around his wrist tightened. Tentacles drew him deeper into the cupboard. In raw terror he swung his left hand and clubbed the creature with the brick. There was a cry of pain and the grip relaxed for a second. He lashed out with his foot and managed to squirm free. Evading the arms clutching at him, he darted into the kitchen and threw himself frantically at the back door. He wrestled with the handle. It wouldn't open. It was locked, and he was trapped.

He froze.

Guy blundered into the corridor and stood in the kitchen doorway. The blow had caught him on the shoulder and sheered off. He tried to smother the rage the pain caused.

'Okay,' he said thickly. 'It's all over, Jamie. Come here, please.'

Silence was his answer.

'That's enough, I said! Now, be reasonable. Show me where you are.'

More silence.

'*For Christ's sake, Jamie!*' he roared.

The boy was desperately trying the windows. Finding himself sealed in, he began darting about the room like a trapped animal. But the kitchen wasn't the place to apprehend him; he only had to keep the table between them and he could escape. No, his exit had to be sealed. Then the house could be combed from top to bottom. Sooner or later he'd be caught.

As he turned and made off down the corridor to lock the study door, he heard a small *click* behind him.

The kitchen light going on!

*

The boy pressed himself up against the wall behind the door. Through the crack, in the light from the kitchen where he was, he could see the man stop in his tracks. If he could entice him into the kitchen, he could toss something across the room to distract his attention and then slip out and escape the way he'd come in.

Guy hesitated. He had to think fast. Turning, he went back inside the cupboard and slammed the mains electricity switch off. To make sure, he pulled out the main fuse and put it in his pocket. The house was back in darkness. Balance was restored.

He padded fast down the corridor to the study and locked the door, taking the key out. Then he slipped into the sitting-room. He'd herd the boy into an ever-tighter space. He'd force him upstairs and corner him in one of the rooms.

He waited. The seconds grew into minutes. Not a sound came from the kitchen. He'd made so much noise himself, had the boy slipped past without his realizing? His heart pounded. How had the game got out of hand? Reason and sense had fled; this was open warfare and there was no turning back now.

Tapping on the window-pane. Only the loose aerial.

A floorboard creaking upstairs. Upstairs? Impossible! The old house easing its joints again.

And then, quite distinctly, a footstep in the kitchen. And another, perhaps in the doorway.

Silence, but for the pumping of his veins.

Then, quite suddenly, *clap, clap, clap, clap*!

Four claps, and at once the key-ring in his pocket started bleeping. He had to get rid of the goddam thing! He flung it into a corner, where it continued its unremitting chime. But even as he did so, he heard

Jamie come darting down the corridor. The door-handle of the study rattled frantically. He burst out into the corridor. With a cry of fury, the boy dashed upstairs and sped across the landing into his den, slamming the door shut behind him.

'Don't come in!' he yelled wildly. 'You're not allowed!'

Guy followed up the stairs. He stood outside the door, clenching his fists to prevent himself charging in and invading the boy's private area. He was out of breath and in pain, but at last it was all over. He had got him in a corner where he could deal with him. Now was the time to calm down, to defuse the drama, to mend bridges.

'Jamie? Jamie, it's all right. I'm not coming in.'

He felt overwhelmingly tired. During those last hours, he'd been strung out on a rack of madness. How could it have happened that a man and his son should end up fighting like that? He breathed a vast sigh of relief. Even if he had to sit there all night and all the following day, he was safe. In due course, over time, he'd break down the boy's resistance. They'd talk it through. He'd tell him things he'd always kept to himself. They'd forge a new understanding. Out of the crisis, a new beginning would emerge. The worst was over.

'You know something, Jamie,' he said quietly. 'Football isn't the same without you. It's no fun dribbling up and down with no-one to pass to.'

There was no response from inside the den.

He sat on the floor. Lighten the tone he thought.

'What a pair we must look! Me sitting out here on my butt, and you in there, a couple of feet away, twiddling your thumbs.'

There was a rustling movement going on inside. Wanting to appear trusting, he went on talking. It was

not until he heard a loud clatter far away that he realized the boy had climbed out of the window, jumped
down onto the shed roof and escaped.

The cry from the garden confirmed it.

'I won't let you do it, Dad! Just don't try!'

CHAPTER TWENTY-FOUR

The sound was soft, insistent. A hissing, like a punctured tyre. It dragged him to the surface when he only wanted to sink back into sleep. It tugged at the inside of his brain, refusing to let him go. He stirred uncomfortably in the armchair. Pain stabbed his head and shoulder. For a moment, the hissing stopped, then started again.

Whispering! It was not a hissing but a whispering. The radio. He must have left the radio on in the kitchen. But no, it couldn't be that: the radio worked off the mains, and he'd shut off the house supply. Besides, he'd probably broken it when he knocked it over.

A tiny whispering. Where was it coming from? Inside his head? Was he hearing voices? He sat up sharply and turned his head from side to side. No, it had direction: it was outside. He clambered painfully out of the chair. He took a few steps forward, but the sound now came from behind. Gradually he focused in on the source. On the table, just by the chair.

Gingerly he reached out his hand. His fingers met a small, plastic object.

The ear-phone!

Slowly he raised it to his ear, plugged it in and listened.

'Dad!' it whispered.

He started violently.

'Wave if you can hear me,' the tiny voice whispered.

A bolt of sick panic shot though him. Last night had been real after all. Jamie was still out there, at large.

Watching from the tree-house through binoculars. In control.

Aligning himself against the back of the chair, he faced the window. He couldn't bring himself to do it. Yet he had to. He'd tried his own dialogue and it had failed.

He half-raised his left arm.

'Come closer.'

He took a step closer to the window.

'Right up, where I can see you.'

God damn the boy! But he went forward until he touched the window-sill. He stood clenching his jaw as he waited for instructions.

'Did you do it last night?'

Guy shrugged. *Do what?* he gestured.

'Did you do the last treatment?'

Guy thought fast. To lie was dangerous. Maybe the boy knew the answer already and was just testing him. Play along, play it straight, keep the dialogue going: he was a hostage dealing with a captor.

He shook his head firmly. *No.*

'Where have you hidden the hormone?'

He spread his hands. *Search me.*

'It's not in the fridge. It's not anywhere. Go and get it! I want to see you smash it. If you don't . . .'

His temper snapped. Fuck the hormone! He fumbled with the catch and flung open the window.

'Jamie!' he yelled at the top of his voice. 'Talk to me down here! I haven't seen the hormone. I'm never going to use it anyway. Jamie! Jamie? Can you hear me?'

But the click in his ear told him that he'd been switched off.

Collecting his keys from the mantelpiece, Guy tramped through the house and left by the back door.

Okay, Jamie would see him leave, but he couldn't stop him checking up on Lisa. He'd catch her either at her flat or at work. The journey between only took a matter of minutes.

The birds were in full song, the air was crisp and a heavy dew soaked his shoes. It must still be early. He slipped into the McVeys' house. The grandfather clock confirmed that it was not yet seven.

Lisa was not at her flat when he phoned.

He went into the kitchen and laboriously felt around the unfamiliar lay-out to make himself a cup of coffee. He sat down and waited. He'd wait until after nine and call her at work.

The boy was alerted by the sound of a van coming up the main drive on the far side of the school grounds. He followed it through the binoculars. The postman. The red van stopped at the main school building, but then drove round the back along the route that led up the old drive to the cottage.

He had to intercept it.

Shinning swiftly down the rope ladder, the boy flagged the postman down as he approached. He smiled nicely as the man reached into his bag.

'Just one today,' he said. 'It's for you.'

'Thanks.'

The postman turned round and drove back the way he'd come. He honked and waved as he passed, but the boy hardly noticed him now, for he was immersed in the letter.

This changed everything.

Lisa's office told Guy she'd taken the day off. They didn't know where she was. Could they take a message?

No, no message.

With mounting alarm, he walked slowly back down to the cottage. For a while he stood outside the front door, wondering what new approach he could use. In the back of his mind, the drums beat one degree louder. Things were closing in. He had until the evening . . . Could he really be sure the time-bomb was set to go off then? If he'd had the premonition a day later, would it have been a different one? Could he assume the clock of destiny always ticked with the same measure?

Should he call Donald and Alice? What would he say? Stated plainly, his fears sounded absurd. He couldn't bring them back off holiday just because he had an uneasy hunch. He had to see it through himself. And yet the drums continued to sound their steady beat, counting off the seconds as slowly and relentlessly as the tick of the grandfather clock.

He went to the sitting room. Very reluctantly, he put the ear-phone back in and stood by the window, waiting.

He waited five, ten minutes. At last there was a click and the small voice came on again. Its tone was injured and resentful.

'You're lying!' it hissed.

He gestured his innocence.

'I know you're going to try! But you can't do it! God won't let you. He's made you blind. It's your punishment for what you did.'

Guy stretched out his hands, pleading for an explanation.

'You know very well!' The voice rose in pitch. 'I've kept the secret all this time. I didn't tell anyone what I saw. Or you'd have been put in prison. But God saw, too. He knows. I saved you as long as I could, but I couldn't for ever. He made you blind. He means you to stay blind.'

Slowly a terrible realization began to creep over him. Could it be that, on that hateful morning when he'd taken Sandy in his arms and carried her to that field, the boy might have . . . ?

A note of hysteria crept into the voice.

'*I saw you do it*! You killed Mum, and I saw it. I followed you from the house. You took her to the field. You meant to do it! I *know* you did!'

Oh Christ, he thought. Oh sweet Christ. So that is it.

The voice fell. Its tone switched from mania to quiet menace.

'So, you see, you're meant to be blind. I know what you're planning. Lisa's coming here. You're going to get her to do it for you again . . .'

He shook his head violently. No, Lisa was *not* coming!

'See – you're lying! I know she is. I got a letter from her. She's coming down here. She wants to meet me. I know what she'll say. But I won't let her do it. It's cheating God.'

Lisa lay in bed, listening to the college clocks chiming eight o'clock and thinking about the day ahead.

She'd take Patrick some flowers. While she was at the shops, she'd buy a few things for Jamie, in case he felt like a picnic. If she had time, too, she'd drop in at her old college and see if her tutor was around.

But first, what to wear? Hardly a choice: not expecting to stay over, she only had the white cotton dress she'd worn the day before.

Guy beat his fist against his head. What could he do, the damn useless blind cripple he was? He couldn't do a fucking thing without his sight! He was a husk, a drone, a feeble, groping, helpless blob of flesh.

There was only one thing he *could* do: confront his own fate.

He took one very deep breath.

First, he went to the window and shut it, securing the lock fast. Then he carried on round the house, upstairs and down, checking each window in turn. He bolted both the front and back doors. The strategy was now to keep the boy *out*.

Satisfied the cottage was impenetrable, he went looking for the hormone ampoule. With its power cut, the fridge had defrosted and stood in a pool of water. Jamie was right: the ampoule was not there. Nor was it upstairs in the treatment room. And obviously not in the boy's den either. Where the hell was it?

Lisa had been the last to see it. What would she have done with it? Surely she wouldn't have taken it with her. Knowing it was kept in the fridge, couldn't she have put it somewhere else cold? He checked the larder. He scrabbled around behind the jars of preserves and tins of fruit, but without success. Time was ticking past. She was a bright girl. Where else did you preserve things cold?

A Thermos?

When he found it, he thought: maybe my luck is turning.

The disposable hypodermics were untouched in the bathroom wall-cabinet. He selected one. He had no idea how he'd use it.

He hadn't time to hunt for the scopolamine tablets. He'd have to do without and bear the pain.

Next, sensory deprivation. How the hell could he soundproof his bedroom? If he lay on the eiderdown, propped up with pillows, would that somehow mimic the special couch? And what about the white sound? He went back to the treatment room and fumbled about among the debris until he found the broken instrument panel and, in it, the cassette tape. The wires at the back had been ripped out. Then he remembered Jamie had a radio cassette player in his bedroom. And there was the small ear-phone in the sitting-room.

While downstairs, he went to the cupboard under the stairs and fitted the fuse back into the mains socket. He'd need power for the strobe.

Returning to his own bedroom, he set up the home movie projector on a table at the foot of the bed and plugged the lead into the socket just by his bed where he'd be able to reach it. His hands were shaking and he made several false attempts at feeding the film back onto the spools. He switched it on; the fan started up, the reels turned and the metal housing began to heat up. He switched it off at the wall until he was ready. Would it work? Was the flicker rate right? What if it gave him even more horrific visions? Who was there to save him?

He prepared the bed, padding it with bolsters and pillows, and lay down for a moment to check. With the hiss of white sound playing in through the ear-plug he'd connected to the cassette-player and a wad of cotton wool pressed tight into his other ear, within moments he was beginning to feel the familiar drifting sensation. That, at least, seemed to be working. But would the rest? It was crazy to expect to replicate all that sophisticated instrumentation with ordinary bits and pieces of household equipment.

But he had to try. And he had to hurry: it must already be late morning. He spent precious minutes taping his eyelids open with strips of sticking plaster, then he finally went to the dressing-table on which he'd laid out the hypodermic and ampoule. He shuddered as he picked up the needle.

How did a blind man inject himself in the neck?

He filled the syringe carefully, holding it upside-down and expelling the air until he felt the fluid squirt out. Bending his neck as Patrick had made him do, he felt for the pulse of the artery. He found it, but it slipped away under the pressure of his finger. He located it again and, holding his breath, he angled the needle obliquely and jabbed it in a few millimetres. He missed. Withdrawing it with a stifled cry, he felt for the artery again. This time he hit it and began slowly sinking the plunger. He kept his lips tightly shut against the exploding pain. Just as he felt he was about to burst, the plunger butted against its stop and he jerked the needle out and flung it aside with a roar of agony.

Sick, giddy and vertiginous, he stumbled onto the bed, plugged in the ear-phone and groped for the switch to turn on the projector.

Lisa arrived promptly at one o'clock. She parked her car in the entrance to a field just round the corner and, taking out her shopping-bag and a rug, she walked over the narrow stone bridge, crossed the stile and sauntered along the tow-path that wound along the river bank. Except for a few desultory pigeons and the occasional fish vaulting for a fly, nothing stirred in the afternoon heat. Rushes rose among the lily-pads and nodded sluggishly in the gentle current.

She'd gone twenty yards when she heard the crack of a twig in the undergrowth. She stopped and listened. Silence.

'Jamie?' she called tentatively.

After a moment, the bushes parted some way ahead and the boy came out. His appearance shocked her. His face was white and his eyes wild, his dark hair was awry and a deep scratch ran the length of his cheek. He kept his distance.

'Whatever's the matter?' she asked, taking a step forward.

He darted a glance back at the bushes, as if to check his escape.

'I know what you've come for,' he said, his voice high-pitched and quavering.

She held out the shopping-bag.

'I brought a picnic.'

'I told you not to interfere.'

'Want to see what I've got?' She spread the rug and, kneeling, began taking food out of the bag. 'Come and sit down.'

The boy didn't move. The rug lay open and unused between them. She straightened and smoothed her hands down the sides of her white cotton dress. There was a moment's uncomfortable silence.

'I know what you did last time,' Jamie said at last. 'And that's why you've come . . . Anyway, Dad isn't here. He's away.'

'I came to see you, Jamie. It's time we had a sensible chat.'

'I don't want to talk to you.'

'That's too bad,' she responded sharply, unable to help herself, 'because I have a lot to say to you.'

He took a step back.

'I've got to go. Dad needs his lunch.'

'I thought you said he's away.'

His manner grew more agitated.

'You can't trick me!'

'Come on, Jamie, that was your trick.' She forced him to meet her eye. In a gentler tone, she went on, 'Jamie, tell me: *why* does he have to be punished?'

The boy started violently and his eyes narrowed with mistrust.

'You're tricking me again! You know well enough.'

She spread her hands in a gesture of innocence.

'I don't, I really don't. Who's punishing him? Am I? Are *you*?'

'Go away!'

'Jamie . . .'

He turned towards the bushes. His expression grew wilder.

'Just keep out of it, do you hear? Keep out of it!'

Abruptly he disappeared, leaving her staring into the undergrowth after him, with the mad, feral look in his eyes still burning in her memory.

From his tree-house, the boy focused his binoculars on the upstairs window. Through a chink in the curtain he saw enough to tell him it was already happening.

He shinned down to the ground and in a crouching run skirted the bushes round to the back of the cottage. The kitchen door was bolted. He checked the front door and the windows. All were bolted, too. The place was locked up.

There was only one thing to be done now.

He went round the back to the small garden shed. Inside, he ferreted around for a piece of wood of the right length: ten or twelve inches would do nicely. From the nest of drawers in one corner he selected two bright three-inch nails and sharpened the points with a file. Then, reaching for a hammer, he drove the two nails into the wood and clear out the other side.

He dug into his pocket and took out the man's dark glasses. Holding the sharp spikes against the lenses, he checked that they were set apart just right to do their job.

Lisa drove a few miles slowly down the country lanes

298

before pulling up in the car-park of a small inn. She had to put distance between herself and that place, to give her time to overcome her anger and work out why it had gone so badly wrong.

What in heaven's name was going on in the boy's head?

She sat over a large vodka for thirty or forty minutes, going over their conversation word by word. Why had Jamie tried to pretend his father wasn't there? Why was he warning her off? How did she 'know well enough' why Guy deserved to be punished? When she'd asked who might be punishing him, why wouldn't he give her a direct answer? And what had he meant in his letter that she couldn't change it? What had all this to do with his attempts to sabotage the Blindsight treatments? And what *sense* did it all make?

As she sifted through what she knew, the picture grew increasingly sinister.

The school was empty for the holiday. Even Alice and Donald were away; she knew, because she'd tried to call. Guy, she was sure, was at home. There he was, blind and alone, on a vast estate with a boy who was dangerously mad and whose madness he refused to recognize.

With sudden decisiveness, she started up her car, turned about and headed back to Gorselands.

Guy ripped out the ear-phone and tore off the tapes holding his eyes open. He could hear the film flapping loose on the spool. How long had he been there? Long enough? He tried to climb off the bed but slumped onto his side. His eyes burned like acid as he squeezed them shut. His eyelids felt like sandpaper. Molten lead surged through his head with every pulse-beat. He'd never known such pain. He lay there for a long while, not daring to move. For the moment of truth had arrived.

Very gradually he opened one eye.

Perhaps darkness had already fallen.

He opened the other eye.

But of course, he'd been staring at a bright light for hours. The eye needed time to dark-adapt. It could take minutes.

He waited minutes.

He got up, and promptly fell over. Grappling with the bedside table, he hoisted himself to his feet. He shut his eyes to feel his way to the window better. He drew the curtains and opened a window. A flood of warmth hit him. He fancied he could feel the sun on his face. That would make it about two-thirty. Three hours: was that enough?

Drawing in a full breath, he opened his eyes. This was it.

Nothing!

He could see nothing. Nothing except the familiar, ever-present dark red curtain.

He twisted his head back and forth. The tone darkened or lightened by the merest degree, but *he still couldn't see*!

He broke into a sweat. He'd taken the ultimate risk. He'd invited brain cancer. He'd faced the challenge. All for nothing!

He couldn't believe it. He stood, rocking on his feet, whimpering. The phrase revolved in his head. *All for nothing.* How could it be possible?

He felt his way across the room and sank back onto his bed.

The boy knelt down on the floor of the tree-house in front of the tin trunk. Opening it, he delved among the tissue-paper and mothballs and carefully lifted out a white lacy cotton dress. It had been one of his mother's, just like the one she'd been wearing when she was murdered.

Holding it safely to his chest, he climbed down the rope ladder and dropped lightly to the ground. He looked around him and glanced at the cottage. The curtains in the upstairs window were open, but there was no other sign of life. The heat of the early afternoon was oppressive, and not a leaf or blade of grass stirred. He was quite alone.

He laid the white dress over his arms and carried it down the path that led through the woods to the far field. For a moment he paused in the shade of a beech-tree on the border of the large field and checked his bearings. He knew the spot exactly. Holding the dress so that it wouldn't trail against the green corn, he struck out into the field. After fifteen paces, he stopped and, with his foot, began flattening the corn in a wide circle. When he'd cleared a space, he carefully laid the white dress down, spreading it out as wide as he could. Then he sank to his knees to pray.

Guy dragged himself to his feet. He was defeated. But he still held one small card: foreknowledge. He knew what was going to happen. And he knew where and when.

He'd find the spot in the field and stay there until nightfall. Whatever was to happen, he'd be there and spend the last drop of his blood defying it.

Pausing every few steps to contain the pain, he groped his way downstairs and out into the warm afternoon air. He stood on the doorstep, presenting himself to whatever powers lay out there. Let Jamie see him, too. There was nothing to be lost. If their destinies were to meet at dusk, what did anything in the meantime matter?

He shuffled down the path and out of the gate. Orientating himself against the gate-posts, he struck off half-right onto the winding path that led through the woods to the field of corn.

The boy watched from the bushes. He knew it would soon be time. He saw the man's bent figure fumbling its way into the woods, and he understood how God had planned it.

He slipped into the garden shed and from under a sack he took out the short spar of wood. He tested the two nails for sharpness. He was shivering and couldn't control his hands shaking.

Lisa parked her car up at the McVeys' house and walked down the steep path to the cottage. The back door was locked and all the windows shut. Odd, she thought, for such a hot day. She peered inside. The place was empty. She went round the front and rang the door-bell. There was no reply. Was Guy away after all? Surely he wouldn't have left the boy on his own? Where were they both? Had they gone out in that short time? Or had they just gone for a walk, to the river, or around the woods?

She stood in the driveway outside the house, wondering what to do. If they were together, she couldn't say what she had to. And if they were perfectly all right together, what was there to say anyway?

But if they weren't?

Guy could tell from the widening echoes that he was coming to the end of the trees and the open field lay ahead. He slowed to a shuffle until his foot felt out the old stile that led over a broken barbed-wire fence into the cornfield. He stopped for a moment as the memory of that terrible morning sprang vividly back to life. What kind of divine irony decreed that it should happen *here*? What if it was another trick of fate and it was to happen somewhere quite different, some other cornfield far away?

It was all mad. The world was crumbling about him into madness.

But the same madness, with its seed of hope and truculence, that had impelled him to chance the eighth treatment now drove him to step over the stile, to walk a few yards along the flinty earth at the edge, trailing a stick against the barbed wire as a guide, then to turn and strike off into the deep corn where, after about fifteen paces, he stopped and, finding a wind-flattened area, sat down to wait for nightfall.

As he stretched out, exhausted, his hand touched something strange. It felt like a piece of clothing.

The boy crept through the undergrowth. He slid like a snake in between the trees, tightly gripping the wooden spar with its twin spikes. When the man stopped at the stile, he stopped. When the man started forward again, he moved forward. He hung back in the trees as the man made unerringly for the patch of flattened corn. He'd prepared it as an altar of remembrance; he hadn't thought it was to be an altar of sacrifice.

He waited until he felt the moment was ripe, then he slipped over the stile and, spikes in hand, stole silently through the corn.

Something white. Dark white, as white goes in moonlight. White against black. No, against dark green. It's all scratchy. Flecked. Grainy. Comes and goes.

Guy blinked hard. The nightmare . . . it was repeating itself!

It comes back again. This time it's closer. A *sleeve*! A sleeve of a woman's dress.

Christ, not yet! He wasn't ready. He needed time.

A flash, dazzlingly bright! A complete dress. Vanishes again. This time it leaves an after-image. Glows grey on grey. Now it brightens briefly. Flickers, off and on . . .

Why now? Why so soon? Wait! Hold everything!

Black-out.

Suddenly something different. It's a spike. Two spikes. Jutting out of something. Fingers holding this thing. It fades in and out of focus, drunkenly. Now it fills out, adding more bits. The fingers grow into hands, hands into wrists, wrists into arms. Arms meet chest. On the chest is a head. With dark hair. Ferocious eyes. A pale, oval face.

Jamie's face.

The hands come closer. The thing jabs the air. The spikes glint. He's going to stab . . .

He's going to jab and stab . . .

Guy jerked his head to the side. The spikes flashed past his face and dug into the earth behind him.

The boy pulled the spikes out and stabbed again.

This time he rolled over onto his shoulder. The boy let out a grunt of rage and attacked again, jabbing, slashing, ramming the wood with its vicious nails anywhere at his face. One caught his cheek and gashed deep into it. Another dug into his forearm and for a moment stuck there like a barb.

Guy surged to his feet, throwing the boy off. He grabbed at him, but the boy squirmed out of reach and scrambled away into the deep corn.

Guy blundered after him. Where? How? He didn't know. His mind was full of sparks and flecks of light. Somewhere among them there seemed to be a figure, etched in silhouette, darting and dodging just ahead of him. He threw himself forward and, tripping, caught the boy's heel, tearing off the shoe.

The boy escaped. Like a hare, he swung round in a wide arc back towards the cover of the trees. Guy saw this (he *saw* it?) and swung round in a tangent to cut him off. For a moment they were heading for collision. The boy sensed this and veered in a sharper angle towards the woods. Guy adjusted his own course.

The boy fell. He disappeared beneath the corn. Guy stopped. An artillery battery pounded away in his head. He felt like vomiting. As he stood there, he suddenly realized he was surrounded by complete silence. He looked about him (looked about him?). The corn stretched in an unbroken sea in all directions. The boy had evaporated.

None of it had ever happened.

But he could see (he could see?) a patch some way ahead where the heads of corn weren't waving like the rest. A flat spot. Slowly he moved towards it, understanding that the boy's strategy was to lie quite still. A blind man (a blind man?) could only detect sound, not movement.

He stopped twenty feet away. For a long moment all was still. Then, very gradually, a head emerged out of the corn. It looked at him. He stayed utterly motionless. Shoulders followed the head. Slowly the boy rose to his feet, taking extreme care not to make a sound, but keeping his eyes constantly fixed on the blind man's. Very cautiously, an inch at a time, he began to back away.

Guy pounced.

He pounced with such speed and accuracy that the boy let out a cry. He caught the boy after four paces. He tripped on a stone and the boy kicked himself free. But a second later he was after him again. He saw (he saw?) terror in the boy's face. When the boy jinked left, he jinked left; when he darted right, he darted right. He shadowed him, closing in all the time, until finally, just as they broke out onto the flinty track, he lunged at him and brought him to the ground in a flying tackle, where he lay on top of him, smothering all resistance.

He held him as if never to let him go. He lay there, coughing and choking, his face jammed into the earth, smelling the dry metallic soil and Jamie's sweat-drenched hair. The boy had lost all his fight. He was shaking from head to toe. Holding him tight in his arms, Guy finally drew him up and clasped him to his chest. Tears filled his eyes.

'It's all right, Jamie. I understand everything. I know what you saw. Yes, I did do it. I did it because it was right. Because she was in terrible pain. You can't conceive of the pain she was in. She hid it from you, because she loved you. She didn't want you to suffer. She pleaded with me to help her end it. She longed to be free. I had to help her go.'

The boy buried his head further in his father's chest.

'Jamie, I loved Sandy more than I have ever loved anyone. More than I could imagine loving anyone. Sandy and I made you, and I love you very much. More than Lisa. Yes, I love Lisa, and she could be great for both of us. But no-one will be Sandy again. Whatever happens with Lisa, she'll never replace Sandy in our lives.'

The boy jerked his head sideways to speak.

'But you killed her!'

'Yes, I helped her go. *Because* I loved her. I couldn't bear to see her in such pain. You'd do the same for something you really loved. If you found a dying rabbit, you'd put it out of its agony. That's a kindness, not a crime.'

'It's against God's law!'

He gripped the boy by the shoulders.

'What kind of God is that that makes people suffer like that? Is that your God? He's the one who made her suffer! What did she do to deserve that? I helped her ease the pain, and then I go blind. Is that your God, too? Blinding me because I save the person I love?'

'You cheated him.'

'I'd cheat the devil!'

The boy drew in a breath to speak, but stopped.

'Your God,' Guy went on, 'killed Kathy. Why? Just for helping me? Your God crippled Patrick. Why? For trying to get me my sight back? Jamie, that can't be right! That God is an evil God!'

Jamie choked on a cry.

Guy lowered his voice to a whisper.

'Your God killed Sandy! Not me.'

The boy was weeping convulsively now. His body had grown limp and great sobs racked his thin frame. Guy sat there, rocking him back and forth and all the time keeping his head pressed against his chest.

After a while, he looked up.

Looked up?

At that moment he had a vision. Scratchy, grainy and flecked with shooting stars.

A figure in a white dress stood a few feet away, close by the trunk of a tree. Sandy!

But it was not a ghost.

It was Lisa.

How did he know if he couldn't see her?

She came forward. She had seen and heard everything. She held out her hand and it linked with his. Their eyes met; in hers he saw uncomprehending delight. And understanding. And love.

The boy knelt in the empty chapel. Dust hung motionless in the shafts of evening sunlight filtering through the stained glass window.

God?

A board creaked in the cooling air. Rooks cawed in the distance.

God? Please?

His arms outspread on the pew in front, face pressed into his knuckles, eyes screwed shut until they hurt, Jamie cried out from his soul. The echo rang achingly in the hollow chambers of his heart.

Love?

Only his own despairing call.

God?

There was no love here. No love, no message of any kind.

He rose to his feet, and walked unsteadily up to the altar rail. For a long moment he stood gazing up into the face of Christ.

He saw there neither gratitude nor displeasure, neither indulgence nor wrath, neither forgiveness nor judgement. He saw nothing. For there was nothing to see.

Stepping forward, he felt behind the foot of the wooden cross and retrieved the wedding-ring he'd placed there as an offering. This was not the house where such things belonged.

He cast a final glance up at the empty idol, then turned slowly away. In the doorway stood the man. For a moment, neither moved. Then, with a small cry, he rushed forward and threw himself into his father's arms.

CHAPTER TWENTY-FIVE

The ambulance drove slowly through the country lanes from Cambridge, avoiding bumps and taking corners gently. Although the wheelchair was locked in position, any sudden lurch might disturb the healing of the brain tissue. Guy sat in silence, a car-rug over his knees and his hands folded in his lap. His open eyes stared sightlessly down the ribbon of the road behind.

From time to time he reached up to his head to relieve the pressure of the bandages. Three weeks had passed since that terrible day. Back at the cottage, he'd admitted to Lisa he'd given himself the eighth treatment and she'd immediately rushed him into Addenbrooke's. Within twelve hours he was on the operating table. Fortunately, they'd caught the tumour before it could spread and do serious damage. For several days he was in intensive care, receiving lumbar punctures and frequent brain-scans to ensure the hormone was now inactive and further malignant growth had been arrested, and then he was moved to a recovery ward.

Alice brought Jamie to visit him on his half days and at weekends. Sometimes she'd leave him there while she went shopping. The change was extraordinary. From being a silent boy, he now couldn't stop talking – about the cricket team he'd been picked for, about plans for the holidays, about friends he'd invited back home. The first time Lisa had brought him, too, he'd sided with her in a frivolous three-way argument and he'd ended up sitting on the end of the bed with her, teaching her the Braille alphabet.

By the sound of changing gears, Guy could tell they'd reached the steep hill that lay just a few miles away from the school. He remembered watching the sun setting behind this hill one evening before he'd gone blind. As the ambulance laboured to the top, he found his thoughts returning once again to the puzzle of that final afternoon.

One question ran endlessly through his mind: if he'd allowed the premonition to run its course, what would he have foreseen? Jamie actually spiking his eyes out?

He almost wanted to answer Yes, for that would mean he'd altered the course of his fate; will would have triumphed over destiny, humanity over pre-determination. But could he say that? The vision, as it had come to him, had been seen *through his own eyes*, with the graininess and blurring of his actual sight, just as he had indeed briefly regained it – so dim, even, that he'd believed the crisis was to take place at twilight. Was, then, his decision to take the eighth injection that gave him sight also predetermined? How much further back did he have to go? To the decision to meet Patrick? To the football accident which made him go blind? To something earlier? To some moment of original sin, as Jamie would have it?

He remembered pressing Patrick for an explana-tion and being offered some way-out theory to do with sub-atomic physics. Every particle has its anti-particle, his friend had told him, only you don't know which it is until you've caught it. Capturing it actually *gives* it its value. For every event, likewise, there's its anti-event. Precognition is merely the capturing of an anti-event; until that moment, anything at all could happen, but from then on that particular event *must* happen.

The note of the ambulance engine changed and he could feel they were going downhill. He frowned, thinking of Patrick's neatly scientific explanation. It didn't feel right; it didn't feel *human*. Surely being human was in essence to be illogical, contradictory. To want the comfort of a grand plan and at the same time the freedom to evade it when one chose. He certainly *felt* he'd made a genuinely free choice. The simple fact was he'd taken the chance and lost. That was all there was to it.

Right now, he had his life to get on with.

He was still blind. At the final hour, triggered maybe by the sheer force of his desperation, the axons had briefly joined up and he'd regained a glimmering of sight. He'd seen Jamie. He'd seen Lisa, too. Blurred, flecked and distorted though the images were, nevertheless he'd seen them with his own eyes! For an hour he'd had his sight back. And then, gradually, the dull red curtain had drawn closed again, leaving only a scattering of tiny pinpricks squirming in the corners of his vision, and even these had been extinguished before the night had fallen. Though he'd impressed their faces indelibly on his memory during that hour, all hope of properly seeing again the ones he loved was forever dead.

The ambulance slowed down and turned in through the school gates. Not wishing to be seen from the classrooms, he directed the driver to take the right fork round the upper track. As the tyres scrunched on the gravel outside the McVeys' house, he wondered if he'd lost all hope of taking over the school, too. Was a blind headmaster quite out of the question? He took a deep breath. What was life without something to live *for*? He'd damn well give it a try.

Lisa stood in the sitting-room and stared out of the

window. On the sill stood the box Jamie had made at woodwork classes that she'd filled with geraniums. The mid-day heat shimmered off the flagstones of the newly-weeded front path. Some way down the drive a freak midsummer storm had blown away one side of Jamie's tree-house. It lay unrepaired.

She went slowly round the cottage. The smell of fresh paint still hung in the air; Jamie had wanted the stairway repainted, insisting it should be yellow. He'd shown her the proper places for all the furniture and ornaments throughout the house. In the kitchen, where she'd laid lunch for three, she'd set out the glasses and cutlery exactly as Jamie had taught her. She'd stocked the cupboards with food, marking the jars and tins in Braille with punched tape, and she'd sat patiently while he went through the daily routines he'd established. Nothing was clearly stated but, by implication, he was handing over the running of the household. Guy was coming home today; she'd see how he reacted. She had her letter of resignation from the BBC in her handbag, ready to post.

Upstairs, she paused for a moment at the door of the small room where Guy had undergone his treatments, now redecorated as a spare room, and she thought back to the moment of breakthrough two weeks before. She'd taken her annual holiday to come down to Gorselands, using the place as a base for visiting Guy and staying, along with Jamie, in Alice and Donald's house. One afternoon when she'd brought him back from a visit to the hospital, he'd led her down to the cottage and invited her in. He'd taken her upstairs to this room. She'd been astonished to find it had all been cleared and a bed and wardrobe put there.

'Your room, if you want it,' was all he'd said.